Praise for the B

"The future shows much success for this series! Fun, vibrant characters (as well as a sexy smolder or two for good measure) give the novel just the right tone."

—*RT Book Reviews*

"I loved the protagonist, Cass. She and her friends were very well developed and felt like a group of people I'd like to get to know."

—*The Book's the Thing*

"The book starts off on a fast pace, and is a quick page-turner. Readers will love the charm, wit, and feelings that these characters show."

—*Bibliophile Reviews*

"It has so many great characters and just enough intrigue to keep me on the edge of my seat. The setting was quaint and the author made me want to live there. The mystery is well written and keeps readers guessing till the end."

—*Texas Book-aholic*

"I love a good cozy book right before bed, and this charming story about psychic shop owner Cass Donovan did not disappoint. I stayed up far too late into the evening because I couldn't put it down. A well-crafted mystery with a quirky cast of characters, and plenty of twists and turns to keep you guessing to the end."

—*The Mysterious Ink Spot*

"This engaging series just keeps getting better!"

—*Cozy Up With Kathy*

Books by Lena Gregory

Bay Island Psychic Mysteries

Death at First Sight
Occult and Battery
Clairvoyant and Present Danger
Spirited Away
Grave Consequences
A Spirit Seeks Asylum

All-Day Breakfast Café Mysteries

Scone Cold Killer
Murder Made to Order
A Cold Brew Killing
A Waffle Lot of Murder
Whole Latte Murder
Mistletoe Cake Murder

A Spirit

Seeks Asylum

A Bay Island Psychic Mystery

LENA GREGORY

BEYOND THE PAGE
PUBLISHING

A Spirit Seeks Asylum
Lena Gregory
Copyright © 2021 by Denise Pysarchuk.
Cover design by Dar Albert, Wicked Smart Designs

Beyond the Page Books
are published by
Beyond the Page Publishing
www.beyondthepagepub.com

ISBN: 978-1-954717-44-2

A Spirit

Seeks Asylum

Chapter One

Cass Donovan closed her eyes, inhaled deeply, and lowered the mental barrier she'd so recently learned to erect to protect herself from being assailed by voices from the beyond. Now if she could just perfect a shield that would protect her from Bee's incessant whining, she'd be set.

"Well?" Her best friend, Bee Maxwell, poked her arm. If he kept it up, he wasn't going to be her best friend for much longer. "Anything?"

She huffed out a breath and slitted open one eye. "I said I'd tell you if I felt anything."

"Yeah, well . . ." He rolled his eyes in a true diva fashion only he could pull off and shivered daintily, or at least as daintily as a man who was better than six feet and two hundred-plus pounds could. "Standing here waiting for a spirit or ghost or whatever to reach out and say hello is giving me the heebie-jeebies."

Ignoring him, she closed her eye and returned to listening for any hint of an otherworldly presence.

Bee shifted his heavily muscled frame from one platform shoe to the other and sighed.

"Ugh . . ." She gave up, pulled out a chair from the long wooden table in the Old Madison Estate's ballroom, and flopped into it. Truth was, it wasn't Bee's fault she couldn't sense anything. It just wasn't happening.

Peering around the room from beneath his lashes, braced to run at the first sign of anything hinky, Bee hesitantly pulled out a chair. "Are you sure you won't be able to get anything?"

"Yup. Positive." Which was unfortunate, since Bee had gone through the trouble of setting up all his camera equipment to catch a glimpse of a ghost for her first vlog, a venture he assured her would be a great income generator during the cold, hard winter months on Bay Island.

He turned the chair and straddled it, folded his arms on the back, and rested his chin on his forearm facing her. "Nothing at all?"

"Nah. I just can't get a sense of anything. It's as if all the ghosts packed up and took off for the Bahamas . . ." Wind howled, rattling the old windows, as if to prove her point. Heck, if she could, she'd take off to the Bahamas herself. "Or anywhere else warm."

"So . . . what's the problem?"

How should she know, since no otherworldly figures felt the burning desire to hang around and explain it to her? She propped her elbows on the table and cradled her head in her hands. That wasn't fair. It wasn't Bee's fault this wasn't working. He'd set up all of his lights, cameras, even some kind of thermometer that beeped whenever it detected any sudden cold spikes. So far, the only thing to set it off had been a particularly strong gust of wind that had infiltrated the room. And that had nothing to do with ghosts, just windows in the old mansion that needed replacing. "I don't know what the problem is, Bee."

"Okay, okay." He sat up straighter. "No need to get testy."

"I'm not—" Okay, that's a lie. She was totally testy.

"Exactly." He pointed a finger at her.

Yeah, yeah, yeah. Point taken. "So. Now what do we do?"

He shrugged as if their whole plan hadn't just tanked. "Now we enjoy a nice, preferably warm lunch and wait to see if anything presents itself."

Easy for him to say; he'd be able to make his rent and mortgage payments come February and March. "And if nothing does?"

"Then we'll move on to the lighthouse. Even after we eat and I pack up all of my equipment, it should still be light enough to go in there. We just won't climb all the way to the top." Which would make Bee perfectly happy. Climbing up all those stairs in an enclosed tube wasn't one of his favorite activities. Nor was it Cass's. But the view from the top would be amazing and well worth the climb. At least it would be if they were visiting the Bay Island Lighthouse, which they weren't.

"I wouldn't mind climbing to the top of the Bay Island Lighthouse, but no way I'm climbing to the top of Stony Bay Lighthouse in the near-dark." They'd visited the old abandoned lighthouse before settling on the Madison Estate for their first vlogging attempt, and the creep factor in there was ridiculous, even for Cass. Bee'd nearly had a meltdown. "Those stairs are way too creaky and unsteady to climb in the daylight, never mind at dusk."

"We probably should have started there in the first place." Bee sulked.

Cass pinned him with a glare and lifted a brow. "Ya think?"

"Wee . . . eell . . ." He pulled at the silver print silk scarf he wore draped around his thick neck. "What can I say? I figured since you conjured your first spirit in this very room, it would be a great place to begin."

"Mm-hmm. That, and the lighthouse terrified you."

He shot her a grin. "That too."

She laughed. Bee was her best friend in the world, and there was nothing either of them wouldn't do for the other, but Bee's level of discomfort with anything otherworldly sometimes made things difficult, considering Cass's chosen profession.

"All right, I admit it, you were r . . . r . . . ri . . ." He choked on the word.

Cass leaned over and slapped him on the back.

"Right." He winced.

Her gaze settled on the large stone fireplace where the image had hovered last winter. A spirit? Maybe. At the time, she hadn't been sure what she was seeing, still couldn't say with a hundred percent certainty it had been a ghost. But events since that time had convinced her ghosts were real and she could absolutely communicate with them, so she had to figure that first one had been as real as any that had come after. "Not really. Neither of us was right or wrong. This was a good try, and if this place was still abandoned, it probably would have worked. Who knows?"

"I guess," Bee agreed, though only half-heartedly.

The new paisley print wallpaper, bright lighting, fresh coat of paint on the wainscoting, and cheerful music made the idea of spirits lingering less believable than the first time around, when Bee had spent considerable time dingying the place back up after the new owners had done similar renovations. "Wanna make a deal?"

He tilted his cheek onto his arm and studied her. "Does it involve skipping lunch?"

"Well, yes, but—"

"No."

"Come on, Bee." Ugh . . . now she was reduced to whining. When Bee had first suggested the idea of a vlog, Cass had been apprehensive. What if no one was interested? What if no one watched? But the more he'd wheedled her, the more she'd warmed to the idea, and now she really wanted to make it work. If she could get enough subscribers to generate some interest from advertisers, she might be able to keep Mystical Musings, her psychic shop on Bay Island's boardwalk, afloat through the winter until spring brought a new influx of tourists from Long Island and New York City. "How about if I treat you to dinner at the place of your choosing before the group reading?"

"Hmm . . . that's not really fair. Considering it's winter and there's not much open." He studied her for a moment. "But I suppose I could go for a nice juicy hamburger at the diner later."

"Yes! Thanks, Bee."

"Uh-huh." He stood, returned the chair to its place, and took his camera off the tripod. "But since I'm skipping lunch, I get dessert."

"Sure thing."

"And I'm not talking the little dessert that comes with the meal." He started packing equipment into cases. "I'm talking about a nice piece of cake or pie from the display case when you walk in. Those things are always talking to me, but I can never justify wasting the calories."

"That and you're always full after your meal."

He shot her a grin over his shoulder. "That too, I suppose."

Cass helped him load everything into her car then drove the short distance to the Stony Bay Lighthouse. Dark clouds gathered over the bay, roiling, churning, whipping ice-cold wind and spray off the choppy water and casting them across the gravel parking lot. Whitecaps surged over the jetty.

"Are you kidding me?" Bee grabbed his camera from the backseat and hopped out. "This is awesome!"

Thunder rumbled, a deep angry sound that vibrated beneath Cass's feet. A trickle of fear prodded her. Perhaps they should wait for another day. It was getting late, and they still had to go to dinner before the group reading at seven. Plus, Beast, her Leonberger, had already been left alone long enough. Any longer and it was almost guaranteed he'd get into some sort of trouble. Even though she'd take him to the shop with her for the reading, she'd need a few minutes to feed and walk him first.

"I couldn't have created a better backdrop." With the wind whipping his bleached-blond hair wildly around his face, Bee snapped picture after picture of the gathering storm. "Hey, grab my video camera out of the trunk, would ya? I'm not going to set up everything just yet, but why don't we try to get some footage before those clouds let loose all manner of fury upon us."

Cass finger-combed her long blonde hair into a ponytail and tied it with a band she yanked from the glove compartment, then dug out Bee's video camera and handed it to him.

He opened the passenger door and set his camera on the seat, then pointed toward the bluff. "Go stand over there and we'll record your opening segment."

Cass glanced toward the bluff he'd indicated. Wind tore through the trees, their branches, long bare of leaves, swaying and rocking. Granted, it wasn't a hurricane or anything, but what if the wind blew her off the bluff onto the rocks below. Images of another body, broken on the jetty not that long ago, popped into her head. "I don't know, Bee."

"Oh, stop." He rolled his eyes. "It's not like I'm asking you to stand on the edge of a cliff or anything. Just stand beside the lighthouse; that way it'll block the wind a bit."

She huffed out a breath. "Fine."

"Hey, who's the creative genius here?"

She laughed as she walked toward the lighthouse so he could get the shot he wanted. He wasn't wrong. Bee's designer dress shop, Dreamweaver Designs, stood just down the boardwalk from Mystical Musings. At this point, his annual fashion shows drew a good number of buyers from New York City to Bay Island each fall. If there was one thing Bee knew how to do, and do well, it was put on a show.

She positioned herself beside the stairway that led to the front door, settling into a crevice along the stone wall. "Good?"

"Nah, step out a little, so I can get the full effect of the raging storm in the background."

She did as he asked. Ice-cold drizzle hit her face and dripped beneath her coat's collar.

"Okay . . ." He held the camera as steady as he could against the wind. "Three, two, one . . ."

Cass offered her most winning smile with her face already half frozen. "Hi. I'm Cass Donovan. Welcome to Mystical Musings, where today we're going to ponder the existence of ghosts while we take a walk inside the old, abandoned Stony Bay Lighthouse in search of . . . well . . . we'll have to see what we can find."

Bee stopped filming. He held his hand out, palm down, and rocked it back and forth. "Not bad, but we're going to have to work on your opening line a bit. We can tweak it later, though. For now, let's get inside before it starts pouring."

Fine by her. In some ways, the ice-cold rain that was predicted was worse than snow. As soon as the sun went down, the roads would ice over, and driving the winding road back toward town would be a nightmare. The last thing she wanted was to slide off the road. Again.

Bee started the camera rolling again. She had to admit, the footage of her climbing the stairs to the big wooden door with the storm ramping up in the background would be dramatic. Now if she could just summon something once they were inside.

The heavy door groaned as it swung inward. The odor from years of mold and mildew assailed her, instantly clogging her nose. The dampness sent a chill rushing through her. At least she thought it was the dampness.

She moved into the center of the space, stood at the bottom of the circular iron stairway, and closed her eyes. Speaking out loud to summon a ghost seemed kind of weird, since it wasn't how she usually made contact, so she simply opened herself and waited, despite Bee's repeated complaints that it would look boring.

Wind howled through cracks and crevices long in need of repair. Rain pelted the metal and glasswork above them. Floorboards creaked as Bee moved slowly around her, no doubt searching for the perfect spot to capture her expression the moment she sensed something. Of course, there was a better than good chance he'd run screaming into the night if anything actually did appear, but she gave him credit for trying.

This wasn't working. She huffed and opened her eyes.

Bee lowered the camera. "Nothing?"

"Nope. Not a whimper." Maybe she was too preoccupied with thoughts of the evening's group reading. Attendance had slacked off since before the holidays and hadn't picked back up again after. Add the coming storm she hoped would hold off for a few more hours . . . She might be better off canceling and going home to snuggle on the couch under a nice warm blanket with Beast and watch a movie.

"All right. Well, let me at least get some footage of you leaving, and then we'll wrap it up for the day." He repositioned himself at her back, across the room from the doorway. "Want to call Stephanie and see if she and Aiden want to meet us at the diner?"

Cass's other best friend, Stephanie Lawrence, had recently taken on a foster child she hoped to adopt permanently. The four-year-old suffered from autism, though doctors weren't yet sure how severe since years of abuse interfered with their diagnosis. "Sure. You can give her a call when we get to the car. Aiden loves the diner."

"He sure does." A warm smile spread across Bee's face. He pointed toward the door. "Okay, I want you to walk across the room and pull the door open. Hopefully, the clouds out front will show through the doorway, then look back over your shoulder dramatically, keeping your expression serious as you look up the stairway, then turn and walk out."

Ugh . . . Sometimes Bee's flair for the dramatic went too far. "Seriously? We didn't even find anything here. Why bother?"

Bee's attention was already on his camera, though. "Because the outside setting is perfect. We can always come back later and try again. But what are the chances of getting a storm like this next time?"

She hated when he was right. She took a deep breath, waited for his signal, then crossed the room and yanked open the door. Wind invaded the building, whipped into a frenzy through the circular room, then exited at her back, giving her a good shove.

As she stepped onto the concrete platform just outside the door, her foot hit an icy rain-slicked patch of moss and went out from under her. She tried to grab the handrail, missed, and went flat on her bottom. A jolt shot up her spine, and her teeth clacked together.

"Are you okay?" Bee asked from behind her.

She looked up to find him standing over her, his expression caught somewhere between horrified and thoroughly amused, camera still rolling.

Her pants were soaked, but other than that, everything seemed okay. She grabbed the railing and started to pull herself up.

Bee hooked one hand beneath her arm and helped her to her feet. Laughter danced in his eyes, twitched at the corners of his mouth. "You know, Cass, we're going to have to work on your idea of dramatic."

Chapter Two

Cass looked in the mirror behind her office door once more and smoothed her hair, which she'd pulled into a bun for the reading. Since her spill on the lighthouse steps had necessitated a detour home to change into dry clothing before they could go out to eat, and Stephanie had had the speech therapist at the house working with Aiden, they'd decided to forgo dinner until after the reading. The end result of that decision: she'd had to stop off at the convenience store for coffee and donuts to hold Bee over.

Now, two donuts later, Cass was stuffed and bloated and regretting her decision to go ahead with the reading instead of staying home with a blanket and a bucket of popcorn, maybe a good movie, while she snuggled with Beast on the couch. They both knew he wasn't allowed up there, a rule Cass had made after he'd chewed her last couch to pieces, but they both pretended the rule didn't exist.

A small group had already started to arrive, and Stephanie had begun to direct them upstairs to the group reading room. With Beast and Aiden happily playing in the back room downstairs, and Jess, Stephanie's babysitter, keeping an eye on them, everything was just about ready to go. So why was Cass still in her office procrastinating instead of greeting her clients?

Bee cracked the door carefully and poked his head in. "You ready?"

As ready as I'll ever be. She smiled. "Sure. I'll be right out."

He studied her a moment, a small frown marring his features, but left without saying anything more.

She stretched and shook out her arms. *Okay, time to do this.* But she paused with her hand on the doorknob. What if she went out there and nothing happened? She'd spent the better part of the day in search of ghosts at the bed-and-breakfast and then at the lighthouse without so much as a glimmer. What if she went out to do the reading and she couldn't connect?

She shook off the apprehension and swung the door open before she could change her mind. Before she'd realized the extent of her psychic abilities, she'd relied on a combination of good instincts and years of psychiatric training to do her readings. At least that's what she'd told herself at the time. If she had to, she could revert to that again.

But it sure was easier when spirits showed up to help out. Not that they outright told her what she needed to know, but they definitely gave her a nudge in the right direction.

A quick peek down the spiral staircase into the main part of the shop showed no lingering shoppers, which brought a quick pang of disappointment. Without tourists, the only real income she earned was from individual and group readings. While her group readings boasted a decent regular attendance and had become a popular local social event, it wasn't always easy to entice people to come out on a cold winter night. Heck, Cass hadn't even wanted to come out tonight. And she could only give so many individual readings to locals; not that many people lived on Bay Island year-round.

She yearned for the return of tourists who'd flock to her small psychic shop on the boardwalk in search of souvenirs, stones and crystals to ease their ailments, and the novelty of a reading. But for now, winter clutched Bay Island in its icy grip. She shivered.

When Cass entered the reading room, the scent of coffee and chocolate enveloped her, instantly chasing away the chill, despite the wind howling outside and the sleet-like rain pelting the windows. A decent crowd had gathered, though too many seats remained empty. Gone were the days of summer, when the room would be crammed full of smiling, chattering guests, all on vacation and looking to spend money.

As soon as she spotted Cass, Stephanie shot her a thumbs-up and started her introduction.

Cass ignored the routine greeting and overview of the evening's events in favor of searching her audience for those who seemed to need her help in some way, weaving between round tables covered in maroon cloths, trying to decide where to begin, focusing her attention on anything that might stand out.

A woman caught her attention—dark hair, even darker eyes, sitting alone, features strained. Had she come to seek Cass's assistance? Maybe. But Cass wouldn't start with her. She'd keep an eye on her and see if she connected or had just come to watch. Some people attended a group reading first but preferred to return for a more private, individual reading later.

A small arrangement of candles in the center of each table cast a warm glow over the dimly lit room. Guests continued to trickle in as Stephanie spoke, many of the tables starting to fill; not bad considering the cold, wet weather.

Amid the familiar sea of faces were a few newcomers. Good. That made things interesting, changed them up a bit. A middle-aged couple she didn't recognize sat at a table toward the front, a gaping space between their chairs. Trouble in paradise? Something they wanted her help with? She added them to her mental list of potential clients.

Stephanie announced Cass, then handed her the microphone and leaned close enough to whisper, "I'll be back in a few."

Cass caught herself before she could frown and kept her smile firmly in place as she watched Stephanie hurry out toward the stairs. Stephanie never left the room during a reading.

When the applause died down, Cass lifted the microphone. "Thank you all for coming. I know it's not the best weather."

A few of her regulars murmured and nodded. Even though many of the attendees were friends, and most would hang around to gossip and have something to eat after the event—cookies and pastries from Tony's bakery with coffee, tea, or hot cocoa for this evening's treats—people tended to remain quiet and respectful during the readings, allowing her the calm she needed to concentrate on what she might be able to interpret, aware that some people who came to the readings sought painful truths.

Jess Ryan, Stephanie's babysitter, hurried into the room and sat at a table toward the back where her mother, Sara, and Sara's boyfriend, Emmett Marx, who also happened to be Cass's handyman and a good friend, were already seated.

Sara smiled widely, the candlelight reflecting in her big brown eyes and flushing her cheeks.

Emmett's wild mass of unruly long gray hair had been tamed into a ponytail at the nape of his neck. He twisted the red baseball cap he usually wore in his hands. When Cass made eye contact, he grinned, then quickly shifted his gaze away.

Hmm . . . something there. She rounded a table and moved closer.

Sara's smile grew wider.

Emmett kept his gaze firmly on the hat he was mauling. He

didn't seem particularly disturbed by Cass's approach, but Emmett was painfully shy. At his first sign of discomfort at her interest, she'd back off immediately.

Jess bounced in her seat, vibrating with nervous energy. Something exciting, then.

Cass circled the table, then returned her gaze to Jess. "You seem happy this evening, Jess."

She grinned and shifted her long curls behind her back but didn't say anything. Jess had attended enough readings to know how Cass worked, and Sara and Emmett never missed a group reading. They'd give nothing away. Good. A challenge to start the evening.

Cass tilted her head and studied Sara.

Sara stared back, her hands tucked beneath the table. Unusual, since she and Emmett often held hands through a good portion of the reading, though she couldn't well hold his hand while he was busy mangling his hat. Sometimes, Emmett sat with his arm slung around her shoulders. What they never did was sit side by side without touching one another in some way. A lover's spat? No way; they all looked too happy for that.

"Seems everyone's happy tonight. Good news, I think."

But what? Jess had talked about going away to college but never too seriously. She and her mom were extremely close, and neither of them relished the thought of Jess going away. Besides, Jess had fallen head over heels in love with Aiden and currently watched him while Stephanie worked. The timing couldn't have been more perfect.

So, if not college, what could have Jess and Sara so excited? Though Jess had a boyfriend, they didn't seem to be too serious, certainly not yet ready . . . Cass's gaze jerked toward Emmett. Emmett, who was so shy and nervous he'd barely been able to ask Sara out on a date when he'd first started attending readings to be close to her. It hit Cass instantly, the way things sometimes did, and she didn't even need her psychic powers to figure it out.

"Well, it seems someone has exciting news to share." Her first genuine smile of the evening shot across Cass's face and straight to her heart. She held out her hand, palm up, and wiggled her fingers in a come-ahead gesture.

Jess clapped her hands together and squealed.

Sara whipped her left hand from beneath the table and placed it into Cass's.

Candle flames danced in the round, brilliant-cut diamond set amid a cluster of smaller diamond chips. Within the stone, teardrops swirled, the prisms casting an iridescence that lured Cass deeper. An image tried to form, a roiling, sparkling fog deep in the stone's center. *Tanya.*

Cass ripped herself from the vision with a gasp and tried to recenter herself, focus on the present. She took a moment to steady her ragged breathing so she could speak without anyone realizing something had happened. She'd save that for a private moment with Emmett. "Oh, Sara, it's beautiful. Congratulations."

Sara stood and hugged Cass. "Thank you."

Bee hooted from the back of the room, and thunderous applause broke out.

Emmett turned beet red as he pushed his chair back and stood to hug Cass. "Thank you, Cass. If it wasn't for you, we would have never gotten together. We wanted you to find out here, among friends, where we first got to know each other."

"Thank you so much, Emmett. I couldn't be happier for all of you." The death of his wife when their son was a baby had left Emmett heartbroken for far too long.

Tears threatened, but not her own. Well, some of her own, but another's as well. Tears of joy. She hugged Emmett closer. "Do you want to know, Emmett?"

He nodded against her shoulder.

"Tanya is so happy for you, for Joey. It's what she wants, Emmett. Be happy."

He sobbed quietly at the mention of his former wife, who'd come to Cass before when Emmett had needed help, then nodded and stepped back.

Sara looked questioningly at him.

He pulled her into his arms and held her tightly, laid a tender kiss on the top of her head. "I love you."

"I love you too, Emmett."

Cass squeezed Emmett's arm, then wiped the tears from her eyes and moved away, giving them some semblance of privacy. "Wow. What a great way to start the evening, huh?"

Nods and murmurs of ascent slid through the room, the subdued atmosphere from earlier now replaced with a more celebratory mood.

Trying to gain control of her emotions, Cass scanned the room in search of whoever might need her services the most, someone who would be open to her sharing her insights with the entire group.

She searched for the woman she'd noticed earlier, hoping to gauge her reaction to Emmett and Sara's news, but was disappointed to find her seat empty. She must have slipped out while Cass's attention was on her friends' engagement. Cass guessed she wasn't impressed with what she'd seen of her psychic abilities. Not that she'd done anything noteworthy yet, but the woman could have at least given her a chance to get warmed up before walking out.

The couple she'd noticed when she walked in still sat with a rift between them, both physically and emotionally, it seemed. She started toward them.

A cool draft rippled across her skin, as if a cloud had drifted to block the sun. A shadow crept into Cass's peripheral vision, slid over the couple and disappeared into a darkened corner of the room. A fraction of a second at most. A trick of the candles flickering in the dim light? She had no idea, nor was she ready to address it yet. Too bad she couldn't just turn a blind eye and ignore it forever. But she'd done that once, in her previous life as a psychiatrist, before she'd realized the extent of her abilities, and her patient had died. She'd most definitely seek these two out, if not during the group reading then afterward, and warn them they might be in danger.

Chapter Three

A woman a few tables away cleared her throat, diverting Cass's attention.

Cass shifted her focus, keeping the couple in her peripheral vision lest they decide to leave before she could speak to them.

A young woman sat at a table alone, which was not completely unusual, but most people tended to come with friends. Was it the same woman she'd notice earlier? Had she just changed seats?

Cass moved closer.

Long, stringy brown hair partially obscured the woman's face. No. Though she couldn't recall exactly what the first woman looked like, her hair had been shorter, darker, her eyes colder, more penetrating.

Cass approached slowly.

The woman studied her through weary brown eyes, straightening as Cass got closer.

"Hi, there. What's your name?" Cass asked.

She tilted her head. "Can't you tell me?"

Oh, great. Just what she needed, a nonbeliever challenging her on a day she was already having issues. Though the desire to turn and walk away was strong, Cass ignored it. She'd been down this road before, and walking away sometimes made matters worse. "Not unless someone from the beyond happens to be here and recognize you."

That elicited a chuckle from some of her more seasoned attendees.

The woman studied her. Would she engage in a more positive manner or continue to heckle?

Cass held her breath.

"I'm Thea. Thea Newburgh."

Forcing a smile, Cass acknowledged the introduction with a nod. "It's nice to meet you, Thea. Have you come tonight just to watch, or is there something you'd like to know?"

Thea pursed her lips but didn't answer. The woman, younger than Cass first realized, definitely had some sort of agenda; Cass knew that without a doubt. A feeling in her gut, or something more? She had no idea, but she was filled with the certainty Thea Newburgh was there for a purpose.

Thea spread her hands on the table and slowly stood. Her hair fell farther into her face, obscuring Cass's view of one eye, but Thea made no attempt to push it back. "Actually, I did come for a reason, but it's not to seek your counsel. There's nothing you can tell me that the dead haven't already imparted to me themselves."

Uh-oh. Cass had no idea where this was going, but she didn't like it. An up-and-coming psychic trying to make a name for herself at Cass's reading? Lure some of her customers with the promise of a more accurate reading? Could be. It wouldn't be the first time a so-called psychic had tried that ruse. It was better to play along for a moment and see where this was headed than to encourage a confrontation in her shop. After all, Cass wasn't the only one the dead sought and spoke to. And, as she'd recently found out, some were more adept and knowledgeable than Cass. "So, you're a medium then?"

She shrugged one shoulder, the bone accentuated through her thin, smock-covered paisley dress. "Of sorts."

Curiosity won out over any anger or indignation. "And what have the dead told you that you've come to share with us tonight?"

She took a deep shuddering breath. "I've come to warn you, Cass Donovan. I'd have waited until after the reading to speak to you privately if you hadn't sought me out, but I can warn you publicly just the same. Who knows? Maybe it's better this way; there are witnesses to my intervention. Just in case you choose not to heed my warning and the worst comes to bear. I guess some things happen just the way they're meant to, huh?"

Cass remained quiet, waiting her out, because as much as she wanted to discount Thea's advice, pass it off as a stunt to gain followers or notoriety, her gut churned with the cast-iron certainty Thea was going to be right about something. She just wasn't sure what.

Stephanie returned just then, slipped quietly against the wall, took one look around and frowned at Cass.

Cass kept eye contact and gave a small, discreet shake of her head. No, she didn't need anyone to intervene. But, come to think of it, she was surprised Bee hadn't already. Her gaze skipped to where he stood in the back corner, twisting his hands together, bottom lip caught between his teeth. She gave him the same gesture and returned her focus to Thea.

"Oh, well, just a theory." Thea stiffened her spine. She lifted her chin and finally tucked her hair behind her ear with a shaky hand. "I came to warn you, Cass, that sometimes the dead are better left dead."

"Uh . . ." What could she say to that? She wanted to ask Thea to be more specific, to spit out whatever it is her cryptic warning was supposed to mean, but she didn't want to encourage any more interaction in public. She could always seek the woman out later, in private, and ask her to expand on her prophecy. "Thank you for letting me know."

She hadn't meant it to be funny, just didn't know what else to say, but a few snickers rippled through the room.

A smile lifted one side of Thea's mouth as she shook her head. "Well, then. Consider yourself warned."

Cass nodded, and Thea lifted a torn wool coat from the back of her chair and walked out.

Though a few murmurs followed, most of the crowd just waited, fully focused on Cass, to see how she'd handle the confrontation. Which she did the best way she could think of: she ignored it and moved on.

Somehow, she managed to get through the remainder of the hour. She helped an elderly gentleman find an heirloom watch he'd misplaced, dismissed a woman who seemed intent on using Cass to steal her former lover's inheritance from his wife and children with a discreet reprimand, and predicted a snowstorm would be coming by the weekend, despite what forecasters said, for a snowplow operator who was desperately in need of work—much like the rest of Bay Island's businesses during the long winter. Unlike milder winters, this year's cold snap, along with a steady stream of storms, made traveling back and forth over the wind-whipped bay more than just uncomfortable.

When the reading ended and her guests began to mill about socializing and gathering refreshments from a long table at the front of the room, Cass wanted nothing more than to bolt for her office.

Bee nudged her ribs with his elbow and smiled at a couple he recognized, then muttered, "Don't even think about it."

She laughed. "That obvious, huh?"

"Puh-lease, gurhl. I knew you'd want to run the instant Thea Newburgh stood up."

She shrugged it off. Bee could often anticipate her reactions, sometimes before even she knew what to expect, not out of any psychic power but because he was an amazing friend.

"Excuse me, Ms. Donovan."

"Yes?" She turned automatically at the sound of her name.

Bee excused himself and wandered away, but not too far, probably concerned she'd turn tail and run the minute she found herself alone, or maybe he just didn't want to miss anything. Knowing Bee, it could go either way.

The middle-aged gentleman she'd noticed earlier stood with his hand extended, the woman he'd been sitting with at his side.

Cass took his hand. "It's a pleasure to meet you, Mr. . . . ?"

"Anderson, but please, call me Elijah, and I assure you, my dear, the pleasure is all mine." He gestured to the dainty woman beside him. "This is my wife, Evelyn."

Cass took one frail hand in her own, careful not to squeeze too hard. "It's nice to meet you, Evelyn."

Evelyn shook her hand with a tentative grip and nodded.

The shadow she'd hoped she'd been mistaken about earlier rushed back to the forefront of her mind. Was this fragile woman in danger? She'd meant to seek them out, try to talk to them without blurting the fact that death might be coming for one or both of them or someone close to them. No point frightening them over something they might have no control over, though she could try to warn them away if they suggested they were planning to do anything dangerous—though she couldn't picture the pair bungee jumping or mountain climbing. "How can I help you this evening?"

"Actually, your reputation precedes you." Elijah's deep baritone resonated through the room. Hopefully, he didn't want to share any private details. At least Bee wouldn't have to work too hard to *overhear*. "I sought you out, came all the way to Bay Island on that dreadful ferry, hoping to hire you to do a job for me."

Evelyn looked away from her husband's stare and harrumphed. "And I sought you out hoping you'd talk some sense into the old fool."

She reminded Cass a little of Bee in a snit. She bit back a smile.

"Well, now, that certainly sounds interesting. What is it you want me to do?"

Elijah straightened his already perfectly aligned glasses and smoothed his impeccably pressed suit jacket. "I need you to go into the old abandoned Bay Island Psychiatric Center and prove it's not haunted."

Bee gasped then slapped a hand over his mouth. He shook his head frantically back and forth behind Elijah, his eyes so wide Cass was afraid they might pop right out of his head.

Evelyn didn't miss the gesture. She pointed at Bee, and her ice blue eyes, magnified by the thick lenses in her glasses, grew even colder. "See, that's what I'm talking about. The idea is crazy, to say the least."

With her mind already set toward being a psychiatrist when she'd started college, Cass had studied the former Twin Forks Psychiatric Center, along with numerous others. It had opened in the late eighteen-hundreds, and the grounds, which once took up a large portion of the far end of Bay Island, consisted of several buildings that had originally housed some of New York's most dangerous mentally ill patients, most of them criminals, who were never expected to return to society. The idea was to create a self-sufficient compound, known at the time as the Twin Forks Lunatic Asylum, where patients could live out their lives in lieu of serving prison terms while still keeping their communities safe.

Later on, when the budget became a problem, they changed the name to the more appealing Twin Forks Psychiatric Center and took on less violent cases with the hope of easing the burden on the overcrowded asylums on the mainland. It operated through one scandal or another for almost a hundred years before it was finally shut down. It was rumored that the patients were often used for experiments, thanks to its close proximity to the notorious Plum Island, though that was never proven.

That place was most definitely haunted.

Cass opened her mouth to say thanks but no thanks.

"Please." Elijah held up a hand. "I need this done. I purchased the property several years ago with the hope of turning it into a boarding school, one of many I own, but the board of directors is shying away amid pressure from numerous other organizations trying to block development. They say the land shouldn't be used, it's haunted, it's not safe. I've invested a tremendous amount of money in this venture, Ms. Donovan, and I can't afford to have the project stalled for the next however many years it takes to fight it out in court because of this silly drivel. The plans need to move forward, and you're my last desperate hope of convincing everyone involved this is a safe venture. At this point, I'm afraid it's that or bankruptcy."

Bee rolled his eyes, knowing Cass was a sucker for a good sob story, and shook his head more adamantly.

She ignored his bulging eyes and considered her options. Even if the place was haunted, which it most certainly would be, would it be unsafe to open and use the grounds for something good? More importantly, did this have anything to do with the shadow she'd seen creeping toward the couple? If not for that, she might have given it at least a moment's consideration. As it was . . .

Elijah lifted his chin defiantly and raked a hand through disheveled graying blond hair, the only outward sign the man was under any kind of pressure. "I'm willing to pay you twenty thousand dollars."

Bee's head froze mid-shake, and his mouth dropped open.

Cass sucked in a breath. That, in addition to the income she generated from Mystical Musings, would easily get her through the winter and give her time to get her video blog up and running before next winter. "I don't know . . . I—"

"Let me be perfectly honest with you. I'm going to pay someone to go out there and check this out for me. From what I've heard, you have a stellar reputation and are honest to a fault. If you don't take my money, someone else will, and whomever it is may not share your level of integrity."

Thea's antics at the reading skittered through her mind. A true warning, or a play for attention? "What exactly is it you want me to do?"

"I don't know." He shrugged. "Whatever it is you do to prove there are no ghosts lurking around anywhere."

And that would be fine if there were no ghosts, and if her senses were functioning on all cylinders. "But what if there are ghosts?"

He opened his mouth, then snapped it closed again. Apparently, an actual haunting was something he hadn't considered.

"Then you're out the money you invested plus another twenty grand," Evelyn blurted.

"So be it, then." He ignored his wife and kept his gaze firmly on Cass. "I'm not asking you to lie or anything; if you go in and think it's haunted, so be it, say so. But be honest about the risk the ghosts pose. Let's face it, there are lots of haunted establishments, housing everything from bars to hotels to private homes, and their occupants are in no danger. Sometimes the ghosts even add to the appeal. But if you think housing people there would be dangerous, by all means, let me know. I'm not trying to get anyone hurt, but who knows? Even if there are a few ghosts, who's to say they wouldn't welcome guests?"

True enough, she supposed. Though most, if not all, of the places he'd used as examples had never been used to house the criminally insane, torture anyone, or possibly use the occupants for clandestine scientific experiments. She kept her gaze firmly on Elijah, not wanting to see Bee's reaction. "Do you mind if I record the session and use it for a new series of vlogs I'm trying?"

"Not at all, my dear." He shook Cass's hand and clasped his free hand over their joined hands. "Not at all. Just prove my investment is sound and you can use the footage for whatever you'd like."

Evelyn huffed and stormed from the room.

Bee finally caught Cass's gaze, his expression completely neutral, and for once she couldn't tell what was on his mind.

It would be fine. She'd go in during the daylight, take a look around, determine if it was safe or not, give Elijah a detailed report on her findings, and maybe get a decent first vlog out of the whole experience. Plus, she'd gain twenty thousand dollars.

Elijah pulled a checkbook out of his pocket, leaned on the closest table, and wrote a check for the full amount. He held it out to her. "Thank you, my dear, I trust this will be a most lucrative endeavor for both of us."

A strong gust of wind howled, rattling the windows, and Cass shivered as a chill raced up her spine. She ignored it. They'd be in and out in a few hours.

What could go wrong?

Chapter Four

Cass studied the imposing Twin Forks Psychiatric Center's main building, the shell of which now housed remnants of the past perhaps better left alone. Was this what Thea Newburgh's warning had been about? Were these the dead better left dead? Had some of them who'd not been able to find peace during their lives finally found peace in death? Was she about to disturb that serenity?

Bee unloaded equipment Cass had no idea what to do with from her trunk and stacked it onto a dolly beside her car, then paused to look up at the imposing main building that had once housed the dormitories.

"Do you really think we need all of that, Bee?" She picked up some kind of thermal imaging camera from the top of the heap. She had no idea what it was for, but she did know lugging all of it out would make a quick exit, even if necessary, impossible. "I don't even have a clue how any of it works."

"Don't you worry about a thing." He hefted a long black bag over his shoulder. "You just work your mojo, and I'll take care of the rest. The man's paying a good amount of money; the least we can do is give it our best shot. Besides, I've already told you, people will be more interested if you use gadgets like these, give them some kind of visual they can understand instead of asking them to believe you spoke to a spirit no one else could see or hear just because you said so. What are we going to do? Show an hour-long reel of you standing still with your eyes closed and then try to pass it off as a close encounter?"

She wasn't sure she was buying it. She had a sneaking suspicion Bee might be hiding his fear behind the pile of gadgets that would allow him a certain amount of disconnect from what they were actually doing, focusing on the technical aspect of creating the show rather than the fact she'd be trying to contact the dead. Though, she did have to concede, watching her stand there in silence, or even worse, only hearing her side of a conversation, even if she did agree to speak out loud, could get a little boring for a viewer. Ugh . . . now she was going to have to admit Bee was right. "I guess you have a point."

"What do you mean, you guess?" He smirked, knowing full well he was right and she knew it. "Who's the expert showman here?"

"Yeah, yeah." Since she couldn't argue that, she left him to his task and looked around, keeping her shield firmly in place. Wouldn't want to drop it too soon or too quickly and get blindsided by a barrage of spirits desperate to make a connection with someone in the real world.

Fat white flurries started to fall from the gray sky, clinging to the flaking wrought iron gate that hung open from one rusted hinge. The air smelled like snow. She hadn't watched the weather forecast, and that was one tidbit the dead never seemed to share with her, but the gathering black clouds rolling across Bay Island from the south were warning enough a nor'easter would soon hold the island in its thrall. "Come on, let's get this done before it starts snowing heavily."

"It should be all right. I heard we're supposed to get a few inches but not until tonight. This—he gestured toward the sky—"is just a sprinkling."

She eased the gate open carefully and stepped back, allowing Bee enough room to cart all of his equipment through the opening.

"Do me a favor and grab that bag, please." Bee pointed to a gray bag still sitting on the backseat.

Cass grabbed it and slung it over her shoulder, then slammed the door shut and followed Bee up what was once a brick walkway, though many of the bricks had cracked and been displaced by the elements over the years. "We probably should have checked to make sure the front door is open before we carted all of this in. Elijah was supposed to stop out here to open it, but I don't see his car."

"Let's hope he came and went already. I want to get this stuff inside without it getting too wet from the snow flurries." The dolly bumped and swayed over scattered bricks and rutted ground. A box balanced on top of the pile slid, and Bee reached out to catch it with lightning-fast reflexes. Despite his size, and his signature platform shoes, the man could move when he wanted too. She just hoped he didn't get spooked and hightail it out of there before she could find out what she needed to know. The last thing she wanted was to have to come back again, next time with Stephanie instead.

The path led straight to thick, weathered double metal doors. No porch or patio to soften the entrance, make it more welcoming. She figured maybe the Twin Forks Lunatic Asylum hadn't often entertained guests.

Graffiti covered the outside of the brick building, though she had no idea how someone had managed to paint as high as they had without scaffolding. Who knew? Maybe they'd built it. They certainly could have gone undetected in such a deserted, remote location long enough to do so. She shivered. Their complete seclusion was a reminder she didn't need.

Cracks ran throughout many sections of the brick façade, worn by time, battered by windswept sand and salt from sitting so close to the bay. Many of the windows on all six levels were broken or completely missing. Some were boarded over, spray-painted slogans and logos layered over one another covering every square inch.

Wind tore across the open field, lashing at her coat and whipping her hair into a frenzy, obscuring her vision. She shoved her hair behind her ears.

Bee parked the dolly beside the front door. He shivered and pulled his wool coat tighter around him, then rubbed his hands together and blew into them while he waited for Cass to open the door.

"You're sure you're okay with this, right, Bee?" Though his penchant for drama bordered on diva status, she'd never want to push him to do something he was actually uncomfortable with. At least not too uncomfortable.

He looked around and pinned her with a gaze, his expression caught somewhere between carefully neutral and horrified. "As sure as I'm going to get, so let's get it done before I change my mind."

He didn't have to tell her twice.

She pressed the latch on the door and held her breath as she pushed. The door stuttered inward with a loud screech, a bit foreboding considering the circumstances. She winced and stared straight ahead, careful not to meet Bee's gaze.

She took a few steps into the large open room, just enough to allow Bee room to move the equipment inside, then she stopped and stood perfectly still. The building itself groaned then heaved a sigh at the intrusion. Enough light spilled through the uncovered windows for her to make out her surroundings.

Though the exterior had been battered by time and the elements, the inside of the building had fared much worse. Litter covered most of what had once been an institutional-green room—if the flaking paint on what was left of the cinder-block walls was any indication. Broken furniture lay scattered everywhere, a bed frame broken and discarded against the far wall. It wasn't likely this room had been home to the bed in the first place, so Cass figured someone must have lugged it downstairs sometime over the years since the last of the residents had been relocated.

A carpet of broken ceiling tiles, pipes, paint flakes, and piles of some kind of powder—crumbled cement, maybe—strewn among newer garbage, fast-food bags, beer and soda cans, torn and stained bedding, sent a niggle of fear up Cass's spine. The dead were one thing; coming across violent drug addicts or a group of homeless people afraid she was going to interfere with what might be the only protection they'd have against the winter cold was something else entirely. She should have asked Elijah if he'd had the place cleared out, maybe even asked for security.

Time to get done and get out of there. Trusting that Bee would get his equipment set up and get whatever shots he needed, Cass closed her eyes and lowered her shields. "There's evil here. And pain. And fear."

"Heck, you don't even need to be psychic to sense that." Bee shivered and rubbed his free hand up and down his arm, keeping the small handheld video camera trained steadily on her.

A jolt of pain pierced her brain, and the shields shot back up on their own. Cass staggered and reached out a hand to catch herself against the doorjamb.

"Hey? Are you okay?" Bee frowned and lowered the video camera. "Cass?"

She straightened and nodded. "Yeah, sorry. Just a headache."

"Yeah, well, don't say that once I get the camera rolling again. That was the best footage I've gotten so far."

She bristled. "You filmed that?"

"Of course." He checked the camera for something, then hefted it back up again. "I film everything. We can always edit out what we don't need later."

Fair enough. But for some reason, the thought of capturing that moment of pain and sharing it with the world didn't sit right in her gut, as if it wasn't her pain to share. She could always argue with him about it later. If that brief moment of pain was any indication, Bee should have more than enough interesting footage by the time they were done here. With any luck at all, he'd be willing to let that one moment slide. If not, she'd just have to overrule him.

"All right, come on. Let's get started so we can get out of here." Which Cass wanted to do as soon as possible. As much as she needed the hefty paycheck, some things were better left alone. She had a feeling this would prove to be one of them. Her mind was already racing with ways to tell Elijah Anderson he'd laid out twenty thousand dollars only to prove his critics right.

"All right . . ." Bee pointed toward the door. "Stand there as if you just walked in and start your introduction."

Cass bit back the urge to argue and did as instructed. The faster they could get through this, the better. Plus, he was right about getting everything documented. She could always look through the footage later, see if she'd missed anything, and reserve editing rights. "Hi, I'm Cass Donovan, coming to you from the site of the former Twin Forks Psychiatric Center, where I am attempting to reach out to any former residents to determine the feasibility of reopening the property as a boarding school."

Bee rolled his hand out of sight of the camera, gesturing for her to move forward.

Keeping her gaze split between the camera and the mounds of debris coating the floor, Cass picked her way farther into the room. "While the physical prospects seem almost perfect—an enormous six-story building, the top five floors of which could be dedicated to dormitory-style housing, numerous outbuildings for classrooms, some not only suitable but already designed as labs, and a full commercial-grade kitchen, complete with cafeteria—critics argue the property holds too much pain and anguish to be repurposed as a school. That's what I'm here to determine."

Bee held his hand out in a stop gesture.

She paused at the foot of the stairs and looked straight into the camera. "To prove one way or the other if the spirits will cooperate with putting the buildings and grounds to a better use."

She'd phrased it that way purposely, alerting whatever ghosts might be lingering to her purpose, letting them know her presence was benign. She meant them no harm and was there with the sole purpose of hearing their pleas and respecting their wishes.

"Okay, hold up now." Bee paused the camera and set it aside on the pile of boxes still sitting on the dolly, since there wasn't a clean spot to put anything down on. He lifted the digital thermometer and pushed a button, then frowned.

"What's wrong?"

He tapped the button a few times. "It doesn't seem to be working."

"It was working fine at the Madison Estate yesterday." Not that it had helped in any way.

He frowned. "Yeah, well, it's not now. It's stuck on zero and won't go up or down."

Ice-cold tendrils of fear crept up Cass's spine. Her breath fogged when she exhaled. "It's working fine, Bee. Get the camera."

"Huh?" He glanced up, preoccupied at first, until he caught sight of her expression. He nodded and set the thermometer aside, then grabbed the camera.

A sense of urgency filled Cass, despite the shields she kept solidly erected around her mind.

"What's happening, Cass, can you tell us?" Bee prodded.

The statement was meant to serve as a gentle reminder that her audience wasn't privy to her internal thoughts or conflicts, but it didn't matter. She couldn't make sense of what was happening unless she dropped her shields, which she was loathe to do.

"I don't know . . . I . . ."

"Well, you're not going to get anything with your shields up."

While she couldn't argue with that, though she was surprised Bee realized it, she was still reluctant to open herself up to whatever might exist in this place. "I'm not sure that's such—"

A white haze erupted from everywhere around her at once, filling the room, cutting off her view of Bee. Her mind begged to drop the shield, even as her gut insisted it remain intact.

"Cass?" A tremor shook Bee's voice. "What's happening?"

"I don't know. Something . . . Can you see the fog?"

"How could I not? It's filling everything. At first, I thought it was powder, like if the wind blew through the room and tossed the concrete dust from the floor into the air, but it's not thick to breathe."

Cass inhaled, tentative at first, then more deeply. "No, it's not."

So, if not powder, what? Snow blown in through the broken windows? Maybe, but she didn't think so.

"So, now what?" To his credit, Bee hadn't fled screaming from the room. That was a plus.

"Just stay quiet a minute, and I'll see if I can figure out what's going on." She closed her eyes and lowered her shield, making sure the jolt of pain in her head wouldn't be repeated before settling more comfortably.

Soft sobbing drifted through her mind. Not in the present. At least, she didn't think it was. A woman, though she couldn't say what made her so certain. The sobs surrounded Cass, filling her with anguish and pain, though not the sharp pain from earlier. This was more of an emotional pain. She searched deeper, tried to reach out to the woman whose emotions had overtaken her own.

A loud pop from the back of the building somewhere shattered the connection, and the soft sobs vanished along with the fog.

Bee's gaze shot toward the sound, and he jerked the camera to the side. "What was that?"

"I don't know, but I think we'd better find out." She hurried toward the back, where a row of low windows, few boarded, most broken, lined the wall.

The sprinkle Bee had predicted had grown into a full-blown raging storm. Wind whipped across a field at the back of the grounds, painting the world in a fog not unlike the one that had filled the building only moments ago. Through the snow, she spotted a dark figure.

She yanked out her phone and focused the video camera on the fleeing figure.

A person, in dark clothing, fled toward the woods. She tried to enlarge the image, but it was no use; the swirling snow interfered with the focus, though it did seem the figure was carrying something in its right hand. As the man or woman—there was no way to tell from the back with all the thick black clothing it was wearing—disappeared into the woods at the far back of the property, Cass gave up. She scanned the area. The camera caught on a pile of something gray and black. Rocks? Cass zoomed in. No. A person lay crumpled in a heap in the snow.

Cass sucked in a breath and shoved her phone back into her pocket as she started to search for a back door.

"What are you doing?" Bee yelled

"There's someone out there lying in the snow." There was no door she could find quickly, but she wasn't about to leave someone laying in the storm.

"Hurt?" Bee set the camera aside and pulled out his phone.

"I don't know, but I have to find out."

"Of course you do." He rolled his eyes and dialed.

She started to climb onto one of the crumbling window ledges, the glass panes long gone. "Someone might be hurt, Bee."

"I know. Come on." He grabbed her arm and yanked her toward a door he had spotted as he relayed their location and what had happened to the nine-one-one operator.

Cass shivered as she ran outside, though it was considerably warmer out there than it had been inside. As soon as she'd tended to whomever was injured and spoken to the police, she'd contact Elijah and inform him her decision was made. No way should this place be opened and used to house children. Or anyone else. Ever . . .

Chapter Five

Cass drank from the thermos of coffee her boyfriend, Detective Luke Morgan, handed her, then handed it back out the driver's side window to him. It was only lukewarm, but it would do until she could wrap her hands around a hot foam cup from the deli — if they ever let her leave the psychiatric center. She adjusted the car's vents to face her more fully, pulled her sleeves down over her hands, and held them open in front of the heaters, allowing the warm air to race up her arms. It did nothing to relieve the chill. Or the guilt.

"Can we leave yet?" Bee was perilously close to whining, and if it was anyone other than Luke and Tank keeping them there, she had no doubt he would have. Not that she could blame him. He leaned forward to look past her at Luke. "We've already answered your questions, all of them, several times. No, we didn't see Elijah Anderson when we arrived. No, we didn't see whomever killed him, unless it was the dark figure running toward the woods, then we only saw him, or her, I suppose, from the back through a whirlwind of snow. Yes, Elijah was already dead when we reached him. Yes, Cass tried to revive him. And no, she wasn't successful, unfortunately, or we'd all be somewhere warm right now. Including poor Mr. Anderson."

The sun had already begun to set, and trucks carrying huge floodlights had just arrived. The phone Cass had used while filming someone running from the scene of the crime had been confiscated by the police. Bee was understandably cranky.

Cass's stomach growled, and she covered it with her hand as if that would block the sound.

Luke lifted a brow.

"Sorry . . ." She offered a half smile, the best she could do under the circumstances. "I haven't eaten all day."

"Join the club," Bee muttered.

"Don't worry about it." Luke smiled back, and her heart warmed just a little. Fat white snowflakes clung to his shaggy dark hair and the thick lashes framing eyes as deep and blue as any ocean. "I'll get you out of here in a few minutes. I'm just waiting for Tank to give the go-ahead."

Bee sighed and flopped back against the seat but didn't say anything else.

"Did you find any clues to who might have killed Elijah?" Since she'd seen the bullet hole in his chest herself, had even tried to stem the flow of blood, she didn't need to ask what had killed him.

He looked up into the worsening storm, glanced over his shoulder at the lights being unloaded several feet away, and turned his attention back to Cass. "Even though the snow remained fairly light all day, it was consistent enough to accumulate. It'll take time to go through everything. They were able to follow a trail of snow-covered footprints into the woods where you saw someone take off, so maybe something'll come from that."

Luke's radio sounded and he stepped away from the window.

Bee turned his head to look at Cass without lifting it from the seat back. "I'm sorry."

"For what?"

"For being a class-A . . . well . . ." He grinned. "You know."

"You're not being anything, Bee, just tired."

"And upset. You know how I am about death."

She did know, and her heart ached for him. Bee was one of the most sensitive people she knew. He had a difficult time dealing with death, or anything unpleasant really.

"Okay, not that I want to, but I have to ask, since Luke and Tank didn't." He squeezed his eyes closed without looking away. "Did Elijah speak to you? You know . . . after . . . ?"

"No. Nothing." She shifted one hand away from the heater and took his ice-cold hand in hers.

"Oh, that feels good." A tentative smile formed on his lips, the first since they'd found Elijah. "You'd think those two would know to ask that by now."

"You'd think." She didn't dare tell him she'd had to slam up her shields a moment or two before they'd reached Elijah, unable to repel the barrage of emotions battering her as she ran across the field — fear, sadness, elation, anticipation. In those moments just before she reached him, she'd already known what she would find.

"All right." Luke leaned into the open car window, startling Cass.

She jumped.

He kissed her cheek. "Sorry. Didn't mean to startle you. You guys can get out of here for now. We know where to find you if we need anything else."

"Yeah, at the diner, drowning my sorrows in roast beef and gravy followed by a nice slab of chocolate cake." Bee looked pointedly at Cass.

She didn't expect anything less. Everyone knew Bee was a stress eater. Plus, the diner was the only place to get gossip on a Sunday evening in the dead of winter. "I just have to stop home and take care of Beast first. He hasn't been out all day."

"That's fine. Just be quick, and I'll bring him home a bacon cheeseburger afterward to make up for leaving him again."

Cass turned to face him. "You're coming home with me after?"

Bee simply shrugged, but his gaze darted to Luke and back.

She looked back at Luke. "What's the deal?"

"Bee's going to stay with you for tonight until we get a better idea of what happened here." Though he made the remark lightly, as if it were no big deal, the strain lines bracketing his mouth gave him away.

"I never mind Bee staying with me, he's always welcome, but why do I feel like you two aren't telling me something? Oh." The pieces fell into place without either of them having to say a word. She and Bee had been at a crime scene where someone had been brutally murdered. Whether or not they'd actually seen anything, or managed to catch anything on film, was irrelevant. They were still potential witnesses. Even with most of Bay Island's rumor mill shut down for the night, that word would spread like wildfire. And she and Bee could both be in danger. "Right."

Luke leaned close, his warm breath against her neck a stark contrast to the cold emanating from his face, and whispered, "Keep an eye on each other, and stay out of trouble."

The "keep an eye on each other" part was a no-brainer, it was the "stay out of trouble" they both knew was questionable at best. "You bet."

Cass watched him stuff his hands into his pockets and hunch his shoulders against the wind as he walked away, watched the increasingly heavy snow swallow him up, then rolled up her window. "It's starting to snow heavier, and the wind is really picking up. Are you sure you want to go to the diner, Bee?"

"Do you have anything in the house to cook?"

She ran a quick mental inventory. Since she rarely ate at home, she didn't keep much in the house in the way of groceries. She knew for sure she had American cheese, because Beast loved it, and she probably had eggs, though she'd have to check the expiration date. "I think I could make a cheese omelet. Maybe. Or a can of soup. I might even have some stale crackers."

Bee lifted a brow and shook his head, then took out his phone and scrolled through his contacts.

Cass focused her attention on the road. Snowflakes swirled in a dizzying array, reducing visibility to near zero. "Who are you calling? Stephanie?"

Since taking in Aiden, Stephanie had started doing actual weekly grocery shopping, with healthy foods and everything. But the last thing Cass wanted was to involve the two of them in this mess.

"Nah. I don't want to bring trouble to her and Aiden." He pressed a button and held the phone to his ear. "I'm calling in a take-out order to the diner. We have to pass there on the way home anyway, so we may as well pick something up on our way. Then we can stay with Beast once we get there, and he won't have to be left alone ag . . . uh, hey, Elaina, are you guys still open?"

"You caught us just in time." Elaina's voice broke up as she spoke, but Bee had the volume loud enough that Cass could still make out what she was saying over the spotty connection. "We're just getting ready to close down the kitchen and then the dining room as soon as everyone's done eating."

"Can I place a quick to-go order?"

"You bet. Go ahead."

Cass tuned out the conversation. Bee knew enough about what she liked to order her something she'd enjoy. Probably something with gravy and carbs given the day's events. At the moment, she really didn't care as long as she got something in her stomach to quell some of the burning.

With silence raging around her, Cass crept along the narrow winding road. The fact that trees bordered both sides made it easier to stay on the road, though whether she was in her lane remained questionable.

Fairly confident they were safe on the level street, as long as she didn't speed up, Cass allowed her thoughts to wander. She hadn't dared try to lower her shields at the psychiatric center, but now — "

"Stop the car," Bee said, pulling her from her thoughts.

She gently pumped the brakes until the car came to a stop on the empty road.

Bee climbed out and went around the front, then opened Cass's door and stood back. "Move over."

She did as he said, contorting herself to climb over the center console rather than brave the storm to walk around. "What's the problem, Bee?"

He got in and slammed the door, then shifted into gear. "If you're going to be trying that nonsense, I'm driving."

Her cheeks heated. He wasn't wrong. Her attention should be fully focused on driving, especially in such horrible conditions. "Sorry, Bee, you're right."

"Of course I am." He snorted and released his tight grip on the steering wheel to wave a hand. "Now, let me concentrate while you do whatever it is you need to do to try to find Elijah's killer."

"Fine." Bee was a better driver in this weather anyway. He actually enjoyed driving in the snow, as long as it wasn't his Trans-Am he was driving.

Leaning back in the seat, Cass closed her eyes and allowed her mind to drift. Bee was right. She shouldn't have even tried to lower her shields while driving. She should know better. She did know better. Her recklessness could have gotten them both killed.

Anger poured through her, simmering, boiling, erupting.

She jerked upright, and her eyes shot open.

Bee swerved but recovered. "What's wrong?"

"Nothing." She shook her head, unable to explain how she could actually feel someone else's emotions as if they were her own. She leaned back again and tried to relax. Wind howled around them. Tires crunched over ice and the layer of salt that had already been applied in hopes of lessening the accumulation on the roads.

Soft sobs intruded. Elijah? No. A woman. She couldn't say how she knew, but she did. The same woman she'd heard crying inside Twin Forks. Sadness filled her. A deep sadness she'd carried for a very long time.

Determination flowed through Cass, shoving aside the helplessness she'd felt at not being able to help Elijah, to save him, to warn him sufficiently he might be in danger. It nudged the guilt aside. She wiped the tears that had tracked down her cheeks.

She might not have been able to save Elijah, but she would do whatever she could to find out who killed him. And then, she'd figure out who this woman was and do what she could to ease whatever burden had brought such sadness through her life . . . and death.

Chapter Six

Cass held on to the diner's front door handle and stomped snow from her feet onto the salted walkway—for all the good it did amid the slushy mess—and pulled open the door.

Bee sat with the car idling at the curb so neither of them would have to cross the icy lot.

She stepped inside and the scent of homemade food, or as close as Cass usually got to homemade food, welcomed her. She smiled as she loosened her scarf and approached the hostess stand. "Hey, Elaina, how's it going?"

"Going okay, but I heard the roads are getting pretty bad." The young waitress, who also worked cleaning rooms at her uncle's hotel, called to the back for Cass's order. "Did you drive, or did Bee?"

"Bee did, thankfully, since everything's definitely starting to ice over." It was not unusual to have a nor'easter that couldn't figure out whether it wanted to snow or rain, so it continued to dump a slushy mess across the island.

"Well, I'm glad we're closing early then." She smiled at an elderly couple who approached the register, then rang them up and wished them a safe trip home before turning back to Cass. "I hate driving in this."

"Me too." Living in New York City for several years, she'd become used to relying on public transportation or walking and had gotten rusty at driving in the snow. Then, last winter, she'd slid off the road in a bad storm and had been reluctant to get behind the wheel during another ever since. If she was going to live on Bay Island year-round, though, she'd have to get used to it at some point, as Bee was wont to remind her. "Make sure you drive carefully."

"I will, and Raul offered to follow me home, so that'll make me more comfortable."

"That's good. He's a nice guy." The cook was a kind older man who'd make sure Elaina got inside safely before he left to make his own way home. Otherwise, Cass would have waited and had Bee see her home. "And a great cook."

She grinned. "That's for sure."

Another customer approached the counter to pay his bill, and Cass stepped aside. Only a few cakes remained in the usually overflowing display case—apparently snowstorms made people take home dessert. She chose a chocolate cake she knew Bee would love and had Elaina add it to their order. Even though only a few customers remained, Cass waited out of the way by the door while Elaina boxed up the cake and went through the bag to be sure everything was there.

The front door opened, and cold wind whipped in and stole her breath.

Emmett, his cheeks red from the cold, took off his hat and shook it out the door before entering. "Oh, hey, Cass. What are you doing out so late?"

"Just on my way home now. How about you?"

"Plowing out all the people who got caught up in the storm unexpectedly, since we were only supposed to get a dusting."

"Instead, we got this snowy, slushy mess."

Emmett, a man of few words, just shrugged. "Oh, hey, sorry about that trouble this afternoon. Terrible thing that."

Caught off guard, Cass didn't know how to respond. He couldn't possibly be talking about her finding Elijah at Twin Forks. How would he have found out so quickly?

"Oh, yeah . . ." Elaina held out the bag to Cass. "I heard about that. How are you holding up?"

"Uh . . . I'm doing okay, just sorry I couldn't save him." Jeez, Louise, did everyone on Bay Island already know? She took the bag. "How much do I owe you?"

"Don't worry about it. Bee already took care of it when he placed the order, and the cake's on the house." She caught her bottom lip between her teeth, and her gaze skipped past Cass to Emmett and back.

Cass looked over her shoulder.

Emmett's cheeks had reddened even more. From the cold? She'd have thought so if he didn't lower his head and take a sudden interest in his boots to avoid eye contact with Cass.

She turned back to Elaina. Something was definitely up, and her gut told her she wasn't going to like it. "Okay, whatever it is, just say it quick and get it over with."

"Well." Elaina looked around the mostly empty diner and moved closer to Cass. "Rumor has it that Thea Newburgh warned you something was going to happen, that you shouldn't mess with the old psychiatric center."

"You have got to be kidding me." Cass resisted an eye roll; even with only a few diners present, Bay Island's rumor mill was apparently not slowed by the weather, and she didn't want to add any fuel to the fire. She turned to face Emmett. "You were there, Emmett, she didn't say anything about Twin Forks, just some random vague comment about the dead being better left dead, or something like that."

"That's how I remember it, and I'll say so to anyone who says different . . ."

"But?"

He shrugged. "Ain't nobody listening to me when Thea's carryin' on all over how she tried to stop you, and how Elijah Anderson won't be the only one to die now that you opened up a bridge to the past."

Great! This is not what she needed tonight. And on top of everything, if she didn't get moving, their food was going to be cold before they got home. Still, rumors like that had the potential to destroy the reputation she'd worked so hard to build, so she had to at least try to stop them. And if that didn't work, she'd just have to send Bee out in the morning to hit all his favorite gossip hot spots and set the record straight. "Look, Elaina, I'm telling you, she never said anything about any of this."

"Yeah, well, in the midst of an unexpected winter storm that has people running into all the local stores in their rush to get home, and then trapped inside with their cell phones and social media once they do get there, what's more appealing to talk about, the fact that Thea didn't say anything like that, or the fact that she bested you, and you didn't heed her warning, and now a man is dead?" Since Elaina was a good friend, Cass appreciated the straightforward honesty. Besides, how could she argue with the truth?

A man pulled the front door open, bringing a rush of cold and flurries.

Hmm . . . seemed the storm had flip-flopped back to snow again. Time to get going.

"Sorry to bother you," the man who'd just entered said, "but does anyone know who that plow out front belongs to?" If his slacks, soaked nearly to the knees, dress shoes, and suit jacket were any indication, he was one of the many caught unprepared by the storm.

"That'd be me." Emmett offered a hand.

"I'm Cam Parker." The man took Emmett's proffered hand and pumped eagerly, then slicked his short salt-and-pepper hair back, sending drops of water cascading down his neck and face. "Oh, man, am I glad to meet you. Any chance I can hire you for an hour or two to get me to the other side of the island? I tried to get out there, but I'm sliding all over the place, and I'm not familiar with the roads."

"Sure." Emmett shrugged. "Where do you need to go?"

"I have to get out to Twin Forks Psychiatric Center." He gestured toward the parking lot. "I could leave my car here, if you'll drive me out there, wait a few minutes, and bring me back?"

"All right." Emmett slapped his cap back on his head and started for the door. "See ya later, Cass."

Just like Emmett to have no curiosity at all about how someone dressed for business ended up on Bay Island in the middle of a snowstorm and needed to get someplace that has been abandoned for years but just so happened to host a murder that very day. And it wouldn't matter how many hours he spent in the cab of the truck with him, he still wouldn't know anything more. Unless Mr. Parker happened to be chatty, then Emmett might pick up something. But probably not.

Cam held the door open and started out behind Emmett.

"Are you part of the investigation?" The words shot straight through Cass's head and out her mouth before she had a chance to censor them.

Cam Parker stopped in his slushy tracks, turned to her, and frowned, deepening the creases around his eyes. "Investigation?"

Oops.

He held up a finger for Emmett to wait and let the door drop closed. "What do you mean? What investigation?"

Oh, well, the cat was already out of the bag. Besides, with the rumor mill up and churning at an alarming pace, he'd be able to find out that much at any business he walked into. "A man was murdered out there earlier today."

His gold eyes narrowed, and for just an instant Cass was reminded of a snake. "Who was killed?"

She wasn't sure what reaction she'd expected, but the cold, calculating stare currently leveled at her was not it. "Elijah Anderson was killed there today."

He continued to stare.

"He was found on the grounds." No need to mention she'd been the one to find him. Cass squirmed beneath his steady gaze.

"Okay." He turned to Emmett. "Thanks for the offer, but I have to make some calls."

Emmett shrugged.

Cam Parker stormed out without another word to anyone.

"Hmmm . . ." Emmett scratched his head as he watched him go. "Weird."

"You're not kidding." She wouldn't dare voice her opinion in the diner, despite the lack of customers. She knew too well the walls themselves had ears.

A horn honked out front.

"Sorry, I'd better run." *And thank Bee for the excuse to escape.* "Seems Bee is getting impatient."

"Drive carefully." Elaina held the door for Cass and waved to Bee.

"You too." Ducking her head to keep the ice pellets from hitting her face, Cass hurried down the steps, stuck the bag of food in the backseat, and hopped into the passenger seat.

"About time. That other guy went in way after you, and he's out already." Bee hooked a thumb over his shoulder, then looked into his rearview mirror and started to pull away. "What took you so long?"

Cass turned to look out the back window in the direction Bee had indicated. Though Bee had kept his windows clear while he waited, Cam Parker's windows had fogged over while he'd been in the diner. Through the one small space he'd cleared on the driver's side of the windshield she could see him with a phone pressed against his ear. If not for how bad the roads were, she'd have told Bee to wait and follow him, just to see if he tried to get out to Twin

Forks after all. As it was, she just wanted to get home.

Plus, she'd left Beast alone most of the day, and it wasn't fair to him. He needed to eat, and he needed to go out. Not to mention he'd once chewed apart half the living room in less time than she'd left him alone today.

"Earth to Cass." Bee chanced a quick glance in her direction, then returned his full attention to the road as he pulled out of the lot.

"Oh, sorry, Bee." She loosened her scarf. Sitting idle had warmed the car to the point of being uncomfortable. "Do you want the bad news or the weird news first?"

"May as well start with the bad, and if the weird has any woo-woo involved, you can just keep it to yourself." He shifted in the seat, sitting up straighter as he navigated the slushy roads.

Cass squinted. The headlights reflected off the icy drops in a dazzling array, creating the illusion of flying through space. "This slush seems harder to drive in than snow."

"But better than driving on ice."

"True enough." Either way, she was glad Bee was behind the wheel. "Anyway, bad news is, word has already spread that we found a body out at Twin Forks."

He shrugged it off. "You had to figure that was coming."

"I guess, but I didn't figure word of Thea's warning at the group reading about leaving the dead alone would spread just as quickly. Nor did I figure it would be construed as a warning that someone would be killed at the psychiatric center if I did as Elijah asked." Because that was not at all what Thea had said.

"Ah, man. Seriously?"

"Yeah." She slumped in the seat and sulked. While the guilt she felt for not warning Elijah he could be in danger weighed heavily, she bore no responsibility for ignoring such a vague warning from a stranger, especially when it had come before Elijah had asked her to work for him. How could she have known what Thea meant? Although, the thought did occur before she'd gone in. Still . . .

"It's not your fault, Cass." As usual, Bee could sense her thoughts.

"I know that." Mostly.

He pinned her with a quick stare and lifted a brow.

That brought a small smile. "In my head, at least. I just wish I would have warned him he could be in danger."

"You can't save everyone, Cass, no matter how much you'd like to." He lay a warm hand over hers. "If you'd have thought he was in danger going to the psychiatric center, or if you'd have thought warning him would save him, you would have."

"I suppose." She turned her hand over and gripped his for a moment. "Thank you, Bee. You always know just what I need."

"Of course I do, dear."

"And you know what I need right now?"

"What?"

She let go of his hand. "For you to put your hand back on that wheel. You're scaring me to death."

He laughed but returned his hand to the wheel. "Just because you're scared to drive in this doesn't mean everyone is."

She lay her head back against the seat. The scent of roast beef and gravy wafted to her from the backseat, and her stomach growled.

"So, that's what people are saying? That Thea warned you? Is that the weird part you were talking about?" Bee eased onto the brakes well before the intersection.

Gray slush was piled along both sides of Main Street where the plows had gone through. Store lights reflected from drops of rain and ice clinging to the windshield, even with the wipers going full force.

"Actually, no." She sat up straighter, interested in Bee's take on Cam Parker. "The man that came out of the diner before me; his name was Cam Parker. He went in because he saw Emmett's plow out front and wanted to know if he'd drive him out to Twin Forks."

"For what?" He came to a full stop before the intersection, then crept forward an inch at a time.

"That's just it, he didn't say. Just said he had to go out there, but his car kept sliding off the roads. Then, when I asked him if he was one of the investigators, he didn't know what I was talking about."

The light turned green, and Bee looked both ways before slowly accelerating. "He didn't know Elijah had been killed?"

"He didn't seem to, and yet . . ." Something about his behavior had seemed off, too calculated. "Something didn't seem right. His pants were soaked up to his knees, kind of high for just having walked across the lot from his car."

"Yeah, but you don't know where his car was parked before he got to the diner, could be he had to wade through a mess to get to it."

"Maybe." After all, he had been dressed as if headed to a business meeting, not as if he'd intended to wade through snow and slush at the psychiatric center. Then again, the storm had been unexpected. Maybe he was supposed to meet with Elijah. Had they met?

"What else did he say?" Bee asked, pulling her from her thoughts.

"Nothing, really. Once I told him there'd been a murder out there, he thanked Emmett and told him never mind, he had phone calls to make." She hadn't mentioned anything in the diner, but if she asked Bee not to say anything, no matter how much he loved gossiping, he'd keep his mouth shut. She didn't want to risk damaging a perfectly fine man's reputation with conjecture based on nothing but a gut feeling.

"But?" Bee hit the signal and turned onto her road. "What aren't you saying?"

"I don't know exactly, he just struck me as off. Somehow not genuine, you know what I mean?" She studied Bee's profile, searching for his reaction.

"So . . . what are you thinking?"

"Well, just between us, what if he just showed up in the diner so people would say they'd seen him and he wasn't able to make the drive across the island because of the roads?" If he had already met with Elijah, had killed him even, what better way to throw someone off his trail?

"You think he was looking for witnesses? Creating an alibi?"

"I don't know." Did she? She wasn't sure. "Maybe."

He pulled into the driveway and shifted into Park but made no move to get out. "It does make sense, I guess. Especially if he's a stranger in town and doesn't know anyone who could vouch for him."

"Maybe he saw people in the diner and decided to stop. You didn't happen to see which way he was coming from when he pulled into the lot, did you?"

"No, sorry, I wasn't paying attention. But it can't hurt to mention it to Luke and Tank when you see them."

"If I see them." Since Luke had confiscated her cell phone to use the video she'd recorded of the fleeing figure as evidence, he couldn't contact her until she got home.

"You will." Bee waggled his eyebrows, like two fat black caterpillars jumping rope beneath his bleached blond bangs. "Luke called while you were in the diner, said he'd stop by later. Just to check up on us."

With that came the reminder that a killer could be after her. That brought another thought. Had Cam Parker been looking for her? Could he have followed her and Bee from Twin Forks to the diner? She glanced in the rearview mirror, searching the road behind them to see if anyone had followed them.

Chapter Seven

Cass hurried as fast as she could up the back walkway, shuffling along to keep her feet from sliding out from under her. As much as she wanted to get in to Beast, it would just take longer if she took a spill on her way in. As soon as she could reach, she gripped the railing with both hands and hoisted herself up the three steps to the back deck, then propelled herself across the slick surface and grabbed the doorknob.

Even as she inserted the key, she peeked between the slats of the blinds to see what Beast had gotten into while she was gone.

"Well?" Bee asked, leaning over her shoulder to get a glimpse inside.

"Good news is, I can't see any damage." She straightened and turned the key in the lock.

He took a step back. "And the bad news?"

"I can't see Beast either." She shoved the door open, spilling slush that had accumulated against the door onto the tile floor, and stepped inside.

With that, over a hundred pounds of excited-to-see-her tan and black fur barreled through the doorway from the living room, skidded around the kitchen table, and made a beeline straight for her.

"Beast, no!" Cass held her hands out in front of her and planted her feet, hoping to brace herself for the impact against her chest. Despite numerous tries at training, Cass never could curb his enthusiasm upon her return home. "Stop!"

Beast's paws hit the slick tile and slid from under him. He scrambled to regain his footing but ended up on his back end just as his body crashed into her legs and knocked her feet out from under her.

With no way to regain her balance and nothing to grab on to, Cass belly-flopped flat onto the wet floor and just lay there, stunned, heaving in deep breaths of the damp air.

Bee bent over her. The least he could do was pretend not to laugh at her, but he didn't even bother. "Are you all right?"

Was she? She took inventory. Since she'd managed to get her hands beneath her just in time to keep her chin from smacking the floor, she counted herself lucky and sat up. "Is Beast okay?"

"He's fine, quite contrite, actually." He gained a few points by holding out a hand to help her up, and a few more because he'd already made sure Beast wasn't hurt. "I don't know, Cass, two spills in one day. What are you trying to do, break a record?"

She chose to ignore him.

Beast sat in the doorway, head down, peering at her from big brown eyes amid a black mask.

"It's okay, boy." She grabbed Bee's hand to steady herself and let him help her up, then held out a hand to pet Beast's head. "It's not your fault, sweetie."

"You're right." Bee gave her a pointed glance. "It's not his fault. The fault lies with she who didn't train him properly."

It wasn't for lack of trying on her part. She'd never owned a puppy, or any pet, before Beast, and she had no clue what she was doing. After a rough start, she'd gone to Herb Cox, who she now had on speed dial, for training, and Beast listened well to him. And to Bee.

Cass just had a hard time putting her foot down and creating boundaries, but he was an angel when she took him to Mystical Musings every day, properly greeting customers who showed an interest in him and leaving those who didn't alone. So he was definitely smart and capable of learning. She just didn't have the heart to stop him from greeting her so enthusiastically. What she lacked as a trainer she more than made up for in loving and adoring him. And as long as she didn't leave him alone long enough to get bored, things were fine.

But a lecture about her failures as a pet owner was the last thing she needed right now, so she did what any self-respecting coward would do: she brushed herself off and changed the subject. "Anyway . . ."

"Mm-hmm . . ."

"Why don't you set the food out while I take care of Beast?" She ran the water and picked up Beast's bowl. Her hands stung, though whether from the cold or smacking the floor she had no idea.

Beast trotted up beside her, head high.

Since Bee spent so much time with Cass, he knew just where she kept everything and started to set the table. "Diet Pepsi?"

"That's fine, thanks." After filling Beast's water bowl, she scooped one cup of food into his bowl. He'd usually eat two, but Bee had ordered him a bacon cheeseburger, which she knew from Elaina going over the order with her, unless Bee was eating a hot open roast beef sandwich and a bacon cheeseburger—not that the possibility was out of the question. Bee might have a firmer hand while training, but he was a big softie when it came to treats.

The house phone rang, and she answered it while Beast ate. "Hey, Luke, what's going on?"

"Not much, unfortunately, considering we're knee-deep in a murder investigation." His smooth Southern drawl seeped in and eased some of the tension from her muscles.

"You didn't find anything?" she asked.

"Not really. The tracks we were able to follow through the woods ended at a dirt road where someone had a vehicle waiting, so that was a dead end. For now at least."

"Bee said you're going to stop by? Do you want something to eat?" Not that she had much in the house, but she could split her roast beef with him.

"Nah, thanks. Someone brought out some sandwiches earlier, but I'm not going to make it tonight. Tank and I have to go in to fill out some paperwork and speak to Chief Rawlins." He hesitated, only for a moment, but long enough for her to know she wouldn't like what was coming. "She'll want to speak with you."

"Tonight?" She couldn't help the squeal. No way was she going back out on those roads.

Luke laughed. "No, not tonight. But in the morning on your way to Mystical Musings if you can swing it."

Could she? Probably. But did she want to? Chief Rawlins had come from a parish in New Orleans where psychics were often turned to, and she was a firm believer in Cass's abilities. But she was a tough taskmaster and expected Cass to have answers even when she didn't.

True? Maybe. Or maybe a bit harsh. If she were honest with herself, Cass would admit Rawlins had a lot more faith in her than Cass had in herself. And she pushed until Cass worked to her full potential. "Fine, I'll stop by on my way in. Is it going to take long? Should I leave Beast home and come back for him?"

"Yeah, probably."

"Ugh . . ." Cass groaned. Not pretty, but there you have it.

"If I can get done early tomorrow, maybe I'll come by and make it up to you."

Hmm . . . now that sounded promising. "And how do you propose to do that?"

"I'll pick up some steaks and barbeque."

She opened the door for Beast and stepped out onto the back deck, careful to hold on to the railing. No sense going down again. "Throw in some dessert and stay for a movie, and you've got yourself a deal."

"It's a date. Now, make sure you lock up and Bee stays with you, and I'll see you in the morning."

"Sure thing. See ya then." Thankfully, Beast was quick about it, since she didn't like to leave him alone outside after he dug under the fence and escaped a few times. "Come on, boy."

He charged across the yard and up the steps to the deck, then danced back and forth while he waited for her to open the door.

She grabbed his collar to keep him from bolting into the house and hitting the slick floor. Bee had spread a couple of towels over the puddle left from her earlier spill and left another hanging over the basket where she often tossed her mail, which she used to dry Beast off. "Thanks, Bee."

He sat at the kitchen table hunched over her laptop, the food still in the bag from the diner. "Uh-huh."

"Is everything all right?" It wasn't like Bee to set food aside for anything, especially when he hadn't eaten all day.

He frowned and scratched his head. "I'm not sure."

Leaving her shoes on one of the towels by the door, she rounded the table and leaned over his shoulder. A still shot of the inside of the psychiatric center was up on the screen. It crept forward one frame at a time. "What is that?"

"I uploaded the footage from earlier at Twin Forks."

She leaned closer to the screen. "Luke and Tank didn't take it?"

"Nah. You had the video of whoever was running from the crime scene, but there was nothing on my camera worth showing them." He scratched his head. "At least I didn't think there was."

"And now?"

He hit a button and the video paused. He pointed to the time stamp in the bottom right corner. "Here. This is when all that creepy fog started rolling in."

He resumed the video, letting it play at normal speed for a moment then stopping it again.

"I don't see any fog."

"Exactly. Because it's not there." He rewound the video and played it again.

"Well, maybe it was at a different point in the video." Not too concerned, she left him to his viewing and grabbed a couple of paper plates. They'd have to throw the food in the microwave at this point.

He was already shaking his head. "I looked at the time when it started, and it's not here. I've gone a full minute past it, and nothing."

"So let it play a little longer." She didn't know what time the haze had started to fill the room, but if she remembered correctly, the sobbing had begun around the same time. "Do you have the volume turned up?"

"Yup, why?"

"Because right around the time the fog showed up, I remember hearing a woman's sobs."

He looked up and lifted a brow. "Define woman."

"Well, at the time, I would have thought the sobs were . . . uh . . . in my mind." That was the best she could do to sugarcoat it for him.

"And now?"

"I don't know." She transferred food from foam containers to paper plates. "But being that we found Elijah a few minutes later . . . What if the sobs were real?"

Bee set the computer aside but left it playing on slow motion, then opened his soda. "I didn't hear anything."

The thought that someone could have really been crying and Cass had ignored the sobs sat like a weight on her chest.

"Seriously, Cass. I didn't hear anything, and I think I would have. It was pretty quiet out there, and I was . . . well . . ." He shrugged, red creeping into his cheeks. "I was paying attention, in case, you know, I had to make a hasty retreat."

Cass laughed. She couldn't help it; Bee made her happy, just by being him. She set his plate in front of him and put hers into the microwave.

Bee unwrapped Beast's bacon cheeseburger. "Sit."

Beast plopped down instantly.

With a satisfied smirk at Cass, Bee gave Beast his treat.

"Smart aleck."

He shrugged. "And?"

"Just making sure you know."

"Of course I do." He shook salt and pepper onto his roast beef and mashed potatoes. "What did Luke have to say?"

"He's not stopping by tonight, and he said you are to stay with me and keep the doors locked. Other than that, nothing of interest."

Bee paused, fork halfway to his mouth. "Honey, with that drawl of his that man could keep me riveted just reciting a shopping list."

She couldn't argue with that. "I meant they didn't find anything."

"So he says." He took a bite and moaned. "Mmm . . ."

"That good?" After grabbing her plate from the microwave, Cass sat across from him at the table. The aroma drifted up to her as she added salt and pepper, and her mouth watered. Not only was she starving, the food smelled amazing.

He swallowed and filled his fork again. "Better. Plus, I'm starved, so . . . huh—"

"Bee?"

His fork clattered to the plate, and his eyes practically bulged out of his head. He nudged his plate aside and pulled the computer closer, then hit a couple of keys and frowned at the screen.

"Is something wrong?"

When he finally looked up at her, after his fingers flew over the keys a few more times, his face had gone pale.

"Are you okay?" Abandoning her dinner, she got up and went to stand behind him so she could see over his shoulder to whatever had him so worked up.

The video moved forward again, and he pointed to the screen. "Watch right here."

"What am I looking for?"

He played the video one frame at a time. "Don't worry, you'll know it when you see it."

Even with the volume turned off, Cass knew exactly where in

the video they were. A shot of her standing in the middle of the room as she finished her intro then frowned, her eyebrows drawing together. That was the instant she'd heard the sobs. She kept her gaze on the spot he'd pointed out on the screen. He enlarged the section a bit, pushing her more to the side and drawing her focus to the row of windows along the back wall. Her eyes widened on the screen, and she whipped her head toward the back windows, reacting to the pop she distinctly remembered shattering the illusion of the fog, only in the video, the room was perfectly clear, offering a direct view out the window into the storm.

Through the swirling snow, which wasn't as thick on the video as she remembered it, a black figure—Elijah?—fell to the ground. An instant later, three figures came into view. One of them trudged to Elijah and looked down. The other two kept their distance as they waved him toward them, then turned and fled into the woods. After leaning over Elijah for another moment, the black-clad figure took off into the woods after his, or her, companions, what appeared to be a long coat flapping in the wind.

Bee flopped against his chair back. "Do you think they killed him?"

"Either that, or they just happened to be hanging out in the woods when Elijah got shot and ran out to see."

Bee just lifted a brow and replayed the scene. "What would they have been doing hanging around the woods in a snowstorm?"

"Who knows? But it's not impossible. Maybe they were homeless and waiting for us to get out of there so they could get in out of the storm."

Bee chewed the inside of his cheek as he considered. "Possible, I suppose, but those snowsuits and boots they're wearing, even from a distance and through the falling snow, don't scream *I've been sleeping in the woods or an abandoned psychiatric center.*"

She watched the replay several more times, paying close attention to each figure. Fear. She could tell that much from the frantic gesturing from the two trying to flee the scene. But of what? A killer they'd just witnessed commit murder? Or fear of getting caught for a murder they'd just committed? Was the lone figure checking to see if Elijah could be saved—and Cass had been able to tell instantly he couldn't be—or making sure he'd finished the job?

Bee swallowed hard, his Adam's apple bobbing with the effort. "Looks like you're going to be seeing Luke tonight after all."

Chapter Eight

As expected, Luke had dropped by the night before and taken a look at the video, and then promptly confiscated Bee's video camera.

So, now, equally as expected, Bee sat across the table from Cass at the diner, sulking over his meat lover's omelet and home fries. He bit into his rye toast, then dropped the rest of the piece onto his plate.

"He said he'll get it back to you as soon as possible." Cass took a bite of her western skillet and chewed slowly, savoring the flavor. On a brighter note, Chief Rawlins had been forced to postpone their meeting due to unforeseen circumstances, which Cass wished she'd known the night before so she'd have slept better.

"I know, but I can't do anything without my camera." He pushed his food around the plate without taking another bite. "I wanted to edit the video this morning."

"Look at the bright side. At least you still have your phone." She'd already reached into her jacket pocket at least three times this morning looking for hers. Hopefully, they'd get what they needed off it and return it before too long. As it was, she hadn't even checked her messages at the shop this morning.

Bee seemed to consider that for a moment, then took a bite of his omelet.

Besides, he wasn't going to be editing the video this morning anyway, at least not until Cass got permission from Evelyn to use the footage they'd taken. After she returned the check Elijah had written. No way could she keep that money now. But she'd break that news to Bee later, when he was in a better mood.

At least he'd started eating. When he finally lifted his gaze from his plate and glanced past her shoulder, the smile that brightened his big brown eyes and lit up his entire face could only mean one thing.

Cass turned in her seat and grinned. "Hey, there."

Bee jumped to his feet and held open his arms to take Aiden from Stephanie, but he didn't reach for him. "Hey, little one. Want to come to Uncle Bee?"

The adorable four-year-old Stephanie and Tank were currently in the process of adopting stared at Bee for a moment, fully focused on his face.

Bee simply waited until Aiden checked things out and then, apparently deciding Bee was safe, reached for him and snuggled into his embrace. "There you go, baby."

Tears threatened, as they always did when she thought of this incredible child being treated poorly. But he was thriving with Stephanie and Tank, with all the love they, along with Cass and Bee, could shower on him.

Aiden lifted his head and grabbed both of Bee's cheeks, then smiled. "Bee Bee."

"You want to sit with Uncle Bee Bee?" Bee beamed. His relationship with Aiden was amazing, though not surprising, considering Bee was the most compassionate person Cass had ever met.

"Yay." Aiden flapped his arms. "Bee Bee."

Cass kissed Aiden hello, then switched hers and Stephanie's plates so Stephanie could slide into the booth ahead of her and sit across from Aiden. "We got you a western skillet and Aiden pancakes, but we can do something else if you want."

"Nope, that's perfect." Stephanie reached into her bag and pulled out Aiden's favorite purple cup.

Since Aiden liked to eat as soon as he arrived, Bee and Cass often went ahead and ordered so the food would arrive before he got there.

When Stephanie reached for his plate to cut up Aiden's pancakes, Bee waved her off. "No worries, you. Uncle Bee's got this; you go ahead and eat, chat with Cass, and relax for a bit."

Stephanie went straight for the coffee. "He slept two hours in a row last night, so I'm considering that an accomplishment."

Aiden smiled at Stephanie and rocked back and forth while he waited for Bee to put syrup on his pancakes and cut them into pieces.

Cass handed him a small plate with three strawberries from her fruit salad.

"Yay, Ca," he responded and dug in.

"He seems to be doing great. He's definitely put on a few pounds." Aiden had been painfully thin when they'd first gotten him. His shiny blonde hair, once dull and limp and hanging down his back, was still long, but once washed curls had sprung up along the ends.

"Two pounds, the doctor said." Stephanie started on her omelet, no doubt wanting to get some down before Aiden tired of Bee and wanted his Ma Ma.

"That's awesome, Steph. I'm so thrilled." Once the moment of sadness passed, the thought of anyone having hurt this amazing child still sent a surge of anger rushing through her, so she shoved the reminder away and decided to focus on the positive. If not for the past, he wouldn't be here with them now. And he had filled all of their lives with so much joy already, Cass could only view the whole situation as a blessing.

"So, anything new on Elijah?" Stephanie shifted her frizzy brown hair behind her shoulder so she could look at Cass while they talked.

"I haven't heard from Luke since he picked up Bee's camera last night. Have you heard from Tank?" Stephanie's husband, Tank, and Luke had been partners since Luke moved to Bay Island to be closer to Cass.

"No, not a thing." Stephanie sipped her coffee, then closed her eyes for a moment, then opened them and shook her head. "I don't think coffee's going to be enough today. I may need an infusion of caffeine."

Cass just laughed. No matter how tired Stephanie was, motherhood agreed with her. She was happier than Cass had ever seen her, and they'd been friends for a very long time.

"What did you decide to do about the vlog?" With a quick check on Aiden's progress, Stephanie set her coffee down and returned to her skillet.

Bee's ears perked up at the mention of her vlog. No matter how involved Bee was with something else, he had a natural radar when it came to gossip. "What's that now?"

"Oh, uh . . ." Stephanie's gaze shot to Cass and she mouthed *sorry*.

"Don't worry about it; I was getting ready to talk to him about it when you got here. I wanted to talk to you both at once so we can make a decision."

"A decision about what?" Bee asked.

"First, should I run the vlog at all, considering Elijah was killed, most likely during its filming. And two . . ." She swallowed hard to keep from choking on the words, then blew out a breath. "I have to give the money back to Evelyn."

Bee's eyes went wide. "What? Why?"

"Because she was already worried about finances, and with Elijah gone, well, I just wouldn't feel right about keeping it." Even if, technically, she had done what Elijah had hired her to do, determined that Twin Forks should never be repurposed as a school.

"If you hadn't done the job, I'd agree wholeheartedly, but you did do the job, at great risk to yourself, I might add." Bee pointed his fork at her, then dug into his omelet.

She couldn't argue that, and still. "What do you think, Stephanie?"

She sighed and smeared jelly on a toast triangle. "If I were you, I'd talk to the widow and ask her if she wants you to go back out there and continue investigating where you left off."

"Which I already know she won't." She'd made that perfectly clear when Elijah had hired her. She hadn't wanted him to spend the money in the first place, and if he'd listened, he might still be alive right now.

"Well, as far as I'm concerned, you did the job you were hired to do. It's haunted. End of story. Collect your paycheck and go home." Bee smiled down at Aiden then looked back up at Cass. "Oh, wait, you already collected your paycheck. All you have to do is deposit it."

A dull throb began at her temples.

"And for the record, I am not going back out there," he added.

"Well, right now it doesn't matter. Going back out there isn't even an option, since the police have everything closed down for the investigation." Not that it would matter, since all Cass had to do was ask, and Chief Rawlins would certainly grant her access to the crime scene. She'd even accompany Cass and, in her own way, try to push her toward an answer.

"Hey, Cass, Bee, Stephanie." Gina, who owned the bakery with her husband, Tony, leaned over and smiled. "Hello there, Aiden."

Aiden smiled around a mouthful of pancake and bounced in his seat, sending his curls springing up and down, but he didn't respond.

"If your Ma Ma has time later, you tell her to come on by the bakery so I can give you a cookie." Since Gina understood he most likely wouldn't answer, she returned her attention to Cass. "I was so sorry to hear about the trouble you ran into, Cass."

"Thank you." She had no doubt Gina and Tony had gotten an earful the minute they opened their doors at six this morning, but Cass had no intention of elaborating. Gina was a sweetheart, but she spent the majority of her day gossiping from behind the counter at Tony's. "Where's Tony? Working?"

"Nah." She gestured toward the front door. "He's parking the car. He dropped me off at the door so I wouldn't have to cross through all the puddles out there."

"It sure is a mess," Bee agreed. Most of what remained of the night's storm had melted the instant the sun came up.

"Ah, here he is." Gina waved to her husband. Apparently, she still wanted to chat. Hopefully, not about Elijah's murder, though Cass doubted anyone on Bay Island was talking about much else this morning, especially since the storm hadn't had any lasting effects.

Tony wiped his feet on the mat by the front door and joined them. "Good morning."

"Hi, Tony." Bee grinned. "Any chance you want to make up some cannoli balls this morning?"

Tony just laughed. No matter how hard Bee tried, Tony still only made cannoli balls on Sunday mornings.

Bee slid his empty plate aside. "One of these days you're going to surprise me and say yes."

"You can always hope," Tony said.

The hostess held up two menus to get Tony's attention and set them on the table next to theirs. At least they'd saved her from any further discussion about the check she was most definitely going to return.

"So, nasty business out at Twin Forks yesterday, huh?" Tony took his wife's coat and hung it on the hook beside the booth, then removed his own and hung it as well.

"Sure was." Cass knew from experience if she just agreed Tony would keep on going, with Gina jumping in every now and again to elaborate.

He slid into his booth and opened his menu, then frowned. "Funny thing, though, that's not the first murder out there."

With her interest suddenly piqued, Cass sat up straighter. "What do you mean?"

"Well, back about . . . I don't know . . ." He looked to Gina for help. "What, four or five years ago?"

Gina nodded confirmation. "About that."

"A groundskeeper turned up dead out there under unusual circumstances."

"Murdered?"

The waitress stopped to fill all of their coffee cups and take Tony and Gina's orders.

As soon as she walked away, Tony continued as if he'd never been interrupted. "They never did find whoever killed him."

"Was he shot?" Try as she might, she couldn't figure out what a groundskeeper getting killed four or five years ago could possibly have to do with Elijah's murder. Coincidence? It didn't seem likely.

"No, not shot." Tony frowned at the menu as if it held the answers he was searching for. "If I remember correctly, he was hit over the head or something like that."

"And they never found the murder weapon either," Gina added. "Or the killer."

"Unless, of course, he just took an unfortunate fall with no one around to help him." Tony was quiet for a moment while they all pondered the likelihood of that scenario, then snapped his fingers. "You know who would know more about it, if you're interested, is Liam McAlister."

"Who's that?" The fact that people sometimes forgot Cass had been gone for seventeen years after college before returning to Bay Island just last year always brought a smile. No matter how long she'd been gone, she was still accepted as a local. And that was one thing about locals, they talked about people as if everyone on Bay Island knew everyone else, which they mostly did. Especially those that had lived there most of their lives.

"Liam McAlister, heads up the historical society." Gina blew on her coffee and took a sip, then added a little more milk.

"You can always find him out there at his office by the lighthouse," Tony finished.

Cass had seen the sign out in front of the small building surrounded by a white split rail fence often enough, since it sat just down the hill from the Bay Island Lighthouse, but she'd never gone in.

"Trust me, he'd be more than happy to chat about it," Gina said. "There's nothing about Bay Island's history that man doesn't know."

"And he'll talk your ear off if you give him the time." Tony laughed, a deep rich sound that carried through the diner, drawing attention as the breakfast crowd grew.

Aiden looked up from where he was lining sugar packets in a perfectly aligned row.

Cass slid her mostly empty dish aside. "Are you guys ready to go?"

"Go, go, go." Aiden bounced with each word.

Cass grinned and stood so Stephanie could get up. "I guess someone's had enough."

Bee moved out of the way so she could clean Aiden up.

When Stephanie started to clean up the sugar, Aiden yelled, "No."

"Aiden, honey," Stephanie started.

Bee lay a hand over hers to keep her from putting any more away. "I'll take care of it. It's fine, right, Aiden?"

He popped his thumb into his mouth and rested his head against Stephanie.

Stephanie lifted him into her arms and held him close.

They had no idea what was on Aiden's mind, but it wasn't a matter of just not wanting to clean up after himself. He was actually quite good about putting his toys away after he played, always putting his things just so in the toy box Cass had in the back room of Mystical Musings for him. But sometimes he liked to line things up, sugar packets, toy cars, Beast's chew toys—much to his dismay—and he needed them left just so.

Cass gave Stephanie a quick hug and kissed Aiden's cheek. "Later you can come play with Beast if you want."

His pale blue eyes went wide with joy.

While Cass went to pay the check, Bee waited for Stephanie to leave, then cleaned up the packets. When he was done, he met Cass by the door and held it open for her.

"Thanks, Bee." She pulled her coat tighter around her to ward off the damp wind. "What are you doing now?"

He rolled his eyes. "Well, I *was* going home to bed, but I have a sneaking suspicion I'm headed out to the historical society to see Liam McAlister with you instead."

"Thanks, Bee." She hooked her arm through his, loving that they were so often on the same page. "You're the best."

"Yeah, well, don't you forget it."

"Never." And since he was the best, she'd wait until after they left the historical society to tell him she was going to have to go back out to Twin Forks.

Chapter Nine

Bee held the historical society's door open for Cass.

"Thank you." She preceded him into the main room of the small cottage near the base of the Bay Island Lighthouse.

A faint mildew odor hung in the air, along with the not unpleasant scent of old paper. Glass-topped cases ran along all four walls and an island in the center of the room, holding everything from collections of local insects, to plant life, to shells from a variety of sea creatures that made their homes in the waterways on and around Bay Island.

Two closed doors stood side by side at the far end of the room, but no one came through either.

"Hello?" Cass browsed the cases. One in particular caught her attention, fully documenting in minute detail the hurricane of 1938, which had destroyed much of eastern Long Island's south shore and had some lasting effects on Bay Island's coastline.

"What can I do for you?"

Cass whirled toward the man's voice.

He stood behind her, his graying hair sticking up in tufts around his head, glasses slipping halfway down his nose.

She had no idea how he had moved so quietly that neither she nor Bee had heard, or even sensed him, but one of the doors stood open, so she assumed that's where he came from and resisted the urge to reach out and pinch him to make sure he was real. "Mr. McAlister?"

"Liam, please." He shook her hand and then Bee's.

"It's a pleasure to meet you, Liam," Cass said.

"So, what can I help you with?" He pushed his glasses up his nose, and they promptly slid back down. "Are you looking for something in particular or just come to browse?"

"Tony and Gina from the bakery sent me to see you. They thought you might be able to help me."

A warm smile emerged. "They are the kindest couple."

"Yes, they are," Cass agreed.

"Please . . ." He gestured through the open door toward a small office at the back of the room. "Come sit, and I'll see what I can do for you."

Cass followed him into the room with Bee on her heels.

Liam lifted a stack of papers from one of the two chairs in front of the desk, then searched for somewhere to put them down amid the clutter that was a stark contrast to the meticulous organization of the showroom. "Hmm . . . seems I'm always in the process of organizing but never can quite get there."

Cass had once lived that way, but her divorce and the death of one of her patients had left her with an uncanny need for order. She needed everything in its place. Not that she'd ever examined the need too closely, but she was pretty sure it came from a time when everything else in her life was out of control and she had the burning need to control whatever she could. The state of disarray in Liam's office was enough to bring on a full-blown anxiety attack. At least, it would if the mess was her responsibility.

"Sit, please. Let me just put these in the storage closet, and I'll be right back." True to his word, he returned a moment later and took a seat behind the desk. He pulled his gray cardigan sweater, complete with brown suede elbow patches, tighter around his frail form.

From the corner of her eye, she noted Bee's smile, his inner designer obviously approving of Liam's fashion choices. The man was, for lack of a better word, adorable.

And, despite Cass's offended sense of order, she had to admit, the space suited his absentminded professor look to a T. "Thank you for taking the time to sit with us."

"Of course, dear. It always brightens my day to sit with a beautiful lady and her equally handsome companion." He leaned back in his chair, resting his elbows on the arms. "So, tell me, what brings you by on this dreary winter morning?"

Though she took an almost instant liking to Liam McAlister, she would have to walk a fine line between getting information from him and not revealing too much about what had happened. Even though she wanted to know more about the groundskeeper who was killed, she couldn't compromise an investigation by trading information. Tank and Luke could always come back if anything he shared proved relevant to their investigation. "I'm hoping you can tell me a bit about Twin Forks Psychiatric Center."

With a sigh, he took off his glasses and massaged the bridge of his nose. "You and everyone else, it seems. I really don't understand the sudden interest in a place that's been shut down for so many years."

If Elijah had done his research and asked around, which made sense if he was going to try to do business on Bay Island, and if Tony and Gina were right about Liam's knowledge of the old compound, it made sense someone would have directed Elijah to the historical society, but who else had sought his advice? "Do you mind if I ask who else inquired about Twin Forks lately?"

"Oh, you name it, they've been here." He waved a hand, cleaned his glasses, and put them back on. "In the past month, I've spoken to a man who wanted to turn the old place into a school, of all things, another who was interested in demolishing the entire compound and building condos on the property, and, get this, a woman who wants to turn the whole place into some kind of macabre museum of death, complete with displays of ancient torture devices once used in the name of science."

Bee shuddered so hard his chair shook.

Cass's mind raced. No doubt Elijah Anderson was the man who wanted to turn the building into a school, but who were the other two, and did either of them have anything to do with Elijah's murder?

"And then there's Thea Newburgh. Good old Thea, who contacts me at least once a day to remind me of the atrocities committed there, and to push her agenda that Twin Forks should not only never be sold or developed, but should instead be burned to the ground, lock, stock, and barrel. So . . ." He sat back with a sigh and folded his hands over his nearly concave stomach. "What's your angle?"

"Oh, uh . . ." It probably wouldn't hurt to tell him Elijah had hired her, especially if he already knew he was looking to use the property as a school. Besides, if Liam knew Tony and Gina, he'd know all the gossip before long anyway, if he didn't already. "Elijah Anderson hired me to try to find out if the property was haunted and if it would be safe to house children there."

"And?" He quirked a brow. "What did you find? Is the old place haunted?"

"Of course it is." She had no idea if he believed in ghosts, so she simply waited to gauge his reaction.

He nodded slowly. "Yes, I would imagine so, all things considered."

Now she'd given him a few tidbits, hopefully he'd be kind enough to share whatever he could, and then she could press him on the groundskeeper who'd died. "So, aside from Elijah, do you mind if I ask who else specifically has paid you a visit regarding Twin Forks?"

"Not at all." He sat up and shuffled through a stack of haphazardly piled papers on his desk, then came up with a torn scrap of printer paper and a napkin. "Ah, here we go. Aside from Mr. Anderson, whose tragic death I was very sorry to hear about, I had a visit from a Mr. Cameron Parker and Ms. Mercedes Dupont."

"They both came to see you recently?"

"Within the past month or so." He set the napkin aside and read from the scrap of paper. "Mr. Parker didn't seem at all interested in the history of the psychiatric center. As a matter of fact, when I tried to share a few tidbits I found interesting he shut me right down, said he didn't have time for that drivel."

"What did he want to know?"

"He asked about the previous owners and, more specifically, Mr. Anderson. Now, I had already spoken to Elijah and knew he was very set on opening a boarding school out there, and I said as much to Mr. Parker, but he dismissed me with a smirk and a wave of his hand."

No surprise, if he was the same arrogant man she'd witnessed in the diner.

"He said that was no place for a bunch of kids to be playing around."

Cass pretty much agreed, no matter how much she hated to agree with Cam Parker. That property was no place for children. The negative energy associated with the place would not be conducive to learning, and she couldn't see it as a place for sports, dances, parties, or any of the other joyful social events associated with kids attending school.

"Not that I didn't agree with him there, but he was very intent on demolishing the place and building condos. I ask you: do kids not live in condos? Because at the end of the day, I don't see the difference."

Bee shifted in his seat, leaning forward a bit, not very discreetly trying to get a glimpse of something on Liam's desk.

She willed him to sit back before Liam noticed too. "Why did Mr. Parker come to you for that information? It seems he could have simply googled that much and saved himself the trip."

"True, but he couldn't find out from an internet search who was going to oppose his proposition. Or who he might find to support his position."

"But he could find that out from you?"

"Yes indeed." He set the scrap of paper aside and held up the napkin, which was covered in sloppy abbreviated notes. "I can tell you exactly who would oppose developing that land. But first, let me tell you about Ms. Dubois."

"Is she the one who wanted to turn the property into a museum?" Cass asked.

"Not only a museum, she wanted to completely restore the place to its original plan. I don't know how much you know about the place . . ."

"I've actually studied it before," Cass admitted.

"So you know the complex originally housed the most severely ill patients, many of them criminally insane. Murders, or deaths at least, were a regular occurrence there."

"Rumor had it some of those deaths had to do with Plum Island." Though Cass had never really believed that. Plum Island, which was actually an animal disease research center, was the subject of more rumors and conspiracy theories than Cass could count.

He waved her off. "Nah, none of that was ever proven, probably just local lore to be honest. But still, it wasn't a good place, and they did a lot of terrible things there in the name of science, things Ms. Dubois wants to showcase and charge admission to share with the world."

Cass shivered. "Wants to?"

"Yup, heard from her just yesterday morning asking for my backing."

"Yesterday morning? You mean before Elijah was found murdered?"

He was already nodding. "And I had already told her the current owner was planning to develop the property, but she didn't care one iota. Said she planned to make him an offer he couldn't refuse."

A phone rang in the other room, and Liam stood and frowned. "Excuse me a moment, please, I never can remember where I left my darn phone."

He was barely through the door before Bee jumped out of his chair and leaned over the desk, then snapped a couple of pictures, opened a coffee-stained manilla folder and snapped a couple more, then shifted through a few pages, clicking away seemingly randomly.

"What are you doing?" Cass looked over her shoulder to see if Liam was watching them.

He stood with his back to them, facing the hurricane display. Even though the place was tiny, he kept his voice too low for Cass to eavesdrop.

Bee stuffed his phone back into his pocket, stuffed the folder back together, and flopped into his seat. He heaved in a deep breath and let it out slowly. A bead of sweat trickled down his temple. "This detective stuff is not for me. My nerves are not cut out for spying."

With a quick glance to make sure Liam was still occupied, Cass whispered, "What did you find?"

"The folder is marked *Twin Forks Psychiatric Center*, so it caught my interest, especially when he was sorting through the papers in search of that torn printer paper and napkin."

"The napkin with the notes all over it?"

"Yeah, except the notes on the scrap of paper are a shopping list. The napkin I couldn't read."

"So you think—"

"I think he was just moving papers around to hide the folder that was sitting right in plain sight on top of the pile."

"Hmm . . . I—"

"Sorry about that." Liam strode back into the room and grabbed his coat from a rack beside the door. "I have to run over to the high school, seems one of the history teachers had an emergency and had to leave, so they need me to sub for him. I told them I'd be right over. I hope you understand."

"Of course." Cass stood.

"Please, feel free to come back anytime. I don't often get visitors who are interested in hearing centuries-old gossip, but I'd be happy to chat again if you'd like."

"Thank you for your time, Liam." Cass shook his hand. If he thought he could get off the hook that easily, he didn't know her very well. She'd be back, and she'd push him to follow up on who would oppose developing the land as well as asking him about the groundskeeper she never got the chance to bring up, if Bee couldn't find out more about it online when they got back to the shop. "I might just do that."

He grabbed a battered briefcase and ushered them out the door, then locked up behind himself and headed for a silver Mini Cooper at the far side of the lot.

"Liam," Cass called after him.

When he stopped and turned she hurried to him before he could get away. "Do you mind if I ask you one more quick question?"

He glanced at his watch. "What's that?"

"In your opinion, what should be done with Twin Forks?" She didn't know why it mattered so much, but her gut told her it did, especially since he seemed so intent on getting rid of them quickly.

He took a deep breath and looked out toward the lighthouse. "Some things, Ms. Donovan, should be neither celebrated nor forgotten. That place is one of them."

Apparently, Mr. McAlister topped the list of those who thought the land should never be developed. She nodded and thanked him again for his time then turned to Bee. "So, what do you think?"

"I think he's hiding something."

"Do you think he was involved in Elijah's death?"

Bee frowned after him. "I'm not even sure he knows. I think he might suspect something he told someone could have been a contributing factor, though."

"What makes you say that?"

He held his phone out to her, which displayed one of the pictures he took of the folder. "Because the utterly disorganized Mr. McAlister has a folder neatly marked *Twin Forks Psychiatric Center*, and inside he has detailed notes on each person he's spoken to regarding the property and what he discussed with each of them. It looked suspiciously like a suspect list to me."

Cass knew better than to take the bait, the fact that Bee had been a suspect on Cass's list once upon a time still too sore a memory. "Too bad he hurried off."

"Yeah, because the top page was regarding his conversation with Thea Newburgh. I'm assuming that was the most recent one he had, and one of the things they discussed stood out like a neon sign to me."

"Oh, what's that?"

He reached over and enlarged the picture on his phone, then pointed to a line. "*E set to hire CD.*"

Chapter Ten

After a quick stop home to pick Beast up, Cass unlocked the front door to Mystical Musings and ushered Bee and Beast inside before the cold air could rush in. She turned up the heat a bit, then set about opening the shop. Only an hour and a half late; not too bad. It's not like she'd expect many locals to stop by right when she opened on a winter morning, unlike the summer months, when early risers would already be out and about on the beach and cruising the boardwalk.

"I'm going in back to print these pages out, see if we can read them more clearly. Then I'll grab the laptop and see what I can find out about another murder out there." Without waiting for an answer, Bee strode toward the back room, which was actually located on the side of the shop since the shop had two entrances, the front from the boardwalk and the back from the beach, and was separated from the main room with red crushed-velvet curtains.

Beast unearthed a bone he'd hidden beneath a corner of the rug and lay down to chew. Cass had learned a long time ago not to disturb the toys he hid, since he always remembered where they were and went back for them as soon as they arrived. On the few occasions her driving need for order had her picking up the toys and putting them in his toy basket, he'd sat where he expected to find something whimpering.

First order of business, coffee. She started a couple of pots, just in case she got busy, along with a pot of hot water for tea and hot chocolate. Anyone who braved the damp chilly temperatures to come in this morning deserved something hot to warm them up. It had been an odd winter so far, with temperatures all over the place, dropping from the sixties to the twenties in a matter of hours, then hiking back up again, only to plummet a day or two later. She figured by this evening, once the sun began to set on the melting slush from the previous night's storm, the cooler temperatures would ice the roads over. Better to be home before that happened. Maybe she'd close early.

With coffee brewing and Bee and Beast both entertained, Cass opened the register and started taking inventory. She'd have to place an order soon. She hadn't been selling many crystals lately, since most of her regular customers had already chosen those they needed, but she was almost out of the scented bath balls and candles she'd used to make up baskets for the holidays. She'd have to replenish.

The wind chimes hanging above the door signaled a customer, and she turned and lowered her pad.

A young woman stood in the doorway, wringing her hands.

Cass smiled and held out a hand. "Good morning. I'm Cass Donovan."

The woman took another tentative step into the shop and shook her hand. "Hi. I'm Amy."

"It's nice to meet you, Amy." Cass gestured toward a small seating arrangement with a love seat, a chair, and a low coffee table, one of several strategically situated around the shop to allow her privacy to speak with her guests and to give anyone who wanted to wait for a reading a comfortable place to do so.

"Oh, thank you, but I can't sit right now."

"Can I get you anything? Coffee? Tea? Water?"

She shook her head. "No, thank you. I'm already so loaded with caffeine I couldn't take another drop."

Cass lay the pad and pen she'd been using on the counter. "What can I help you with this morning?"

She chewed on her lower lip for a moment and looked around, her gaze flitting from one display to the next. "I'm not sure, actually, but I've heard you can help people sometimes."

Though the woman appeared jittery, for sure, she didn't seem to be in any true distress. Dark circles ringed her bloodshot blue eyes, though, and her hair had been hastily thrown up in a sloppy knot—the same hairstyle Cass went with when she rushed out of the house with too little sleep and not enough caffeine. "That depends on what you're looking for, but I will certainly try."

"I had a baby a few months ago." Tears slid down her cheeks. Not sobbing, so hopefully there was nothing wrong with the baby, but unusual just the same. Amy simply let the tears fall, not even bothering to wipe them away.

"Congratulations, that's wonderful. A boy or a girl?"

A shaky smile emerged through the tears. "A girl. Marissa."

"What a pretty name." Cass sensed she needed a moment to collect herself. "Do you have a picture?"

Amy pulled her cell phone out of her pocket and swiped, then held it out so Cass could see a picture of a smiling infant, one pudgy fist in her mouth.

"Oh, she's beautiful." And she was. Bald as could be with the biggest blue eyes.

"Thank you." Amy beamed, some of her confidence returning.

"So, how can I help you and Marissa this morning?"

Amy took a deep breath and blew it out, fluttering her brown bangs. "I love Marissa more than life. She's amazing, and beautiful, and her smile gives me the energy to drag myself out of bed in the morning . . . no matter how little sleep I've gotten."

Cass sensed they were about to hit on the problem.

"I would do anything for my baby girl, and I want so bad to be a good mom . . . Everyone said I was crazy to try to raise her on my own when her father took off as soon as he knew I was pregnant, but I loved her so much already." She sniffled, and another tear fell. "Anyway, whatever, that doesn't matter now. But what does matter is that I'm exhausted. Beyond exhausted. And I don't know what to do."

"Marissa's not sleeping through the night?" There wasn't much Cass would be able to do about that, short of offering to babysit for a night.

"No, that's just the thing. Marissa sleeps through at least six hours, has for weeks now. Everyone keeps telling me how fortunate I am, but I don't feel fortunate, because I can't sleep a wink. I lay down the instant she falls asleep, hoping to get the full six hours, and nothing. I lay there and lay there and watch the clock creeping closer and closer to the six-hour mark, and I just cannot fall asleep. And if I do fall asleep, I just jerk awake again a moment later. On the rare nights I do manage to sleep, I wake up with bad dreams. I don't know what to do, but I can't keep going like this."

"Come on and sit down, please." Cass took her arm and guided her toward the love seat.

Amy flopped down, rested her elbows on her knees, and lowered her face into her hands. "I feel like such a failure."

"Do you know how many young mothers I get in here with the exact same problem?"

Amy's gaze shot to her, eyes wide, and Cass was struck by how young she appeared. If she had to guess, she'd say early twenties at the most. "Really?"

"Yup. All the time."

"Thank you for that." She let her head fall back against the cushion and finally relaxed. "I thought it was just me."

"Not at all."

She laughed and shook her head. "I had myself convinced there was something wrong with me. I only work part-time, but I also go to school to be a teacher, and I'm having a hard time keeping up."

"Well, first off, let's look at your schedule. Instead of falling into bed the instant Marissa closes her eyes, why don't you try taking some time for yourself. Do you have a bathtub?"

She nodded eagerly. "I do, a nice deep one. I hate those walk-in shower things they make now. Give me a good old-fashioned clawfoot tub any day."

Ain't that the truth. "Perfect. Tonight, when Marissa falls asleep, run a nice warm bath. I have scented bath balls that will help you relax."

"But then I won't get the full six hours of sleep. Everyone says I have to lay down when she does."

Since Cass didn't have kids, she couldn't speak from experience, but she'd been through this with customers often enough to know the routine should help. "When you get into bed worried about getting to sleep, chances are you won't."

Now, that she had experience with.

Amy considered her, then nodded.

"Giving up half an hour to help you relax and unwind enough to fall asleep will be well worth it. I'm also going to give you some crystals. You'll put them beneath your pillow at night, and they will help you get a good night's rest."

"Oh, thank you." She sighed. "Sadie said you were amazing."

"Sadie?" Sadie's grandmother, Grace, was one of Cass's best customers.

"Yes. We've been friends since we were kids, and she told me to come to you. She said you'd be able to help." A pink flush crept up her pale cheeks. "I have to admit, I was somewhat skeptical, but I was so desperate I was willing to give anything a try. No offense."

"None taken." Some of Cass's most loyal customers hadn't believed in her ability to help when they'd first come to her. "Now, let's see what we can do to help you out. Where's Marissa now?"

"With my mom. She watches her while I work, but I called out this morning. I was just too tired and emotional to go in."

"Excuse me, Cass?" Bee stood beside her, practically vibrating with nervous energy. "I'm sorry to bother you, but I found that information you needed."

Since Amy was looking right at her, she avoided leveling Bee with a death glare for interrupting her with a customer and simply took the Post-it note he held out and glanced at it quickly. The note said *Salvatore Marcuzzio, groundskeeper, found dead, unusual circumstances.*

Torn between the need to help her customer and the desire to know more about Salvatore's death, Cass folded the paper and slid it into her pocket. "Do you know when?"

Bee nodded. "Five years ago."

"Okay, thanks. I'll take care of it as soon as I'm done here."

Bee grinned, apparently pleased he'd discreetly gotten her attention when he couldn't wait any longer to share what he'd found. She couldn't blame him; her mind was already running through the possibilities at a frantic pace.

Shifting gears, Cass led Amy to a display case. She pulled out a small leather pouch and a tray of crystals. The first stone was easy, since she knew exactly what she wanted. She held up the deep purple stone. "Okay, first off, let's start with amethyst."

"Okay, I'll bite." Amy leaned closer and stared deep into the transparent crystal. "What's that for?"

"Amethyst is a protective stone." Cass placed it in the pouch. "It provides relief from stress and anxiety."

"That's one thing I definitely need."

"Plus, once you do relax and fall asleep, it may even aid in bringing pleasant dreams."

Amy relaxed a little and offered a genuine smile. "I wouldn't mind pleasant dreams."

Cass returned the tray to its spot, then pulled out another. Rose quartz, her most popular selling stone. She held up the crystal for Amy to see.

"What does that one do?" She tilted her head to study the light reflecting from the translucent crystal. At least she seemed interested, so maybe this would work for her. In Cass's experience, those who believed in the power of crystals to help heal them often found relief from their ailments.

"Rose quartz emits love, harmony and peace. Its soothing, calming effects should offer tranquility, which will allow you to fall asleep. Then it will help to bring gentle, pleasant dreams." She held the stone out to Amy. "This one won't remain in the bag. You'll hold it in your hand before bed and focus on your problems, almost like sharing your troubles with worry dolls."

"Oh, hey . . ." She took the stone from Cass. "I've heard of those. Supposedly, you tell the dolls your problems and they solve them while you're sleeping, or something like that. So, this little pink stone is supposed to take my worries away?"

"It's supposed to help ease them for you." And if the crystal itself didn't help, surely focusing on your problems then setting them firmly aside before bed certainly would. "Once you are done focusing on your problems, you'll set the stone beside your bed and relax."

She seemed to consider for a moment, then nodded. "What do I do with the others?"

"The rest you'll keep in the pouch and place under your pillow at night." She chose black tourmaline next.

Her gaze shot to Bee, who'd quietly returned to the far side of the room and was now spreading pages across the table. He paused a moment, his concentration fully on the task at hand, and absently petted Beast's head.

She'd given him a black tourmaline once when he'd been going through a particularly rough patch, a period that had brought back his past and reignited former suffering. He'd cherished it, a gift from a friend, even if he didn't believe in all the hocus-pocus, and she knew he still carried it in his pocket every single day.

A smile tugged at her as she showed Amy the stone. "Black tourmaline also has protective qualities. It absorbs negative energy and transforms it into positive. It's one of the most powerful crystals for anxiety and should help you get a peaceful night's sleep."

Amy kept her gaze on the pouch and chewed on her bottom lip

for a moment, then looked up at Cass. "Are these crystals expensive?"

"Nope." Especially not for a new mother desperate for some sleep who also happened to be friends with Sadie. Even if the crystals were expensive, Cass would have discounted them significantly—much to Stephanie's chagrin, since she handled the bookkeeping. "These are all common crystals and all quite inexpensive."

"Oh, wow, thank you. I need sleep, but I'm a single mom and don't have a big budget."

"No problem. Two more should do the trick." She slid open the moonstone tray and chose an opalescent blue stone. "Moonstone helps reduce stress, as well, and was used in ancient times as a sleeping stone. It's great for treating insomnia and promoting lucid dreams."

"It's beautiful."

"It is, isn't it." She shifted the stone so Amy could see the opalescent quality. Then she placed it in the bag and chose a clear selenite, used to battle insomnia and provide a clear, calm mindset before bed. Once done, she wrapped the pouch in tissue paper and put it into a bag, then rang Amy up and handed her the purchase and hesitated. "Do you mind if I make one more suggestion?"

"Not at all."

She kept her tone gentle so Amy would know she wasn't criticizing. "Stop worrying so much about what everyone else thinks. You seem to have a good head on your shoulders, and there's no doubt you love Marissa and want the best for her, even put her needs ahead of your own. Start trusting yourself, and I bet it will do wonders for your sleep habits."

Amy smiled, though tears shimmered in her eyes. "Thank you for that. I've been so worried I'm going to do something wrong, I seem to second-guess every decision I make."

"Well, I can't promise you'll always make the right decisions, but if you make them for the right reasons, things usually work out well enough in the end."

"You're right, thank you. I'm going to take your advice. All of it. I'm going to use the crystals you gave me, and the thought of a nice warm relaxing bath is giving me goose bumps, and I'm going to stop worrying so much about what everyone else thinks I should do."

"Good for you." She paused. "Oh, except for Sadie. You should definitely listen to Sadie. She's a wise woman, that one."

"Obviously, since she sent me to you." Amy laughed. "I'll be sure to let her know you said that."

"And please tell her I said hello."

"Will do." She saluted and hefted her purchase.

"Don't forget to let me know how it goes."

"I definitely will, thank you." She said goodbye and left with a spring in her step she hadn't had when she'd come in. Good. Hopefully, that meant she truly believed she'd be helped by the crystals, and so she would.

Cass made sure to put everything back in place, then went to see what Bee was studying so intently. "What's up? More on Salvatore Marcuzzio's murder?"

"Not yet. Actually, these are the pictures of the papers that were in Liam's folders."

"Well?" She sat down across the table from him and scanned the pages. Nothing jumped out at her. "Anything of interest?"

Bee grabbed a page from the center of the spread and handed it to her, then pointed to the line he'd shown her earlier. *E set to hire CD.* "This is the one I told you about."

Cass read the hastily jotted notes Liam must have taken, either while speaking to Thea or hurriedly scribbled afterward. Any doubt she had about her being the *CD* Liam referred to fled right out the window. Cass's name was scrawled crookedly across the top of the page and underlined twice. Nearby were the words *psychiatrist*—which Cass had been once upon a time—and *psychic* with a question mark. "So he knew who I was before we arrived today."

"Yes." Bee frowned and tapped his perfectly manicured nails against the table. "But I can't recall if he seemed to recognize you when he showed up. I was startled by his stealthy appearance and don't remember. Do you?"

She shook her head. "No. He definitely didn't make a big deal of knowing who I was. Then again, we're on Bay Island in the dead of winter, where everyone pretty much knows everyone, or has at least heard of them."

"And yet, you hadn't heard of Liam McAlister before Tony and Gina mentioned him."

Touché.

"Plus . . ." Bee sat back with his hands wrapped around his warm coffee mug. "Mr. Disorganized had obviously done his research where you were concerned. Look toward the bottom of the page."

She did as he suggested, skimming his notes on the schools she'd attended, the name of her former psychiatric practice, the time and date of the group reading Thea Newburgh had attended, and even Luke's name, and sloppily scrawled across the bottom was the phrase "Problem or possible ally?"

Chapter Eleven

Bee took his promise to keep an eye on Cass seriously, dozing on the couch in the back room, arm dangling over the side to rest on Beast's back.

Beast snored softly beside him, a koala missing half its stuffing tucked between his crossed paws.

Cass just shook her head and laughed at her protectors, then took an afghan from the back of the couch and lay it over Bee. Since he was often up most of the night working on his dress designs, when he was least likely to be interrupted, noon was well past his bedtime.

Leaving them to sleep, and hoping they wouldn't snore too loudly, Cass headed back out to the shop to replenish the tray of cookies and make a fresh pot of coffee. Not that she'd had many customers after Amy, but the gentleman she'd just finished a private reading for had eaten the entire tray and washed them down with a nearly full pot of coffee. Oh, well, at least he'd left happy, confident his life was headed in the direction he intended and he would soon realize every one of his dreams. That wasn't exactly what Cass had told him, but it was what he'd heard just the same.

She surveyed her shop. A psychic shop on Bay Island's boardwalk had been her dream from the time she was a teenager and had begun doing readings for tourists on the beach, first for fun, then to earn some extra money. The polished driftwood countertop gleamed in the sunlight streaming through the front windows. A variety of seating options scattered throughout the space amid a number of display cases lent a cozy atmosphere as well as providing guests with some semblance of privacy while they waited. A large round table with velvet-covered seats sat tucked into the back corner overlooking the beach, with a beautiful view of the Bay Island Lighthouse. The fact she'd been gone for seventeen years to go to school, get married, and open her own psychiatric practice barely registered anymore, since Bay Island felt more like home than New York City ever had.

The tinkle of wind chimes pulled her from the past, and she smiled as she turned toward the sound, then stopped short when her gaze landed on Evelyn Anderson. "Mrs. Anderson, I'm so very sorry for your loss."

"You can call me Evelyn." She nodded toward Cass but made no motion to move closer.

Cass gestured toward a nearby love seat. "Would you like to sit for a moment, have something to drink?"

She dismissed the offer with a wave of her hand. "I really just came in to find out what you plan to do?"

"Uh . . . I'm not sure what you mean? Do about what?" She didn't want to be rude, but Evelyn was going to need to be a little more specific if she wanted her question answered. Unless, of course, she expected Cass to be able to figure it out on her own, as skeptics sometimes did.

She studied Cass, her angular jaw clenched tight, then relaxed. "Since you took my husband's money and must already have been to Twin Forks, since you were the one to find his body, I assume you plan to provide some sort of report to the board of directors."

"Uh . . ." She actually hadn't thought of that. She hadn't thought past returning the check to Evelyn.

"So, I'm curious, what do you plan to tell them?" She shifted her weight and cocked a bony hip. This was a much more formidable version of Evelyn Anderson than she'd met the night of the reading. "I'd think it's pretty much a no-brainer that the place is unsafe, given that Elijah turned up dead out there."

"Actually, Evelyn, whether or not the place will be able to open and when isn't up to me. There's an active murder investigation going on out there," which she shouldn't have to remind Evelyn about considering her husband was the victim. "It will be up to the police to determine if and when to release the crime scene."

"Yes, of course, but you and I both know that's not what I'm talking about." She lifted her chin and straightened her glasses. "I want to know if the place is haunted, which I assume you will say it is, and with whom you plan to share that information. As far as I'm concerned, that place can't be sold fast enough. It's already cost a tremendous amount of money and my husband's life, and I don't need a local psychic carrying on publicly about it being haunted. His life insurance won't last forever."

Taken aback by the vindictiveness in her tone, Cass bristled. So much for her vlog. "I was hired by your husband, Mrs. Anderson, and he approved my recording any sessions out there for use on my video blog."

Not that she planned to release them, at least not before they knew what had happened, and maybe not even afterward. A decision she'd already made along with her choice to return the check, but Evelyn was making it difficult to want to do the right thing.

"As if twenty thousand dollars isn't enough of a profit to make off my husband's death, you need to sensationalize the whole situation as well?"

Tears pricked the back of Cass's lids, but she didn't dare let them fall. If she withered beneath this woman's accusations, Evelyn would no doubt continue to batter her.

A gust of wind jingled the chimes as the back door opened and Thea Newburgh walked in. Great, just what she needed, an audience.

A warm solid hand landed on Cass's shoulder, just for a moment, an offer of support as Bee continued past her to stand toe to toe with Evelyn. He jutted one hip and straightened his scarf.

Cass bit back a smile. No doubt Evelyn Anderson could not appreciate that she was about to meet her match.

Bee smiled. "Mrs. Anderson, I'm so very sorry for your loss."

She nodded once, her teeth clamped tightly together.

"And while I appreciate how stressful and upsetting the situation must be, I'm sure you can understand it wasn't Cass's fault."

She took a breath and started to open her mouth.

Bee held up a finger to stop her. "In a moment, dear."

She harrumphed but remained quiet.

"Now, that said, your husband hired Cass to do a job, which she partially completed. She went out to Twin Forks, determined the place was haunted, tried to save your husband's life, in case you weren't aware, and called the police to alert them about his death. She even provided evidence she hopes will lead to his killer."

Uh-oh. In his haste to defend her, Bee blurted information better kept under wraps. Now how could she stop him without causing a scene in front of not only Evelyn but Thea as well? Easy, she couldn't. He was going to say what he said, and they'd have to deal with the fallout afterward.

"Not only did Cass do all of that, but she already told both me and her bookkeeper that she planned to return the check to you, and if I know Cass, which I really do, she won't be releasing any of that footage, nor will she idly gossip about a murder." He lifted a brow. "*She* has more respect than that."

Evelyn snorted and shifted her gaze to Cass.

Thea leaned a hip against the counter looking slightly amused and didn't even bother to feign disinterest.

"Now, if you'll excuse us, Cass has a customer waiting, and I'm in the middle of something." He nodded to her and whirled away, then winked at Cass before grabbing a seat at the table and gathering the pictures he'd left spread there.

Without waiting for another outburst, or an apology that was most likely not coming, Cass turned her back to Evelyn and mouthed *thank you* to Bee as she hurried to the shelf at the back of the shop and fished the check out of her bag. When she turned, Evelyn was standing behind her with her hand out.

Cass handed her the check, but she had no clue what to say. She'd already offered her condolences, and Bee had made it clear she had no intention of sharing anything she'd discovered as of yet, so . . . "Have a good day, Evelyn."

She tucked the check into her bag, then turned and left without another word.

Ruffled, Cass would have liked a moment or two to collect herself before dealing with a customer, or whatever role Thea was there in, but the sooner she took care of her, the sooner she'd leave so Cass could regroup. "I'm sorry about that, Ms. Newburgh."

"Don't worry about it, and it's Thea. That was quite . . ." She tilted her head and watched Evelyn stride across the gravel parking lot. "Entertaining, I suppose, despite the grim circumstances."

Cass didn't acknowledge the comment. No sense adding fuel to whatever gossip Thea might decide to share. "Would you like to sit for a moment?"

"Yes, that would be nice, thank you." She took a seat at the table next to Bee.

He'd already stacked the pages and turned them over so she

couldn't see their contents. Bee could be discreet when he wanted to be. And when he wasn't consumed with defending Cass.

Thankful she'd get to sit for a moment, Cass pulled out a chair across the table from Thea. "So, what brings you by this morning?"

"Actually, my great, great, great . . ." She rolled a hand. "However many times great-grandmother wanted to meet you, so I stopped by to see if you have time to say hello?"

Interest piqued, despite the confrontation with Evelyn, Cass nodded. "Sure, where is she?"

"Well, see, that's the thing." Thea leaned her forearms on the table and clasped her hands together. "I'm afraid it will take both of us to get ahold of good ole Granny O."

Oh, boy, this was not what Cass needed right now. "Oh, and why is that?"

"Because my grandmother, Ophelia Wilson, is a resident of Twin Forks Lunatic Asylum."

Bee stiffened. "You mean *was* a resident, right?"

Thea shrugged one slim shoulder and slouched back in the seat, the large velvet back of which practically swallowed her up. She kept her gaze on Cass. "Depending on what you believe."

"On that note" — Bee lurched to his feet, taking the stack of pages with him — "I believe I'll go finish my nap."

Once he was gone, Thea smiled. "So, are you willing to give it a shot?"

"I'm curious, how did you know your grandmother wanted to speak to me if you can't contact her alone?"

"Oh, I can contact her alone, but only out at Twin Forks. Here . . ." She gestured around the shop. "I won't be able to conjure her alone."

"How do you know?"

"Because I've tried, and I'm not a strong enough psychic." She drew her eyebrows together, obviously troubled by that fact.

"But you were strong enough to receive a warning, which you then passed on to me at the reading."

"About that . . ." She looked down, studiously peeling her nails, and spoke quietly, a much more demure version of the woman who'd spoken out at the reading. "It wasn't actually me."

"I'm sorry?"

"Well, it was me who spoke out at the reading." She blew out a breath and raised her voice a little. "But it wasn't me who heard the warning. Well, it was, but . . . Ugh, I'm not explaining this right. Okay, I did get the warning from my grandmother, but it was my grandmother who was able to . . . project it to me. She was remarkably psychic. I'm just psychic enough that she's able to reach me."

"But only at Twin Forks."

"Right." She nodded once in agreement, as if the whole situation made perfect sense.

"And how did you find that out? It doesn't seem like the kind of place a young woman would hang out." She couldn't quite put her finger on what, yet, but something about the woman's claim seemed off.

"It wasn't, I mean, it isn't. Not really. A bunch of us went there one time when I was younger, kind of like a dare, you know? Like kids do." She paled. "Before they understand the full extent of the possible consequences of their actions."

Hmm . . . something there. Something in her eyes. Fear, vulnerability. A far cry from the seemingly confident woman she'd met at the group reading.

"Did something happen when you were there?"

She swallowed and lowered her gaze, wispy brown hair falling like a veil over her face, and she suddenly seemed so much younger.

"How long ago was the first time you went out there?" Cass didn't have to wait for an answer. She knew before Thea opened her mouth what she'd say.

"'Bout five years."

Exactly what Cass figured. "And was that the first time Ophelia spoke to you?"

She nodded.

"Have you returned in the past five years?"

She nodded again. "Many times."

"And did she speak to you each of those times?"

"No, not always. Sometimes I would sense her presence, but that was all. She was more apt to communicate with me if I went alone, but I don't really like going alone." She shivered. "It gives me the creeps."

Cass could certainly understand that. The creep factor out there was pretty high. "When did she give you the warning to pass on to me?"

"The night before the reading. She wanted me to find you, to tell you sometimes the dead are better left dead. I sensed she expected you to understand, even if I didn't."

"And when did she tell you she wanted to speak to me?"

"Yesterday." She swallowed hard.

"When yesterday?" Had she been to the grounds before Elijah was killed or after?

"Just yesterday."

"Before Mr. Anderson's murder?"

She pressed her lips tightly closed and stared straight ahead.

Okay, she'd have to try a different track. "Did you look her up, try to determine if she was telling you the truth that she was truly one of your ancestors?"

Thea looked up quickly, her eyes wide.

"As in life, people are not always honest," Cass said gently. A difficult enough lesson to learn about the living, never mind having to learn you can't always trust the dead.

"I didn't think of that." She shivered again and pulled her torn wool coat tighter around her.

"I'm not saying I won't help you, but if it's all the same to you, I'd prefer to do a little research before we try to reach out?" She, at least, wanted to know who she'd be trying to contact before doing so.

Thea hesitated, chewing on what was left of a thumbnail, then nodded. "But after that, you'll help me contact her, so she can tell you what she wants you to know?"

She couldn't commit to that. If Ophelia had been a resident back in the days of the original lunatic asylum, she could not only be a liar, but dangerous. "Did she share what she wants me for?"

"No." Thea frowned, seeming lost in thought for a moment, then sighed. "I can't actually hear like if she's speaking to me, I get more like, impressions, really, if that makes sense."

Hmm . . . Cass wasn't quite sure what to think. Thea claimed she couldn't hear the words, only sense impressions, which Cass could understand, but still, the phrase she kept repeating seemed more in line with something someone had told her to say. Was she trying to scam Cass? Making up the fact her dead ancestor had spoken to her? But for what purpose? Unless a live flesh-and-blood person had sent her to pass on the message. Maybe someone who wanted to scare Cass off, keep her from investigating the psychiatric center. Perhaps someone who didn't want to see it developed?

"It makes perfect sense." And not only would she be researching Ophelia Wilson, she'd also have Bee take a look to see what he could find out about Thea Newburgh. And if she turned out to be legitimate, Cass just might offer to help her out, mentor her, teach her to control her talent and protect herself from those who might seek to take advantage. "Would you be willing to come back again tomorrow?"

Thea slid her chair back and stood. "I could do that."

"Okay, then, I'll see what I can find out and we'll talk again."

Thea nodded and started toward the door, untied work boots clunking with each step, shoulders slumped. Defeated? Weary? Maybe just insecure.

Or was something weighing on her? Something more than just her however many greats grandmother reaching out from beyond. "Thea?"

She stopped and turned. "Yeah?"

"When you were out at Twin Forks five years ago, did you see anything else? Something that maybe didn't take place in the past?" Like the murder of a groundskeeper, perhaps.

Thea stared at her, her big brown eyes wide with something akin to terror. Tears shimmered in her bottom lashes. "I'll see you tomorrow."

"Thea, wait."

But this time she just kept walking, leaving the chimes tinkling in her wake as the door fell closed behind her.

Cass watched her walk away, her tea-length smock dress whipping in the wind. The image of whomever had walked away from Elijah when he'd fallen superimposed itself over Thea and left Cass wondering if the long coat she'd seen flapping in the wind could have been a full skirt instead.

Chapter Twelve

"Enough! Look . . ." Bee stared at Cass, his fingers poised over the laptop's keys. "You're going to have to slow down if you want me to figure out what to research here. Or, if you can't go slower and make your thoughts more comprehensible, at least grab a pen and paper and write it all down."

He was right. Again, though she hated to admit it.

His smirk told her she didn't have to.

Once Thea had left and Bee had returned from being unable to fall asleep again, Cass had recounted her conversation with Thea and started rambling off a long list of things they needed to know. "Okay, sorry, I'm supposed to meet with Thea again tomorrow, so the searches I'll need for that meeting will take precedence over the others."

"Makes sense." Bee started typing. "So, you think she's messing with you? On her own, or you think someone put her up to it?"

"I don't know. I was wondering about that myself." And hoping it wasn't the case.

"Question is, who would she be in cahoots with?" Bee paused, read for a moment, then scrolled without saying anything.

"The only one we can connect her to is Liam McAlister, since he admitted he's spoken to her on numerous occasions."

"And apparently, those conversations, at least one of them, revolved around you." No surprise his thoughts ran similar to her own, since they often did. "But what's the connection between them, if any, other than that Liam heads the historical society?"

Wasn't that the million-dollar question. Cass typed Liam's name into the search engine on Bee's phone, since hers was still confiscated. Though she'd let Bee handle the bulk of the research, since she was still open and Bee was a better researcher than her, it wouldn't hurt to see what she could find. "Liam mentioned he was going to sub at the high school, and Thea appears to be in her early twenties—"

"Twenty-two." Bee frowned at the screen, then started typing again.

"Okay, so only a few years out of high school. And the first time she was contacted by her supposed grandmother, around the same time Sal Marcuzzio was killed, she'd still have been a student, so there is a possible closer connection than just her pestering the head of the historical society."

"Albeit a loose connection." Bee turned the screen to face her. "Liam McAlister is listed in the Bay Island High School yearbook as a substitute teacher the year Thea graduated."

"Hmm . . ."

"And get this." He reached over to switch to a new tab, which held a profile of Liam McAlister from some roster of professionals he'd found. "Liam minored in theater and had a brief connection to the local theater group."

"The group Marge Hawkins ran?"

"One and the same."

She studied him to be sure he was okay, since his own connection to Marge and his interaction with the theater group had been part of the dark moment in his life that had prompted Cass to give him the black tourmaline.

"I'm fine, Cass. It was a long time ago, and my life has become so much richer since then." He reached out and squeezed her hand. "Now, hear me out before you dismiss this."

"Always." And she meant it, because despite Bee's flair for the dramatic, he was an impeccable researcher, had a fantastic eye for detail, and always had Cass's best interest at heart.

He smiled, a touch of red tinging his cheeks. "Anyway, I'm still hung up on that fog, and I can't yet figure out how the camera didn't pick up on it, but what do you think of the possibility someone did it intentionally?"

"You mean like a fog machine or something?"

"Sure." He shrugged. "The how of it doesn't really matter right now, but the fact that it could have been staged does. We already know Liam and Thea knew you'd be there, so they could have had everything in place to try to scare you away."

"Actually, that's not so far-fetched." Her interest piqued, Cass encouraged him to continue. "We don't know when Liam found out Elijah was going to hire me, or who told him, but he could have had time to stage something. Maybe the woman I heard crying was fake as well."

"Could be, though I didn't hear that, so I'm not sure how

someone could have pulled that off." He typed frantically, his gaze caught on Cass. A little creepy, actually.

"But why do that?" To scare her off? Maybe, but if Liam had done any research at all on Cass's psychic abilities and her connection with the police department and more than one murder investigation, he'd know she didn't scare easily.

"Well, we know they both agree the place should never reopen, though I can't imagine Liam would agree to burning the place down, as Thea suggested, what with his inclination toward preserving and documenting history," Bee said.

"True."

"But think about it. Thea comes in to your reading, plants the seed of danger with her public warning, then stages a" —he made air quotes with his fingers —"*haunting*, with the hope you'd tell Elijah the place is too dangerous to be opened as a school."

She had to admit, it did sound plausible. Could she see Thea being involved in a scheme like that? Not on her own. Though she'd seemed confident enough when she'd come in to deliver her warning, the insecure girl who'd sat across the table from her a few hours ago did not pull that off on her own. Cass had misjudged her, seen her as confident and strong, when she was actually quite meek. Could she have been talked into something like that? Possibly. Acting? Could be. And had Thea been the dark figure they'd seen fleeing the scene after Elijah's murder? Possibly. But could she have killed him? Cass doubted that.

Come to think of it, Thea wasn't the only one she'd misjudged, though she was usually a good judge of character. She'd mistaken Evelyn Anderson for fragile the first time they'd met, yet that woman was hard as stone during their encounter this morning. Did Evelyn deserve a place on her suspect list? No, not yet, anyway.

She grabbed a random colored pencil from a basket she kept on the table for color readings. Red. The color of danger. A warning? Hmm . . . She thought of and dismissed the urge to choose a different color. If it was some kind of warning, it was best to heed it. Ignoring the burning in the back of her throat, she took a piece of blank paper from the top of the stack. Just to keep her in mind, Cass jotted Evelyn Anderson on the bottom corner of the page. Next to *Motive*, she put *money* with a question mark, since the amount of cash Elijah was dumping into the endeavor seemed to be a sore spot for her. "Okay, so we add Liam McAlister and Thea Newburgh to the list of possible suspects. Their motive, keeping the psychiatric center property from being developed for any reason."

Bee paused and scratched his head. "That doesn't really seem like a very strong motive to kill someone."

"No, it doesn't, but we don't know why they don't want the land developed, not for sure, anyway. Besides, people have killed for less."

"True enough."

"Okay, then . . ." Cass rapped the pencil against the page, the rhythmic tapping focusing her attention. "Who else could we add?"

"Cam Parker," Bee said with no hesitation as he scribbled his own notes, scrolled, and spoke. The man was like a multitasking genius, at least when it came to gossip or research, which in this case was pretty much just gossip from the internet. Hmm . . . no wonder Bee was so good at it.

"Why Cam?" She wrote the name below Liam and Thea. "What did you find?"

"Apparently, Mr. Parker has a habit of buying up old abandoned properties at a disgustingly low price and building cheap condominiums with substandard workmanship that he doesn't stand behind when things go wrong. And get this . . ." He turned the screen to face her again and pointed out an old newspaper clipping. "Seems Mr. Parker was suspected, however briefly, in the murder of an elderly gentleman who refused to sell to him. Though nothing could be proven, Mr. Parker bought the property cheap from the man's estate after he was gone and built the lovely . . ."

He switched screens to show a dilapidated brick building surrounded by a cracked, weed-choked parking lot, dark storm clouds gathering in the background, casting their shadow and adding to the gloom. "Sunny Acres."

"Well, that's something that should definitely be looked into, especially since he just happened to show up in one of the only open businesses with any customers the night of Elijah's murder, making it known he wasn't able to get out there." She wrote *Cameron Parker*, then under *Motive* added *buy property from estate cheap*, which she didn't think would be a problem, considering Evelyn Anderson's feelings about the place. She'd probably be thrilled to dump it and be rid of it, especially since her husband had died there.

She also made a mental note to mention him to Luke when she saw him for dinner. "Did you find anything about Mercedes Dupont?"

Bee tapped the keys again, then frowned and pulled the laptop closer. "Not yet."

Leaving him alone to work his magic, Cass jotted *Mercedes Dupont* on the page, then returned to searching on the phone. Since Bee was already looking into their growing list of suspects, Cass turned to trying to find out if Thea's great-great-grandmother was actually a resident of Twin Forks at any point. But how to find that out?

She made note of the name Thea had given her on the corner of the page and then typed *Ophelia Wilson* into the search box and scrolled through the list of Wilsons that popped up. This wasn't going to work; the surname Wilson was too popular. There had to be thousands of Wilsons, if not more, just on social media alone. And if Thea was right and Ophelia had been a resident back when the lunatic asylum was open, there might not be too much about her to find. "Hey, Bee?"

"Uh-huh," he muttered, distracted.

"How would you go about searching for someone who could have lived as long as a hundred years ago?"

He stood and arched his back, then reached his hands over his head and stretched from side to side. "Well, in a small community like Bay Island, I'd go to the local newspaper office, if it still exists, and search their records. In a city, that would be a daunting task, but in a small town, not so much. If the person is from a local family who'd been around for generations, you might be able to trace birth and marriage announcements, obituaries and the like, as well as achievement articles, like, you know, so-and-so did some wonderful sports thing in high school, or whoever participated in some charity event. The local papers are full of that kind of stuff, especially back in the day."

Beast propped his head in her lap. His big brown eyes rolled up toward her, and he gave a little whine.

Cass slid her hand into his thick fur. "Sorry, boy, you need some attention, and Mama got caught up in other things."

"Or, you could do one of those family tree sites," Bee added, his attention already back on the task at hand.

"I already tried that, but I couldn't find one I could use for free, and I'm not ready to pay for a subscription." She pushed her chair back and stood, then stretched. "Come on, boy, we'll take a quick walk on the beach."

Beast barked once and bounded toward the back door, nails clacking against the hardwood.

"Just give a yell if any customers come in?" She hooked Beast's leash to his collar.

"Yup."

She figured there was a fifty-fifty chance he'd even notice if anyone came in, as engrossed as he was in whatever he'd found on the computer, though the chimes should alert him.

She didn't bother with a coat, since it was hung in the back room and they'd only be outside for a few minutes, but she regretted that decision the instant she hit the porch.

Wind tore across the open beach, enraging the bay and tossing beach sand and spray from the whitecaps over her.

"Come on, Beast, let's hurry." As she started down the steps, she thought briefly of unhooking him, since the beach was completely deserted, but decided against it. Beast loved the water, and the last thing she needed was him taking a dip in the forty-degree weather. Especially since there was a good chance she'd have to go in after him if he was having fun. No way was that happening. She hooked the leash over her wrist, wrapped her arms around herself, and braced against the cold wind.

Beast bounced up and down as he ran, kicking massive amounts of sand up behind him but getting nowhere fast since he was still tethered to Cass, who could only move so fast through the deep mounds of windswept sand.

"Hurry up there, boy." Cass shivered, the spray making her not only cold but damp too, the kind of cold that went all the way to her bones and would no doubt stay with her all day. She shivered and hunched further into herself. "Hurry up and do your thing there, Beast, before I freeze to—"

A sharp sting tore through her right shoulder. "Ouch, what wa—"

Behind her, the entire back window shattered and crashed to the ground.

"Bee!"

Chapter Thirteen

Drop flat on the sand or run?

Beast danced in circles, barking in every direction at once.

Cass had to get him to safety. She had to get to Bee.

Keeping Beast as close as she could, trying to keep herself between him and whomever was shooting, probably from the lighthouse, Cass ran toward Mystical Musings, fully aware of the target on her back. And Beast's. She had to get him off the beach, where there was no cover. Had to get to Bee inside the shop. Not through the shattered glass covering the back deck, though.

She zigzagged as best she could and headed toward the alleyway between her shop and the next. Fear or cold numbed the pain in her shoulder. She didn't care which, was just grateful for the reprieve.

"Cass!" Bee yelled from somewhere inside the building.

"Oh, thank God," she huffed and sucked in a big gulp of frigid air. He might be injured, but at least he was alive. Now to keep him from showing himself to come after her, if he could hear her over the sound of the wind and his own heart pounding, which she doubted she'd be able to do. "Bee. I'm okay. Stay down."

The instant she ducked into the alleyway, she flopped her back against the wall and ran her hands over Beast. "Are you hurt, baby?"

Beast barked frantically, and she realized he'd never stopped.

"It's okay, boy." Satisfied he wasn't hurt, she heaved in a painful breath and pushed off the wall. She couldn't crash yet. She had to get inside. The fact the shooter hadn't taken another shot didn't mean he wouldn't. He may just be biding his time or changing position since her evasive maneuvers proved so efficient.

Fat chance.

Beast stayed close as they ran toward the front of the shop.

When she reached the corner of the building, she paused. While she could climb beneath the split railing, which would provide some cover in case the shooter had made it to the front, she couldn't get Beast up and through.

"Cass," Bee whispered urgently from the front door he'd cracked open.

"I'm here, Bee. Are you okay?"

"I'm all right, just shaken. Are you hurt?"

"I'm okay." At least she thought she was. Hard to tell when she didn't have much feeling in her shoulder. But even if it was a bullet that had gone into her shoulder, it wouldn't have hit an organ or an artery or anything else vital.

"I called Luke," Bee whispered urgently.

Of course he would have.

"He's on his way." Bee belly-crawled along the front porch toward her.

"What are you doing, Bee? Get back inside."

"I'm not leaving you out here like a sitting duck. Here." He positioned himself flat on his belly and reached beneath the railing. "Boost Beast up to me."

Not wanting to leave him in the open a moment longer than necessary, Cass gave up arguing and did as he said, trying to use her good arm to lift the hundred-pound dog, while using her injured arm to keep his head ducked beneath the slat so Bee could haul him up and under.

Her shoulder screamed, but she ignored it. At least she could feel it now.

The instant Bee had Beast, Cass scrambled onto the porch and through the railing, then, together, the three of them scuttled across the porch and dove through the front door to land in a heap on the floor.

Cass slammed the door closed with her foot. Not that it would make much difference, considering the entire back window was blown out. Not for the first time either. She might consider building a wall this time instead of replacing the window, but then she'd lose her spectacular view of the beach. Plus, she'd gained more than one loyal customer when they'd simply wandered in off the beach to escape the heat. Okay, so no wall, but maybe shatterproof glass.

Sirens screamed in the distance, and Cass rolled over onto her back and sucked in ragged breaths. She kept her arm close to her body to avoid any movement that might send a jolt of pain firing through her, but right now her shoulder had settled into a blessedly dull throb.

"You're hurt." Bee hurried to her and squatted beside her. "Are you all right?"

"Ye—"

"You're bleeding." He peeled her sweater away from the wound.

"I know, I—"

"What happened to your shoulder?"

"I was hit wi—"

"Hit? Hit with what?"

"Shot, Bee. I think whoever was shooting got me in the shoulder and the bullet went right through and hit the back window."

Every ounce of color drained from his face, and his mouth fell open.

"Bee?"

His eyes rolled back in his head.

"Are you ok—"

And he went over like a towering oak.

Cass did her best to break his fall, but he still landed hard on his side. Thankfully, she managed to get her legs beneath his head to keep it from hitting the floor. If he'd been standing instead of squatting beside her, it would have been a different story.

Beast whimpered and licked Bee's face.

"It's okay, boy, he'll be all right in a minute." She petted Beast's head and whispered soothingly, helping to calm his nerves as well as her own.

When he finally settled beside her and Bee, she closed her eyes, just for a moment to gather her wits. Since Bee had fallen in her lap, she couldn't get up to try to get a wet cloth without shifting him off of her. And he'd already said he wasn't hurt, so she'd leave him where he was for a moment and just try to breathe through the ache in her chest.

Everything in her started to quiver as the adrenaline rush subsided. She struggled to control her breathing. Tears streamed down her face as she stroked Beast's head, ran her fingers through Bee's hair, and reminded herself everything was okay. They'd all survived. For now.

Her divorce, after she'd caught her husband in a compromising position with a woman she'd thought of as a friend, the death of a patient she should have foreseen, and the death of her parents, which had also come as a shock, had left her with a driving, almost compulsive need for order and control. The mess of glass carpeting

Mystical Musings was a stark reminder things were currently out of control. She needed to do something to remedy that. And the best way she could think of to do that would be to find Elijah's killer.

"Cass." Luke burst through the front door, gun drawn, with Tank at his back. "Who's hurt?"

"We're okay."

He dropped at her side and felt Bee's neck for a pulse while Tank stepped over Bee's feet and scanned the beach through the broken window.

"He's okay; he just passed out when he found out I'd been shot." She shifted, and pain shot through her shoulder and down her arm.

"Shot?" Luke tucked his weapon away and moved to Cass. "Where?"

"My shoulder." She moved the collar of her V-neck sweater aside so he could get a better look. "Shouldn't be too bad, just a bit painful. Nothing vital there."

"Okay, just sit tight. It just grazed you, but we'll get it cleaned up just the same." Despite his attempt to project calm, the trembling in his hands when he called for an ambulance gave him away.

Cass groaned, but the protest was only half-hearted. As much as she hated hospitals, she knew she needed to be checked out, have the wound cleaned and probably sutured. "Could I just have a sip of water, please?"

Luke grabbed a bottle from the fridge and held it out to her. "Only one sip. You shouldn't really eat or drink anything."

"I know, thank you." Cass tried to take the water Luke offered, but her hands shook too badly to grip the bottle. Cold? The subsiding adrenaline rush? Probably both. The throbbing in her shoulder had begun in earnest, though, so she must be warming up.

Luke steadied her hand and cradled the back of her head so she could get a sip then set the bottle aside. "Can you tell me what happened?"

"Luke?" Bee squinted up at him and rolled onto his side. "You made it."

"Of course we did." Luke gave Bee a hand to help him sit. "Do you really think there's a time you'd call for help and we wouldn't come?"

All the color rushed back into Bee's face and flushed his cheeks. "I suppose not."

"Never gonna happen, buddy." Luke set a hand on Bee's shoulder and looked into his eyes. "Are you okay?"

Cass's breath hitched, Luke's affection for Bee almost her undoing as she battled to control her emotions.

Bee nodded and lowered his gaze. "Sorry, I guess I'm not much of a bodyguard if I passed out the instant I found out Cass was shot."

"All of you are okay, and that's all that matters."

"Cass is okay?" His gaze ran over her even as he asked Luke the question.

She smiled through her tears. "I'm fine, Bee. Thanks to you risking your own life to get Beast and me onto the porch and inside the shop."

"I guess you're more of a bodyguard than you thought, huh?" Luke patted Bee's back, stood, and held out a hand. "Come on, let's get you guys more comfortable if you both feel okay to move."

"I'm fine now," Bee said as he grabbed Luke's hand and let him pull him up.

Together, the two of them lifted Cass gingerly to her feet and led her to a love seat toward the front of the shop, away from the broken glass and out of sight of the window.

"I think someone was shooting from the lighthouse, but then they stopped. Maybe they were trying to get to the front of the shop, I don't know, but do you have someone looking out there?" The last thing Cass wanted was to let the gunman get away so he could try again or hurt someone else.

"We do. Don't worry." While Bee sat next to Cass and took her hand in his, Luke took a seat on the coffee table, caging her knees between his, and took out his notepad and pen. "We have a couple of witnesses who noticed a small recreational boat on the bay around the time of the shooting, and while a large number of individually owned boats travel back and forth to and from the mainland for Bay Island residents who commute, not many would just be sitting out there on a day like today. The cold alone would be brutal, but add the wind and the choppy sea and it would be more than a little uncomfortable."

"I saw that boat and wondered about that," Bee said.

Cass tried to think back. She hadn't noticed any boats. Then again, she'd been freezing and more interested in keeping her head down to stay warm until Beast was done and she could get back inside. Lesson learned; from now on she'd be more vigilant, take the threat to herself and those around her more seriously. But she would not stop investigating. "How did you notice the boat, Bee? I couldn't even get your attention for two seconds before I walked out, you were so engrossed in your research."

He shrugged. "As soon as you stepped out the back door, I put it aside and watched you. I scanned the beach to be sure no one was out there, didn't see anyone but noticed the boat and dismissed it since it was pretty far out."

"Could you give me any distinguishing features?" Luke asked, pen poised above his notebook.

But Bee was already shaking his head. "Nothing, sorry. I mostly kept an eye on Cass. It was one of those small boats you see flitting around out there all the time in the summer, but I'm not much of a boat person."

"That's okay. Is there anything else you can tell me about the moments before the shooter opened fire?"

He shook his head.

Luke shifted his gaze to Cass and lay a hand on her knee. "How about you?"

"I forgot my coat, and I was freezing." Actually, she still was. With the back window blown out, the shop was like an ice box.

When she shivered, Bee moved closer and tucked her beneath his arm.

Luke jumped up and grabbed her jacket from the hook in the back where she always hung it and tucked it over both of them.

"Thank you." She pulled the coat up to her chin. "Anyway, it was colder than I realized, with the wind blowing the spray off the bay and all, and I had just stopped for Beast to go to the bathroom and wrapped my arms tighter around myself to try to keep warm when I felt a sting in my shoulder and the whole back window exploded."

"That pretty much answers my next question, but do you think there's any chance it was an accident of some sort?" He wrote as he spoke.

Cass thought about it, but she already knew the answer. The only question that remained was whether someone was trying to kill her or just scare her off. Had shifting position at that precise moment saved her life or gotten her injured? The gunman would most likely not have been able to see into the shop, at least not clearly enough to make out if there were any customers. He may have just seen her come out to walk Beast and meant to blow out the back window and she just shifted into the bullet's path at the last moment. Or it could have gone the other way: he'd meant to kill her and she'd moved just in time to avoid a bullet to the heart.

Ah, but there was another pressing question. Why hadn't she received any kind of warning? Maybe not a neon sign flashing *a killer has you in his crosshairs*, but at least the hairs on the back of her neck should have stood up, or she should have gotten goose bumps, or some kind of warning she was being watched. But no, nothing at all. Odd.

Unless . . . Recently, another psychic, a psychic more powerful and with more experience than Cass, had been able to shield her from being bombarded by voices from beyond. Could another psychic have done the same this time? Dampened her senses so she wouldn't realize she was in danger? Was it possible Thea Newburgh was more powerful than she claimed?

Luke cleared his throat, not pushing her for an immediate answer, but bringing her attention back to the question.

Maybe she'd give Simone a call later and see what she thought. "No, not an accident. Someone was either trying to scare me or trying to kill me. But if someone was trying to kill me, why not take another shot? It took me a while to get off the beach, even running."

Luke squinted toward the back window. "Could be a number of reasons, fear someone noticed you react or heard the window crash down and called the police, and the shooter wanted to escape before we showed up. Could be he noticed Bee inside once the glass was out of the way and didn't want to hurt a bystander. Or, you have to figure, he had as long as he needed to line up that first shot while you were basically standing still on the beach, and he was on a boat that was rocking and shifting with the sea. If he didn't get you that time, chances were he wasn't going to once you were aware and running."

"So, not a professional then," Bee said.

"Not likely. Which leads me to my next question." He pinned

Bee with a stare. "What exactly were you doing that might have garnered the shooter's attention?"

"Oh, please." Bee grinned. "You can't possibly be naïve enough to believe Cass wouldn't be looking into the players surrounding Elijah Anderson's death, can you?"

"Of course not." He shoved a hand through his shaggy dark hair and sighed. "So, what did you find?"

"Well, we started a list of people who might have had reason to keep Twin Forks from opening." Bee started to get up, but Luke waved him back. "Tank?"

Tank, who'd been staring out the window, his back to them, seemingly lost in whatever he was looking for out there, brushed some of the glass aside and lifted Cass's suspect list out of the mess. Then he grabbed the stack of notes Bee had been working on and the laptop as well.

"Ah, man," Bee whined. "Don't tell me you're going to confiscate the laptop too."

Tank handed Luke the stack of papers.

Luke grinned and tucked his notepad away just as the paramedics arrived. "Nah, but I would like to take your notes, if you don't mind."

"Sure, go ahead, but I warn you, my penmanship when I'm scribbling notes is atrocious."

Luke read through the notes, then looked up at Tank. "How do they do it?"

Tank scowled. "I have no idea, but my money's on dumb luck."

"Sure, buddy, keep telling yourself that." Luke laughed and shook his head. "Where did you two come up with this list of names, some of whom aren't even on our radar?"

Bee did a quick explanation of their theories about each of their suspects.

Luke pointed to the corner of the page. "And what about this one? Who's Ophelia Wilson?"

Bee hooked a thumb in her direction. "You'll have to ask Cass about that one."

"Ophelia is a ghost, an ancestor of Thea Newburgh. Supposedly."

Luke sighed. "And is she a suspect?"

In all fairness, he had to figure there'd be a ghost if she was involved. "I added her name to try to find out if there's any actual relation there or if Ophelia could be a real live flesh-and-blood person trying to take advantage of a vulnerable young girl."

Luke handed the pages back to Tank and looked past Cass's shoulder.

Great. That could only mean one thing.

"Hey, Cass, what happened?" Rick, who owned the deli and volunteered with the fire department, rounded the love seat and squatted down in front of her.

This day just kept getting better and better. With Rick tending her it would only be a very short matter of time before Emma Watson, who worked at the deli and was Bee's biggest rival when it came to Bay Island gossip, got wind of the fact that Cass had been shot. Within the hour all of Bay Island would know.

Chapter Fourteen

"I just spoke to Emma, and she said rumors are already flying that you were with Elijah Anderson when he was killed." Bee unwrapped a stick of gum and stuffed it into his mouth then handed Cass a piece, which she took gratefully, since they'd just spent the past few hours at the hospital getting patched up and hadn't eaten anything.

Cass stuffed the gum into her mouth and shifted to get more comfortable, then stared out the passenger side window. "I wasn't with him when he was killed, Bee."

"Yeah, well, you know that, and I know that, and you already know from past experience I'll do everything I can to squash that rumor —"

"And it won't make one bit of difference."

"Exactly." Bee stopped at a traffic light and looked at her, his eyes filled with sympathy she knew was genuine. "Any time you're present at a crime scene, the automatic assumption is that the victim told you who killed him, and blah, blah, blah. You know the drill."

"If only it were that easy." She sighed, happy to be developing a good reputation, but at the same time weary with the implications.

When the light changed, with no one behind him, Bee rolled through the intersection. "So, where to?"

Wasn't that the question. She wanted to get to the local paper and see what she could find in their archives, but that would have to wait until morning since they'd already closed by now. She wanted to talk to Liam McAlister again, and he was certainly done substituting by now, but chances were he'd be home all tucked up and toasty rather than at the historical society. And she was starved, so a trip to the diner was certainly on the agenda, especially since Stephanie and Aiden had picked Beast up from Mystical Musings earlier and taken him for the night, and Cass was in no rush to go home to an empty house. She'd thought of picking Beast up from Stephanie and taking him home, but she'd never disappoint Aiden like that.

"Cass?" Bee had pulled over just before the next intersection to allow a few cars to pass. "Do you know where you want to go?"

She knew Bee had to be starving, for both food and gossip at this point, but he kept his thoughts to himself, which Cass appreciated. "Would you just do me a favor and run past Twin Forks, then we can go to the diner and get something to eat?"

He frowned. "Are you sure you don't just want to go home? Or you could come to my house? We could even stop by at Stephanie's and see Beast if you want. And Aiden always makes you smile."

Even the thought of that precious little boy made her smile and her insides go all mushy. "If I go see Beast, I'm going to want to take him home with me, and Aiden would be crushed. Besides, I don't want to take a chance of bringing any danger to Stephanie's door."

"No, me neither."

"I will give her a call in a little while, though."

Bee nodded and adjusted the heating vent to blow on her. "You're shivering. Are you sure you're all right?"

She pulled the jacket Luke had wrapped around her shoulders at the hospital tighter around her, inhaling deeply the scent of his aftershave, cocooning her in the sense of safety his presence often brought. "I'm fine. Just a bit tired."

"Does your shoulder hurt?" Tears shimmered in his eyes, tears she knew he'd held back all day so as not to upset her further.

She reached out to him, gripped his hand. "I'm fine, Bee. Promise. A little sore, but nothing horrible, and the painkillers helped."

He nodded, and one tear tipped over his thick lashes and rolled down his cheek.

She reached out and wiped it away. "I'm okay, Bee. Honest."

"I know. It's just . . ." He sniffed and wiped his eyes with his free hand, then looked into her eyes. "I don't know what I'd do if anything ever happened to you. You're my world, Cass. I love you like I've never loved anyone else since my mother . . ."

"I love you too, Bee." Her own tears pricked the backs of her lids. Bee had become so much to her, and the thought of ever losing him brought instant panic, so she understood his fear. She also knew he'd had a difficult time getting close to anyone since his own mother's death had led him to Bay Island. "When my parents passed away and I returned to Bay Island to see to their arrangements, I hadn't planned to stay."

He squeezed her hand, fully understanding what she'd gone

through in that time, since he'd gone through a similar situation upon learning about his mother's connection to Bay Island after her death.

"My life was a mess, Bee. Personally, professionally. I had nowhere to go, nothing left to lose, but then I met you." She and Stephanie had been friends when they were kids and had picked up that friendship as if it had never been interrupted by the seventeen years Cass had spent in New York City. But her connection with Bee had been different. When she'd met him, she'd seen something in him that drew her, a kindred spirit maybe? "We will always have each other, Bee. That's a promise."

"You can't promise nothing will happen to you."

"No, I can't, and neither can you." The thought of losing him sent a blast of cold rushing through her. "But I can promise as long as I'm here, you will be the best friend I ever could have asked for."

"Ah, Cass." He shoved his hair back off his forehead and sagged against the seat back, and a shaky laugh blurted out. "At least if I die first, I know you'll still be able to reach out and chat me up. And I guess since you can talk to the dead from this side, maybe you'll continue to haunt me from the other side when your time comes."

She laughed, couldn't help it, despite the seriousness of the discussion. "Now that's a promise too."

Bee shook his head, scrubbed his hands over his face, and sat up, then shifted into Drive and pulled out. "Twin Forks, you say?"

"Yup. If you don't mind."

"There's no place I wouldn't go with you, Cass." Keeping his eyes on the road, he reached over and patted her hand.

She turned her hand over to twine her fingers with his. "Nor I with you, Bee."

They drove in silence, Cass lost in her own thoughts, some of the past, some of the present, some wondering what the future might bring. It was a jumbled, chaotic reverie, probably thanks to the medication they'd given her at the hospital.

"We're almost there, Cass. But I don't remember the property ever being that lit up. Though I don't often drive out this way, I do occasionally pass by." Bee squeezed her hand once, then released her and sat up straighter, leaning closer to the windshield. "Looks like someone set up spotlights on the property."

"Probably the police to investigate."

He slowed to a crawl as they passed the start of the grounds. "What are you looking for?"

Cass turned a bit to study the grounds out the passenger window. "I don't know, exactly, but I figure I'll recognize it if I see it."

Bee mumbled something unintelligible, then slammed on the brakes.

The seat belt tightened against her. Thankfully, they hadn't been going that fast.

A black-hooded figure stood in the middle of the road, staring up at the main building. Cass leaned forward and squinted through the windshield, which had started to fog. A ghost? No, probably not, since Bee had seen the figure as well and stopped to avoid hitting it. At least, she assumed that's why he stopped. She glanced over at him. If his horrified expression was any indication, he definitely saw the figure.

"What is it?" He swallowed hard.

"A person, that's all. Move closer."

He did as she asked, creeping forward an inch at a time. He stopped far enough back to allow room to go around if need be and shifted into Park. "Well, now what?"

"We wait." She didn't know what for, but she had no burning desire to confront the figure. Nor did she feel the need to flee. So . . .

After a moment, the figure turned toward them and lowered its . . . her hood, letting her dark hair flow behind her in the wind. Her black cloak billowed around her, once again bringing to mind the figure Cass had seen standing over Elijah. Perhaps it wasn't Thea Newburgh after all.

Bee shivered.

"It's okay, Bee. It's just a woman."

"I know." He chanced a quick glance at Cass before returning his gaze to the woman in the road in front of them. "It's Mercedes Dupont."

"What?" Cass had no idea who she expected the woman to be, though the possibility it was Ophelia Wilson had flitted through her head, but Mercedes Dupont had never entered her mind. "How do you know?"

"I had just started researching her when you went out to the beach, had just pulled up her picture when I stood to keep an eye on you and Beast."

"And you're sure it's her?"

"Oh, puh-lease, girl." He rolled his eyes. "Would I say so if I wasn't sure?"

No, he wouldn't.

"She had that same look in the computer image: dressed all in black, long raven hair, eyes so dark you can't distinguish iris from pupil."

"Come on, Bee, you can't possibly tell that from this far away."

"Well, you have to admit, those eyes staring us down right now are pretty dark. And they were downright creepy in her picture."

"A look it seems she fosters with the black hooded cape." Cass took a deep breath and let it out slowly. She'd been hoping for a conversation with Ms. Dupont at some point. No time like the present. Cass gripped the door handle and pulled.

Bee grabbed her arm. "Are you crazy? Where do you think you're going?"

"She's a woman, Bee, nothing more. And I had hoped to try to speak to her anyway."

"Yeah, well, woman or no, how do you know she's not carrying the weapon used to shoot you earlier?"

That stopped Cass short. Why had she assumed a flesh-and-blood woman held no threat? Had the medication dulled her thinking? That's why she never took anything stronger than ibuprofen and should have refused the stronger painkiller at the hospital. Or was that just an excuse?

Her instincts hadn't seemed to be working right ever since the night of her group reading when she'd first spoken to Elijah. No, wait. Actually, her abilities had been on the fritz even before that. The thought occurred again that someone could be blocking her, interfering with her abilities. Thea? Maybe. Or, perhaps Ophelia was strong enough to reach out from beyond and block her? Could Mercedes Dupont be psychic?

A call to Simone was definitely in order, since she had a lot more experience than Cass did. It would be too late by the time they returned home tonight, but tomorrow morning, first thing, for sure. "You stay here, Bee, and I'll be right back."

"Fat chance that's happening." He grabbed his door handle.

"Please, Bee. I don't think she's a threat."

"Then why hasn't she moved?"

"Who knows?" Had she frozen like a deer in the headlights at their approach? "But she has no way to know who's in the car, since our headlights are on and she's standing on a fairly dark stretch of road, even if she would recognize me, which I doubt, since she has no reason to even know who I am."

Unless she was the psychic Cass suspected was dampening her abilities.

"Please, wait here. I think she's more likely to talk to a woman alone. A large man striding toward her on a dark, deserted stretch of road, in front of a defunct home for the criminally insane, could be a bit intimidating."

He harrumphed but let go of the handle. "Fine. I can see your point. But don't walk between her and me, and if that woman makes one move to reach for anything inside that cloak, I'm running her down."

"It's a deal." Though she hoped it wouldn't come to that. Cass got out of the car slowly and started toward Mercedes, keeping Bee's instructions in mind. But what to do? Let her know she recognized her, or play dumb? "Excuse me."

A slow, lazy smile spread across the woman's face. "Well, I'll be. Cass Donovan. I've been hoping to run into you. I've been wanting to talk to you."

Taken aback that the woman recognized her, Cass slowed. Well, then, since they were being honest with one another. "Well, it looks like you'll get your opportunity then, Mercedes."

Just a flicker of surprise in her eyes, so brief Cass would have missed it had she not been watching for a reaction, and then it was gone.

Mercedes's black-lipstick-lined lips stretched into a smile. "Would you like to stand out here and talk in the cold, or perhaps go somewhere warmer, more private, more conducive to a discussion of death?"

Fear skittered up Cass's spine. A threat? Or just a woman who wanted to talk about someone who'd died?

Chapter Fifteen

Having agreed to meet at the diner, which was warmer but definitely not private, Cass had gotten back into the car and argued the merits of meeting with this woman at all as she and Bee followed Mercedes to the diner. "Remind me why I'm doing this again."

"Because you wanted to speak with her anyway, and it's better to meet in a public place than to go somewhere alone with a possible killer," Bee said patiently.

"Oh, right." Still, she could be home in a nice warm Epsom salt bath, tending muscles too unused to running on the beach while tensed for more gunfire. She tried to stretch her legs in the cramped footwell, ease some of the soreness in her back.

"Besides, aren't you at all curious what Mercedes was standing in the middle of the street contemplating in the dead of night?" He glanced at her and grinned. "Pun intended."

Cass laughed, which helped ease the tension knotting her muscles better than stretching had. "I suppose I am curious; I'm just tired right now."

"And a bit cranky." He lifted a brow. "You might want to curb the attitude a bit when you talk to Mercedes if you want to get her to confide in you."

Getting people to confide in her had never really been a problem. But Bee was right, though in her current state, the thought rankled. She sighed and relaxed her shoulders. "Sorry, Bee. I guess I'm just exhausted, between running and the medication they gave me at the hospital. Thanks for the gentle reminder."

"No problem, sweetie." He hit the turn signal and followed Mercedes into the fairly empty diner parking lot. "And when this is over, I'll take you home, run you a nice hot bath, and nurse you back to health."

She had to admit, the thought of letting him baby her for a little while did appeal. She dropped her head back against the headrest and closed her eyes.

Bee shifted into Park. "Are you sure you're up to this? I could just hop out and reschedule, ask her to come into the shop tomorrow for a reading or something."

Ugh, yes, she wanted very badly to do just that. Instead, she sat up and checked her reflection in the visor mirror. "No, thank you. Better to get it over with."

He turned off the car without saying anything.

As much as she'd love to postpone, what if Mercedes disappeared before Cass got to speak to her? Someone had already taken a shot at Cass; what if Mercedes showing an interest in the investigation put her in danger as well? What if Mercedes was the killer and she struck again and someone else died while Cass was lounging in her warm bath? Not a chance she was willing to take.

"I've learned the hard way, more than once, not to put things off." She finger-combed her hair and flipped the visor back up. There was not much she could do to salvage what little makeup she wore.

Bee got out and walked around to her side, then opened her door and reached for her arm.

"Thanks, Bee, but I'm okay. Really." And showing any sign of weakness in front of a potential suspect was the last thing she wanted to do. She took her time crossing the lot in case any of what appeared to be just wet had frozen over into black ice. Thankfully, it hadn't, though the temperatures must be hovering somewhere close to freezing.

Bee held the door for Mercedes, who stood waiting on the stoop, then Cass to precede him into the diner.

As soon as Cass stepped through the door, the low hum of conversation stopped. Diners, some discreetly, others not so much, stared at her as she opened Luke's coat a bit and waited to be seated. Ah, well, no surprise news of her incident had already spread. She resisted the urge to squirm. She'd been the topic of Bay Island's rumor mill too many times to let it bother her.

Lara, the hostess on duty, rushed over. "Cass, how are you? We heard you got shot. I hope everything's okay. You look pretty good."

"I'm fine, thank you." Cass forced a smile. In hindsight, this might not have been the best idea.

"I'm so glad. Everyone was worried." Lara grabbed three menus and ushered them to a booth in the back corner. "Hopefully, you'll have a little privacy to relax and enjoy your meal back here."

"Thank you so much, Lara. I really appreciate that." And with that one kind gesture, Cass's mood improved considerably. And so did her appetite. She slid into the booth.

Bee slid in behind her, caging her in the corner.

Mercedes hung her cloak on a hook beside the table and sat across from Cass. She set her menu aside.

Oh, well, whether Mercedes chose to eat or not, Cass was having dinner. She opened her menu.

Elaina Stevens rushed over. "Cass, oh my goodness, are you all right? Everyone was saying you got shot and had to be taken by ambulance to the hospital."

"I'm fine, Elaina, barely a scratch." She glanced at Mercedes, tried to gauge her reaction. Nothing, the woman's expression remained completely neutral. "I just went to the hospital as a precaution and to have the wound cleaned."

Elaina pressed a hand against her chest. "Well, I'm so relieved. It's good to see you up and around, and Frankie had to run out, but he said to tell you your meals are on the house."

And that was the same caring that had enticed Cass to remain on Bay Island after her parents' funeral. She was sorry to have missed the owner, Frankie Mandola. She'd have to stop by and thank him herself one day during the week. "Please, tell him I said thank you."

"I will, for sure." Elaina lifted the pad. All business and no gossip, which meant either Mercedes was a stranger to her, or she knew the woman well enough not to speak in front of her. Since Elaina gave nothing more than a perfunctory nod and a polite greeting, Cass was betting on the former. "Can I get you all something to drink?"

Cass figured caffeine, even this late in the evening, wouldn't keep her awake at this point, but she didn't want something hot, so she went with a diet soda.

Bee ordered the same.

"I'll have a coffee, black." No surprise there, since black seemed to be her color. From her midnight black hair, almost black eyes emphasized by a thick line of black eyeliner, and the black cloak she'd removed to reveal black jeans paired with a black turtleneck and black boots, to her short black polished nails, the woman was a walking advertisement for darkness.

Question was, was the look a brand to go with her supposed

obsession with opening a macabre museum of death, as Liam McAlister had so eloquently phrased it? Or did her obsession with death and darkness go deeper? Because she was decades past any kind of teenage rebellion, and if the lines bracketing her eyes and mouth were any indication, at least some portion of that jet-black hair came from a bottle.

With Elaina hurrying to get their drinks, Cass got down to business. "So, what were you hoping to speak with me about?"

She rested her forearms on the table and clasped her hands in front of her, perfectly still, and captured Cass's gaze. "I want to help you."

"Oh?" Cass lifted a brow and waited.

"It seems your reputation has been a bit . . . tarnished, shall we say? Thanks to one Miss Thea Newburgh." Her expression twisted in distaste. Apparently, no love lost between those two. "Well, I want to help you restore it."

"Do you now?" Though Cass studied her, the woman gave nothing away. "And why would you want to do that?"

She tilted her head. "Because it will benefit both of us."

Cass was too tired to deal with Mercedes beating around the bush, but Bee's warning echoed in her mind . . . At least, it did right after he elbowed her discreetly in the rib. She counted slowly to ten in her mind, reining in her shortened temper. "And how is that?"

"Okay, hear me out." She scooted up straighter and held up her hands, the first sign of any kind of emotion peeking out as she apparently warmed to her subject. Had she finished feeling Cass out? Or had this been her agenda all along? "I think you and I both agree that the Twin Forks building and grounds should never be used to house children."

Since Cass couldn't argue that but didn't have a clue where Mercedes was headed, she remained silent.

Elaina dropped off their drinks and took their orders. Since Bee and Mercedes both ordered cheeseburgers and fries, Cass just ordered the same. It didn't matter to her, though she did give one wistful thought to the steaks she and Luke were supposed to share tonight as she ordered. No doubt he'd take a rain check and do it as soon as he could, but following any leads on who might have attacked her came first. Which she both understood and appreciated, so here she sat waiting for a cheeseburger and whatever pitch Mercedes had coming.

"Nor should it be razed to build condos," she continued as if she'd never been interrupted once Elaina left to submit their orders. "But why knock the place down, or burn it to the ground as Thea would like to see happen? Why not let it stand as a testament to what came before? Show people the path that led to current treatments for mental illness. Only by opening our eyes and seeing— really seeing—the past can we learn from it."

While Cass couldn't argue with her logic, she also couldn't jump on board with a plan she hadn't even yet heard with a woman she didn't know.

"And if we don't learn, how do we keep from repeating the same mistakes?" Mercedes continued.

Again, Cass couldn't argue. Instead, she lifted her soda and took a sip, letting the blessedly cold drink sooth her dry throat. "What is it exactly that you want to do?"

She sat back triumphantly. "I want to turn the place into a museum, restore it to its original look and feel, return all of the equipment to where it once stood with plaques to notate the purpose of each device, explain how they were used."

Cass was already shaking her head at the image of a display much like that of the Hurricane of '38, which Liam McAlister had so meticulously documented. "While I do agree with some of what you're saying, I don't think that's the best purpose for that land."

Her dark eyes narrowed. "If you agree with any of what I'm saying, then I know you won't go along with developing it, so what then? Burn it down?"

"I'm not saying that." But what did she think? So far, none of the plans she'd heard seemed like the right thing to do.

"Then what are you saying? Exactly?"

She wasn't sure, and she wasn't clearheaded enough to argue the point coherently. "I need some time to think and research some more before I can offer an opinion. Besides, I have no say in what happens to that land. It's up to Elijah Anderson's widow what she decides to do with it."

She wished she could take the words back even as they left her lips. She hadn't meant to set Mercedes on Evelyn Anderson, even if the woman had been rude to Cass.

"And who do you think has the most influence over that decision? Perhaps the woman her husband hired to get answers?"

"Actually, Cass no longer works for the Andersons." Bee had been quiet up until that point, perhaps waiting to see how Cass would react and what she wanted to do, but clearly he was done with the conversation, or at least realized she was. "She returned the check Elijah gave her to Evelyn and that's the end of that."

Mercedes looked appalled. "Why in the world would you return his check?"

"Because I felt like his widow probably needed the money, first of all. And, second of all, I don't want any further involvement with this whole thing." And it surprised her to realize that was true. Not that it would stop her from trying to find out who'd killed Elijah, but as far as the psychiatric center went, she'd leave that decision to others.

"So does that mean you won't be going out there to have a chat with Ophelia Wilson?"

Caught off guard, Cass hesitated.

Mercedes smirked. "Please, you think I wouldn't know what the competition is up to?"

"I'm no competition to you. And this isn't a game. A man is dead."

"Not you. Thea Newburgh. Because only one of us can get our way on what happens to that property, and I can assure you, it won't be Thea." She stood and grabbed her cloak from the rack, then waved Elaina over. "I'll take my burger to go, please."

Elaina glanced at Cass and Bee, then smiled tentatively at Mercedes. "Of course, I'll take care of it right away."

Mercedes slung the cloak over her shoulders. "And, by the way, have you spoken to the poor widow recently? Oh, wait, how could you have? She left Bay Island this afternoon. On her yacht."

Bee watched her walk away and stop to collect her food at the hostess station, then looked at Cass. "I told you that woman didn't need her money back."

"I don't care about that, Bee. The money wasn't mine to keep, whether she needed it or not. What I do find interesting, though, is the fact that she's already gone from Bay Island. I'd think with her husband's death under investigation, she'd have stuck around at least for a little while."

Elaina set their plates on the table in front of them and cleared Mercedes's setting. "Everything okay?"

"Sure, thank you." Cass's mind raced, ricocheting between suspects, all of whom had their sights on their own goals.

"Do you want to switch sides, Bee?"

Bee hesitated, then narrowed his gaze on Elaina and stood. "Sure."

Elaina glanced over her shoulder then slid Bee's plate across the table. She waited for him to take his seat, then leaned over. "I couldn't help overhearing that woman say Thea Newburgh's name, so I figured I'd let you know she walked in a little bit ago, saw you guys sitting over here, then turned around and left without saying anything, even when Lara called after her to let her know we had available seats."

"Thanks for that, Elaina."

She stood and smiled. "Can I get you anything else?"

"Nope, we're good, thank you." Unless she could tell them who'd killed Elijah and how Thea and Mercedes played into the equation.

Chapter Sixteen

A ringing sound pulled Cass from a deep, thankfully dreamless, sleep, and she fumbled her hand across the nightstand in search of the snooze button. Even after she hit it, the ringing continued. She lifted her head, slitted one eye open, and glared at her alarm clock.

Nine o'clock! Yikes! She had less than an hour to get the shop open.

Her house phone screen lit up as it rang again, and the previous day's events came crashing back. She didn't have to get up. She couldn't open Mystical Musings until after the insurance adjuster came and she hired a cleaning crew to take care of the glass and a contractor to replace the window. Thankfully, Luke had asked Emmett to board up the window so no one broke into the shop.

So, why was someone bothering her?

The name Simone Carlson flashed on the display, and Cass grabbed it. She'd forgotten she wanted to speak to Simone this morning, but how had Simone known to call? And how had she known to call her landline when Cass almost never used it, didn't even recognize the ringtone at first?

She'd felt an instant connection to the other psychic when they'd met, and Simone had helped Cass learn to exert more control over her abilities, to shield her mind from intrusion. Had she sensed Cass needed her? "Simone, hey, I was going to call you this morning."

Simone's deep rich laugher streamed through the line and instantly helped Cass relax. "I assure you, my dear, it was no great psychic connection that led me to call you, simply a news alert on my cell phone that Elijah Anderson had been killed on Bay Island, and an attempt had been made on the life of the psychic who found his body."

Cass groaned. It was too early for this.

"At least they didn't mention you by name." Simone's smooth accent and laidback tone held a hint of tropical island tranquility that instantly set Cass at ease.

"Well, I guess that helps." She scooted to sit against the headboard and try to pull herself from the last remnants of the painkiller-induced sleep. "How'd you know to call the house?"

"That was easy: you didn't answer your cell, and I took a chance you might not have left for work yet. So, how are you feeling? Are you all right?" Concern tinged her voice.

"I'm fine, Simone, thank you. And thank you for calling to check in on me. If I realized news would reach the city so quickly, I'd have called you last night." And she should have. Simone had told her more than once she didn't keep regular hours and Cass could call anytime she needed her.

"Don't worry about it, dear, I'm just glad you're okay? And Bee?"

"He's fine too, passed out on my couch if the snoring that's rattling my walls is any indication."

Simone laughed. She'd developed a deep affection for Bee after the two had gotten off to a rocky start, and Bee for her. "Well, then, you said you were going to call me this morning, a catch-up call, or did you need assistance?"

A brief niggle of guilt crept in. When Simone had first returned to New York, they'd kept up regularly, talking several times each week. Lately, the calls had dwindled to once a week, and now she hadn't spoken to the other woman in about three weeks.

"Stop beating yourself up, Cass. It's not a reprimand."

Cass grinned. Psychic connection or not, the only person who could gauge her feelings almost as well as Bee and Stephanie was Simone. Quite impressive, really, considering they hadn't met that long ago.

"I've actually been out of the country on a case for the past two weeks. It came up suddenly, or I'd have called to let you know. So, no worries. Friends understand when life intrudes, and they pick up where they left off when they can. And they always drop everything when called upon to help."

And that was what she loved about Simone. Straight to the truth, no nonsense or beating around the bush. With her, you always knew where you stood. At least, you did if she didn't suspect you of murder.

"Now, get up and get yourself a cup of coffee, let that monster of yours out, and tell me how I can help."

Cass swung her feet over the side of the bed, suddenly energized. "Thanks, Simone, you're the best."

"Hey!" Bee yelled from the hallway and poked his head into the room. "I heard that, and I thought I was the best. If I'd known, I wouldn't have just let Beast out and put on the coffee."

"Sorry, Bee, you're right, of course. You're the best."

Simone blurted a laugh. "Tell Bee I said hello."

Cass passed hellos back and forth between the two for a moment while she stepped into her slippers and finger-combed her hair. She decided to leave on her sweats and T-shirt since she could afford to be a little lazy this morning. She rolled her shoulder. Not too bad, all things considered.

While she went through an abbreviated version of her morning routine, thanks to Bee's help, she brought Simone up to date on everything that had happened, careful not to leave out even the smallest detail Simone might glean something from.

As was her way, Simone remained silent while Cass worked through it all.

"So, you have three potential problems, then, in addition to figuring out who the killer is."

Cass frowned and plopped onto one of the kitchen chairs.

Bee set a big mug of coffee in front of her, and she absently thanked him. "How do you figure three problems?"

"One, the woman you met with last night, Mercedes Dupont. From the little bit of research I was able to do while you were speaking, since you said Bee's initial attempts were interrupted, she seems obsessed with death. Her social media accounts are filled with a macabre fascination with methods of not only death, but torture as well. Though I can't find any mention of her being psychic, or visiting a psychic, or anything like that, anyone who's that obsessed with death has to be curious about what comes beyond, so it wouldn't surprise me if she'd visited a medium in the past."

"Thea Newburgh?"

"Which brings me to problem number two. Is Thea a strong enough psychic to shield you from sensing danger? Is she playing some kind of game?"

Cass hoped she wasn't. Despite the circumstances, she'd felt a certain . . . not pity exactly . . . but compassion for the young girl. She'd hate to think she'd been conned.

"And the third problem, which I see as the biggest threat you're facing aside from the killer, Ophelia Wilson."

"Why is she the biggest threat if she's already dead?"

"For that exact reason, my dear. If you're dealing with a psychic who can still . . . manipulate, shall we call it, events even decades after her death, you are dealing with an extremely powerful mind. One who might well be fixated on revenge."

Cass hadn't thought about that. She probably should have—if nothing else her psychiatric training should have led her to the possibility of revenge—but her developing psychic abilities were too new for her to consider the concept of revenge from beyond the grave as a motive. She lowered her head and massaged her temples.

Bee gave Beast a treat and sat down across the table from her with his own cup of coffee.

"And that's why I'll be there later today," Simone said.

Cass's head snapped up. "What? You're coming out here?"

"Of course. I can't stay long, but I'll at least try to help you figure out what you're up against. If someone is dampening your abilities, you might need some help shielding yourself."

"I don't know what to say, Simone, thank you."

"Of course, dear, anytime."

"And I'd come anytime for you as well. I hope you know that."

"Absolutely. And don't worry, one of these days I'm sure I'll call upon you."

"And I will come, with no hesitation."

"Good. Now, let me go make a ferry reservation and get started. It's a long drive out to eastern Long Island."

"I'll see you later then. Thank you again, Simone." Cass hung up and looked at Bee.

He looked tired, puffy circles surrounding his eyes, his usually dark tan paled by months of cold, cloudy weather. "You okay, Bee?"

"I'm fine." He smiled at her. "Just keep in mind, this is the middle of the night for me."

And he'd gotten very little sleep the day before either.

He slouched back on his chair. "So, what's on the agenda while you're waiting for Simone to get here?"

Cass sipped her coffee. "I would like to go to the local paper, see if I can get access to their archives and find out anything I can about Ophelia Wilson before Simone arrives."

"Good idea. I'll just jump in the shower and get changed." Since

Bee so often stayed over, he kept a few outfits and toiletries in one of the guest bedroom dressers. "I thought I heard Simone mention Mercedes Dupont."

Beast propped his head in Cass's lap, and she twined her fingers through his soft mane. "She was able to find a little on her while we were talking, says she's obsessed with death."

"I got that much from our conversation at the diner last night." He sipped his coffee. "But I'll try to look into her more while you're inside the paper. Probably better if only one of us goes in."

Cass wrapped her hands around her warm mug, not looking forward to going back out in the cold. She'd much rather curl up on the couch with Beast and watch a movie or read a book. But none of them would be safe until Elijah's killer was found, so . . . "Sounds good, and then we can go finish our conversation with Liam McAlister."

"That works." Bee slid back his chair and stood, then patted Beast's head before heading out of the kitchen to get ready.

Cass sat, petting Beast's head, contemplating getting up to top off her coffee mug, and thinking about revenge. She'd been so caught up on Elijah's death having something to do with the psychiatric center, she hadn't given any thought to a more personal motive. And as far as motives went, revenge was a popular one. What if whoever had killed him had no interest in what happened to Twin Forks Psychiatric Center? What if the killer's motives were more personal?

Who would top the list of suspects then?

"Hey, Bee?" she yelled, hoping he hadn't yet gotten in the shower.

A minute later, he appeared in the doorway carrying a stack of clothing and a towel. "What's up?"

"Instead of researching Mercedes, could you do me a favor?"

He shrugged. "Sure. What do you need?"

"Could you research Elijah?"

He leaned one shoulder against the doorjamb and crossed one leg over the other. "Why, what are you thinking?"

"Well, we've been assuming, because Elijah was killed at the psychiatric center, that the killer's motive had something to do with how that property was going to be used. Or not used."

He pursed his lips.

"But what if the killer had a more personal motive?"

"And Elijah being out behind Twin Forks with a storm starting just provided an opportunity." He nodded, and she could see the gears turning. "I'll try to find out who he was close to. Question is, what was he doing out back? He had already unlocked the front door, and I really expected him to be there to greet you, maybe cajole you a little to remind you what he needed."

Cass had expected the same. She'd been concerned he'd make another attempt to pressure her into leaning in his direction. "So, what was he doing out behind the building? Did someone just follow him there—"

"Or did he have plans to meet someone out there?"

"Exactly."

A knock on the back door pulled her focus.

Luke cracked the door open and peeked in. "Hey, got a minute?"

Beast scrambled to his feet and barreled across the room to greet him.

Luke just laughed and caught Beast up, then squatted beside him for a belly rub.

"Hmm . . . I don't know, Cass." Bee looked at her and lifted a brow. "He doesn't greet you with that level of enthusiasm."

"Are you serious? He practically knocks me over when I walk back in from getting the mail."

Bee winked. "I wasn't talking about Beast."

Luke stood and laughed, then crossed the room to Cass and offered a kiss. Not the usual peck on the cheek or temple in greeting, but a deep, soul-searing kiss that seeped into her muscles and eased the tension from all of them.

"Well, then . . ." Since he wasn't yet wearing a scarf, Bee fanned himself with is hand. "Now that's much better, dear."

Heat rushed into Cass's cheeks.

Luke just grinned. "I'm glad you approve."

"On that note . . ." Bee turned to leave.

"Actually, Bee, could you stay a minute. I have something I need both of you to look at." His gaze lingered on Cass. "Unfortunately, this morning I'm here on business."

"Sure." Bee moved farther into the room. "Do you want a cup of coffee? It's already made."

"Thanks, but I can't stay." He was already scrolling through his phone. "I have a better image if you can't tell from this, but in anticipation of Beast's greeting, I left it in the car in favor of the one on my phone."

Cass glanced at Bee, who moved to stand beside her.

Luke held out the phone, a grainy photo on the screen.

"Hey, that's from the video I took." Bee pointed to the dark figure standing over Elijah's body. Only now, the image had been enlarged and enhanced to clear it up somehow, and you could see the woman's face clear enough to identify, with two dark blurs behind her by the woods.

"Do you recognize her?" Luke asked.

Cass's mouth went dry and she nodded. "That's Thea Newburgh."

Chapter Seventeen

Since Luke had gone to question Thea, Cass would have to wait to reach out to her, which she most definitely would do at the first opportunity. No matter what her suspicions might be about Thea's psychic claims, Cass just couldn't see her as the killer. Though she'd been surprised before. You never knew who could be motivated to kill.

She pulled against the curb and parked in front of an old house off Main Street that had housed the local paper, the *Bay Island News*, for the past hundred years or so. Before that, the paper's home was the basement of the local market. "Are you going to come in, or do you want to wait here?"

"I'll wait here and keep an eye if anyone goes in after you, but I want to get started researching Elijah some, see who he connects to on Bay Island," Bee said.

"All right, just come get me if you need me." Leaving the car running so Bee wouldn't freeze, Cass hurried inside, where the air wasn't much warmer than outside.

A woman with hair as blue as the coat she was bundled into looked up from whatever she was typing on an ancient typewriter that might well have been an original from when the paper first began. "How can I help you?"

"Good morning." Cass's breath fogged with each word. "I'm interested in researching articles from the past, do you keep an archive section here?"

She stood and pulled her coat tighter around her. "Sorry, heat's busted. Someone's supposed to come fix it later, but I'm not holding my breath."

"I'm sorry to hear it."

The woman shrugged and held a low gate open for Cass. "Not your fault. Anyway, follow me."

Cass followed her to a room in the back where a row of surprisingly up-to-date computers stood in a row. From the layer of dust coating them, they didn't see much action. "Help yourself. Everything we have records of has been transferred to digital."

"Oh, wow. Thanks." She'd had visions of having to dig through boxes and boxes of dusty old papers in a damp, moldy basement somewhere, or at the least reels of microfilm.

The woman beamed. "I did it myself. Not like there's ever much for me to do around here, so I updated all we had to the computers 'bout ten years back. Makes it a whole lot easier for me when someone requests something. Is there anything I can help you with?"

"Um . . ." Did she really want to involve anyone else? No. But was there some way of getting help without the other woman realizing what she was researching? Maybe, but it wasn't worth the chance. The rumor mill was already going strong enough; no sense fueling it. "I don't think so, but thanks."

"Sure, just give a yell . . ." The squeak of her sneakers against the tile floors followed her back to the reception area.

Keeping her coat on, Cass hung her bag on the back of the chair at the first workstation and sat in front of the computer. Despite the chill in the air, a bead of sweat dripped down the side of her face. Anxiety? Maybe, but from what? She didn't know, so she didn't waste any more time wondering if it was real or imagined or someone trying to warn her off investigating.

She wiped the sweat with the back of her wrist and typed Ophelia Wilson's name into the search bar. A long column of articles popped up immediately. She started with the most recent, a front-page piece on Ophelia's transfer to Twin Forks from a correctional facility on the mainland, where she'd been held throughout her murder trial.

Cass went back to the search results and chose an article from the sentencing: *Long Island Woman Sentenced in Murder of Family.* A quick skim through the article gave a summary of the accusations. Apparently, Ophelia Wilson had been found covered in blood, standing over several family members who'd been murdered.

"No, that's not right," Cass whispered, suddenly certain that wasn't the way the murders had happened. Though she had no clue how or why, she knew in her gut the article was wrong.

The article went on to chronicle the arrest, the trial—where very little physical evidence was produced beyond the way she'd been found—and the sentencing. According to witnesses, Ophelia had a penchant for violence even before the murders.

Cass braced herself for the certainty the witnesses had been mistaken. Nothing. Hmm . . .

Fearing she posed a danger to herself after sentencing, officials transferred her to Twin Forks for observation. She was never released according to a small obituary Cass found from twenty years later.

A black-and-white photo accompanied the text. A plain woman, unusually thin, with straight darkish hair hanging limp in front of her shoulders. Any resemblance to Thea? Not really. At least not that Cass could see from the picture, other than the long brown hair, which was too common to be considered.

"Well?"

Cass jumped at the intrusion and whirled to find Bee standing over her. "Oh, man, Bee, what are you trying to do? Scare me to death?"

"Sorry. I didn't mean to startle you, just wondering how you're making out." He pulled a chair out from the computer next to hers and sat. It squealed beneath his weight.

Cass held her breath a moment, waiting for him to go crashing to the floor, but the chair held. "Apparently, Ophelia was convicted of killing her parents and a sibling, then sent to Twin Forks, where she died after twenty years."

"What did she die from?" He rocked back and forth in the chair to a steady screech, screech, screech.

Cass tried to keep her attention on the obituary. "It doesn't say."

"Hmm . . . Okay, let's see what we can dig up." As he turned to the computer, the seat gave one final squeal of protest. Ignoring it, he wiggled his fingers, cracked his knuckles, and started typing.

Cass left him to it and returned to her own search. "It says here Ophelia's husband and a young daughter moved to Bay Island to be closer to her."

He narrowed one eye. "She was already married and had a child at the time of the murders?"

"Apparently." Which didn't feel right to Cass either.

He rested an elbow on the table and ran a finger over his lips. "Did they say what her motive was?"

"It's not really clear from the article." At least, not at first glance. "Seems there was a dispute between her and the brother over something, and the parents sided with him."

"I suppose people have killed for less, but still. It doesn't feel right. Hey, you got any lip balm in that bag? The cold is murder on my lips." He waggled his eyebrows.

"Ha-ha." Cass just shook her head and pointed to the bag. "It's in the pouch on the front."

"What's the child's name?" Bee smoothed the balm over his lips, which really were pretty chapped and cracked, then dropped the tube back into her bag and opened a new tab. "Does it say?"

"Uh . . ." She scanned the article. "Yeah, here. Husband's name was Samuel Wilson, daughter, Samantha."

"Got it."

Leaving Bee to find out what he could, Cass typed in the name Cameron Parker. She found the article Bee had already shown her and scrolled past it. What was she looking for exactly? She had no idea but figured she'd know it when she saw it. And, bingo, she did.

A search result with the name Cameron Parker along with the name Twin Forks both highlighted. She clicked on the article, a small local piece on the sale of the former Twin Forks Psychiatric Center property to Mr. Elijah Anderson, followed by a paragraph about the board of directors pushing back on his intention to develop the property as a boarding school. "Hey, Bee, look at this."

"Huh?" he answered, distracted by whatever he was squinting at on his own screen.

"You'll never guess who's on the board of directors of Anderson Properties."

"Who?" He glanced over, causing another loud screech.

Cass pointed to the screen. "None other than Mr. Cameron Parker."

"What?" He rolled his chair toward her, then jumped up, shoved it toward another workstation, and grabbed a different chair. "I can't listen to that thing squeal another minute. Besides, how am I supposed to know if someone is sneaking up on us with all that noise?"

He had a point there.

"Okay. Now." He sat and leaned closer to the screen. "Hmm . . . not only is he a board member, but it says here he's the one leading the opposition to Elijah's plan to develop the property."

"So why was he trying to get there on the night of Elijah's murder?"

Bee shook his head. "Unless he had already been out there and, like you suggested, was just looking for an alibi."

Cass contemplated the screen for another moment and wished she'd thought to stop for coffee on her way in. "But where do we go from here?"

"See if you can find out how long he's been a member." Bee returned to his own search.

Now that she knew what she was looking for, the searches were easier, yielding the results she was looking for moments later. "He became a member almost five years ago, after another board member, a Mr. Harvey Potts, disappeared."

"Disappeared?"

Another search brought up an article detailing Harvey's disappearance. "Seems he came to Bay Island to research the property and never returned home."

Bee stopped what he was doing. "A coincidence he disappeared at around the same time Salvatore Marcuzzio, who happened to be a groundskeeper at Twin Forks, was killed?"

Cass shook her head. When you looked at it like that, it didn't seem likely. She went back to the article about Cam becoming a board member and enlarged the photo accompanying the article. A group of people, Elijah at its center, holding glasses up in a toast. She recognized Cam Parker standing beside Evelyn Anderson, his arm hooked comfortably around her shoulders. A gesture of friendship? Or did the two have something more intimate going on?

No way to tell from the picture. But at the least, they appeared to be friendly. Cass looked through several more pages of search results, but she couldn't come up with any other connection between the two. And Cam Parker seemed to keep his head down, until it came time to develop the property, at which time he became quite vocal in his opposition.

"In other news." Bee slanted the screen toward her so Cass could see what he'd found. "After weeding through a long list of birth and marriage announcements, among other things, I've found your woman. It seems your ghost is telling the truth, or at least Thea is. Thea Newburgh is a direct descendant of Ophelia Wilson."

"And Thea was found leaning over Elijah Anderson's body only moments after he was killed."

He tilted his head and studied her but didn't give his own thoughts away. "Do you think she killed him? And really, honestly, deep down in your gut, do you see that girl taking a shot at you and Beast on the beach from a rocking boat pretty far out in the bay? Because that's pretty cold-blooded, if you ask me."

Cass didn't answer, because she didn't know what to think.

He let it drop. "So, where to now?"

Cass welcomed the change of subject. "Well, we can't very well interview . . . I mean talk to, Thea, since she's probably still being questioned by Luke and Tank. And I have no idea where to find Cam Parker, or what I'd say to him if I did find him, and Evelyn, who I'd love to ask about her relationship with Cam, has apparently already left Bay Island."

"And since your last discussion with Mercedes Dupont proved pretty much useless, there doesn't seem to be much sense in seeking her out again." Bee scrolled and tapped away at the keys while he spoke.

"So, where does that leave us?"

"Well, well, well. What have we here?" He lifted one bushy brow and pursed his lips. Then he sat back and gestured toward the screen.

Cass stood and leaned past him to read the article he'd left up.

Being Bee, and loving to impart gossip as he did, he didn't wait for her to even start reading the first line. "Seems Mr. Liam McAlister was arrested a while back."

"Arrested?" She glanced at the picture accompanying the article. It showed a large group of people; some appeared to be yelling, angry, others calmly held signs protesting the sale of the psychiatric center grounds.

Impatient, Bee scrolled to the end.

"Hey, I didn't get to read it yet."

"The beginning of the article doesn't matter. They didn't agree with the sale, protested, and blah, blah, blah . . ." He stopped scrolling and pointed to a list of names toward the end of the page. "See there."

Liam's name was close to the top of the list of protesters who'd been arrested for trespassing on the psychiatric center grounds, though the reporter theorized it was more to get him out of the way at the moment, since he was eventually released, the charges dropped.

"And . . ." Bee rolled his finger for her to keep reading. "Wait for it . . ."

"Mercedes Dupont?"

He surged upright. "Yup, one and the same. Arrested at the same protest as Liam. Coincidence?"

Was it? Maybe. "It says here over a thousand people protested the sale of that land."

He shrugged. "And a dozen or so were arrested. And now two of those twelve are suspects in a murder investigation of the man who bought the property in a transaction they were trying to stop. Plus, Liam was quick enough to mention Mercedes wanted to purchase the land and turn it into a museum the first time we spoke to him, but he conveniently left out the fact they were both arrested protesting the sale of that land in the first place."

"Hmm . . ."

"Hmm? That's it?" He swung his arms out to the sides and flopped against the seat back. It groaned in protest. "You can't be serious. That's a great clue."

"Yes, it is. I'm just not quite sure what to do with it."

"What else would you do with it?" He shrugged and closed the article. "You said yourself you can't question anyone else at the moment, we're at the end of what we can do research-wise, and you can't open the shop because the window hasn't yet been replaced."

Cass couldn't remember a time when she had such a long to-do list full of things she couldn't achieve or even begin to work on yet. "So, what do you want to do?"

"Go visit Liam McAlister and ask him why he and Mercedes were there together protesting and why he omitted it from our first discussion." He waggled his eyebrows.

While Cass would never ask that bluntly, he was probably on the right track. "Okay, we'll go see Liam, but I'm asking the questions."

Bee grinned and cracked his knuckles. "Wanna do good cop bad cop? I've always wanted to try that."

Uh-oh. She might just have created a monster. "Sure, but I get to be the bad cop."

His grin faltered. "Seriously?"

She laughed and patted him on the back, then stood and lifted her purse from the back of the chair. "Okay, fine, you can be bad cop."

"Yes!" He pumped his fist.

Now if she could just keep Luke and Tank from finding out what they were up to, because she was pretty sure they wouldn't approve.

Chapter Eighteen

As they walked into Liam McAlister's office at the historical society, Cass decided she'd definitely created a monster.

Bee strode through the door, his expression hard as granite, his chest inflated.

"Please . . ." Liam gestured to the two chairs at the front of his desk that they'd sat in the last time they were there. "Sit, make yourselves comfortable."

Cass slid out of her coat and hung it on the back of her chair, then perched on the edge of the seat and pulled the chair a bit closer to the desk.

Bee folded his arms across his broad chest, his feet apart. "I'll stand, thank you."

Apparently even bad cop Bee was well-mannered.

Cass bit back a smile.

Liam just eyeballed him as he sat behind the desk and shifted a stack of folders from its center to the floor. "So, how can I help you today?"

"I was hoping to pick your brain a bit more, since you had to rush out yesterday." She smiled what she hoped was a winning smile, the kind that said *It's safe to open up to me, share all of your deepest darkest secrets.*

Bee gave a snort under his breath.

With a quick glance at him from the corner of his eye, Liam focused on Cass. "I'm not sure what else I can tell you, but feel free to ask away."

Great. Now she had exactly what she wanted, his full, undivided attention and a willingness, even if temporary, to answer her questions, and she had no clue where to start. What seemed most pressing, just in case he got a call and had to rush out again? "While I am familiar with the history of Twin Forks Psychiatric Center, I wasn't quite up to date on more recent events. You mentioned yesterday that a number of people wanted to stop the property from being developed, could you expand on that?"

He shifted, seemingly uncomfortable under her gaze.

Since the smile was beginning to hurt her cheeks, there was no way she could up the wattage. She considered fluttering her eyelashes, but that seemed a bit over the top.

He lifted his hands to the sides then let them drop. "Aside from those I already told you about who were opposed, I don't know what else I can say."

"You said you spoke to Elijah, knew that he wanted to open a school, and you implied you didn't agree with his plans. Could you expand on that?"

"What do you want me to tell you? I didn't agree with building a school out there, didn't think it was a good place for kids. Like many other people on Bay Island."

"We could guess that much from the fact you were arrested at a protest out there," Bee said matter-of-factly.

If Cass hadn't been looking right at Liam when Bee had dropped that bombshell, she'd probably have missed the slight widening of his eyes, the instant of fear reflected there, before he recovered and slumped back into his chair. "So what? A lot of people were arrested at that protest."

"True enough," Bee continued as he leaned forward, resting both hands on the back of the chair Liam had offered him. "Now, tell us something a Google search won't."

Liam hesitated and picked at a thread hanging from his sweater while contemplating Bee.

If she were being honest, Cass had to admit, Bee was pretty good at this bad cop stuff. Now, hopefully, he wouldn't push it too far.

"Like why you and Mercedes Dupont were both arrested at the same protest. Is that why she sought you out to discuss her plans for the property? Because you and she were in cahoots."

Uh-oh.

Liam shot up in his seat, hands gripping the arms. "I don't know what you're implying, sir . . ."

"I'm not implying anything . . ." Bee straightened, folded his arms, and leaned a shoulder against the doorjamb. "Just sayin' . . ."

Cass held her breath waiting to see if Liam would take up where Bee left off or throw them out on their—

"Look." Liam sat back and smiled. He might even have pulled off the nonchalant look if his hands weren't shaking so badly. "A lot of people were at the protest that day, and a good number were arrested, myself included, for trespassing. A nonviolent offense, I might add. Apparently, Mercedes was arrested too, if your information is correct, though I never met her there. Nor did I know her before the protest."

"So, why do you think she reached out to you afterward?"

"Anyone living on Bay Island, with an interest in what goes on here, would know that I was opposed to developing that property. It makes sense that others who felt similarly would have sought me out, since I do have some pull with the historical society and could, if I so desired, potentially hold things up."

Cass waited to see if he'd say more. She had long ago learned the value of remaining quiet. Often times, people, especially nervous people, would look to fill any lingering silence with something, anything, just to fill the vacuum. She just hoped Bee had learned that same lesson as she waited Liam out.

"You know what, though?" Liam jumped out of his chair and shoved it in, then pulled open a file cabinet behind his desk. From the amount of papers strewn in a disorganized array around the office, Cass half expected the drawer to be empty. Instead, it was packed so full he could barely shift the papers enough to find anything, but he did yank out a folder and held it triumphantly over his head. Apparently, there was some sort of method to the chaos. "Aha. I've got it."

He returned to his seat and opened the folder on the desk then tapped a page with one thin finger. "See here, this is what I was looking for. Salvatore Marcuzzio, the groundskeeper who was killed out at Twin Forks back around five years ago?"

"Yes?" Cass leaned forward to see what he was pointing at. "What about him?"

He tapped his finger up and down so hard she was afraid the brittle-looking bones might snap. "Camille."

Cass frowned and glanced at Bee.

He shook his head.

"Who's Camille?" Cass tried to read what was written after the name. It looked like an address, but Liam's finger blocked the house number.

"Marcuzzio." He grabbed a Post-it pad, then rifled through the mess and came up with a pen and started scribbling frantically.

"Camille Marcuzzio. Sal's widow. As far as I know, she still lives at this address, but I can't be sure. Maybe you could contact her, see if she can tell you what happened with Sal."

Deflection? Was he trying to shove the attention off him and onto someone else? Possibly, but it still wouldn't hurt to check it out. Maybe Mrs. Marcuzzio had some ideas about who, if anyone, had killed her husband.

"Here." He ripped the top page off and shoved the paper at Cass.

Curious why Liam had the information at hand, Cass took the paper from him. "You have a folder on Sal Marcuzzio?"

"I have folders on everything that happens on Bay Island." He smiled sheepishly, and again, Cass couldn't help but like him. A premonition? Just a gut feeling? Or something more? "At least, anything noteworthy. Let's face it, you never know when something will become history, right?"

At least that explained all the papers scattered everywhere, if Mr. McAlister was keeping a detailed log on everything that happened on Bay Island. She didn't even have to turn around to know Bee was probably drooling over the flood of information currently surrounding them. If Liam didn't turn out to be a killer, he might just turn out to be Bee's new best friend.

"Don't worry." Bee leaned over, lay a hand on her shoulder, and whispered, "No one could ever replace you."

She laughed out loud, couldn't help it.

Liam frowned and glanced back and forth between Cass and Bee. "Is there a problem?"

"No," Bee answered, then scowled. "Not yet, anyway."

Liam squirmed, pulled at his collar and nodded. "You'll go see the widow Marcuzzio then?"

Her standing on Bee's friendship list might not be in jeopardy, after all, if Bee maintained his bad cop imitation much longer.

"Thank you, Liam. I appreciate you giving us this information, and we'll definitely follow up on it." Cass stood. Better to put an end to this meeting now, before it got out of hand.

"If anything comes of it, you'll let me know?" He pushed his chair back and stood.

"Of course." Cass held out a hand, which Liam took. "Right after we contact the police."

"Oh, uh." He paled and yanked his hand back. "Right, of course. You would have to contact the police first. I just, uh, just meant, would you let me know at some point, so, you know, I could add it to my notes."

"We'll definitely let you know, Liam." Bee shook his hand as well, his bad cop role apparently over. "Trust me, I know the value of good gossip, and I'd never leave you in the dark."

"Yes." Liam used the back of his hand to wipe the sweat from his forehead. "Thank you. I appreciate that."

She could almost hear Liam's sigh of relief as he ushered them out. Not that they wouldn't most likely be back again after they'd followed up, but the momentary reprieve seemed to be enough to satisfy him for now.

When they stepped onto the sidewalk, and Liam had shut the door behind them, Bee held out his hand for the keys. "I'll drive."

"Sure." Cass dug the keys out of her bag and handed them over, then froze. The hairs on the back of her neck stood straight up, and a chill sprinted down her spine. She looked around. A playground stood empty across the street, swings squeaking as the wind pushed them back and forth. Woods surrounded three sides of the historical center, with a lake peeking through the bare trunks. What little brush remained had dried and shriveled, not offering much concealment. A line of stores down the road a bit boasted second-story apartments, most of the blinds or shades she could see drawn against the dreary day. So why did she have the distinct feeling someone was watching them? Where could someone be hidden?

She looked around, thought for a minute about having Bee stand watch while she closed her eyes and sought answers. But she couldn't risk it. Someone had already taken one shot at her.

"Something wrong?" Bee held the passenger side door open for her and frowned.

With one last look around, Cass climbed into the car. Letting Bee drive would free her up to see what she could find out about the widow Marcuzzio before they went to speak to her, which was definitely on the agenda. Just not yet.

"So?" Bee started the car, turned on the heater, and aimed the vents at his hands. "Where to? Mrs. Marcuzzio's?"

"As much as I'd love to head right there to chat with her, since I do think there's a possibility whatever happened to Sal somehow factors into Elijah's murder, I can't go just yet."

Bee looked over his shoulder and pulled away from the curb. "So, where am I going?"

"I have to stop by Stephanie's and pick up Beast then head into the shop." The insurance adjuster should be meeting her there around lunchtime, and Luke had promised the cleaning crew and contractor would be there soon after.

"Do you think it's safe to have Beast there with all the glass?"

"Are you sticking with me today?"

"Like glue," he answered.

She paused to study his serious expression. Despite having fun with questioning Liam, and his enjoyment for good gossip, be it new or centuries old, Bee was concerned for her. Worry was etched deeply in the lines between his brows and bracketing his mouth. "You're the best, Bee, thank you. No matter what, you always have my back."

"Of course I do. Just do me one favor?" He slowed to stop for a light and glanced over at her.

"Anything."

"Try to stay out of trouble."

"Yikes." She laughed. "You're quoting Luke and Tank at me now?"

One big hand fluttered to his chest. "Oh, my goodness. You're right. What have you done?"

"What have *I* done?"

"Yes, you." He pointed one beefy finger at her. "You've gone and turned me into a grown-up."

"Please." She laughed. "Like that could ever happen."

"Next thing you know I'll be sleeping at night and getting up in the morning." He shivered.

She pulled out her phone to research Camille Marcuzzio but couldn't get service. Maybe once they got closer to town. "If you got up in the morning, we could spend more time together."

He aimed one lifted brow at her. "We could also spend more time together if you'd hire someone to pitch in now and then."

Ugh. They'd been down that road before. Bee was relentless when it came to pushing her to hire help. He loved going to the beach, spending a day on Long Island, even heading into the city for a show, but she could never take the time off. At least, not during the warmer months. And somehow traipsing through the city in the dead of winter, when the wind whipped around the buildings at every corner, didn't quite appeal.

But Cass wasn't ready to cede control of Mystical Musings to anyone else. "We'll see."

"Uh-huh."

"I was almost ready to ask Jess if she wanted a job when I found out she wasn't going away to college, but then Stephanie got her to help with Aiden first."

He shot her a knowing grin. Though the idea had crossed her mind, on any one of the hundred or so times Bee had brought it up, she'd procrastinated until Jess had found something else. "Anyway . . ."

"Uh-huh."

"Let's get Beast and head into the shop. I want to see what we can find out about Mrs. Marcuzzio before we go to see her."

"I don't suppose good cop bad cop is on the table again."

She shook her head, but her attention was diverted by a sinking feeling in her gut. The same sensation she'd had while standing outside the historical society rushed back with a vengeance. "I'm sure there's no need for that this time."

He sulked for a moment but recovered quickly. "I was a good bad cop, though, wasn't I?"

She didn't have the heart to tell him he didn't have it in him to be mean to anyone. His manners alone would have prevented him from playing any sort of bad anything. "You were a great bad cop, Bee."

That brought a huge grin.

Cass was only half paying attention, though, as she looked in the sideview mirror. She didn't see anyone behind them, and yet . . . Why couldn't she rid herself of the certainty they were being followed?

Chapter Nineteen

Cass hopped out of the car, then opened the back door for Beast.

He scrambled out, still excited from his overnight visit with Aiden and Stephanie, who spoiled him to no end. Not that Cass could blame them.

They started across the gravel lot to Mystical Musings. No need to put him on a leash, since the boardwalk was mostly deserted. Apparently, most people didn't find strolling along the boardwalk in the midst of winter's icy bite appealing.

She hitched her bag higher on her shoulder and sorted through her key ring for the key to the front door, neatly labeled for convenience.

Beast stopped and stared at the narrow alley between her shop and the one next door.

Cass paused and searched the shadows but didn't see anything. Still . . .

Beast growled, low and deep, then let out one bark.

Bee was at her side in an instant and lay a hand on Beast's head. "What's up, boy?"

Cass looked over her shoulder to be sure no one snuck up behind them while they were distracted. Other than one couple holding hands and window shopping a few stores down, she didn't see anyone.

Beast barked again.

"Come on. Let's get inside." Cass started forward, but Beast didn't move.

"Do you want to put his leash on?" Bee pulled out the side of Cass's bag and fished out the leash, then just held it in his hand, flicking the clip open and closed.

"Yeah, maybe you'd better."

He clipped the leash to Beast's collar, and the big dog didn't even flinch.

She lay a hand on his thick mane. "Come on, boy, let's get you a cookie."

Beast wasn't much on commands, but cookies he understood perfectly and usually plopped right down to sit in anticipation. This time, he lurched forward and started barking. If Bee hadn't been holding him, he'd have bolted for sure.

As it was, Bee struggled to hold on. "Beast, wait."

He strained against the leash.

"Get him inside, Bee."

"You don't have to tell me twice." He started toward the shop, holding on for dear life, with Beast lunging forward, gaze fully focused on the alleyway between the shops.

Cass ran up the front steps to the deck and unlocked the front door, then paused and held the door open.

Beast pulled against the leash and hurled himself toward the far corner of the porch.

"Hang on, Bee."

Bee narrowed his gaze in the direction Beast tried to go, then held a finger up in front of his lips for Cass to remain quiet.

Unsure what he'd seen, Cass obeyed.

Bee raised his voice louder than necessary for Cass to hear him. "Do you think I should just let him go and see what he's trying to get at?"

Cass held her breath and waited.

"No, please, don't let him go." Thea Newburgh stepped around the corner, hands held high in the air in surrender. "It's just me. I needed to talk to you. Please."

Air rushed into Cass's lungs and she pressed a hand against her chest to ease the ache. "Thea, what are you doing back there?"

"I needed to see you, but I didn't know where to find you, so I was just waiting for you to show up. I figured you would eventually, being it's your shop and all." Her still-raised hands trembled violently.

Now that Thea had emerged, Beast stopped barking. Though he still struggled to move forward in Thea's direction, his tail was now wagging.

"Does he bite?" Thea reached out a tentative hand toward him so he could sniff it.

"Not unless I tell him to," Bee said.

She snatched her hand back.

"Come on in, Thea." Cass held open the door. No sense all of them standing out there waiting for the killer to take another shot, though it would be more difficult to find somewhere to hide on this side of the shop.

Thea kept a close eye on Beast as she rounded him at a good distance and entered Mystical Musings. "Thank you for agreeing to talk to me. I didn't know where else to go."

Cass locked the door behind them, then asked Bee to take Beast upstairs, where there was no chance he'd step on any glass.

"Are you sure?" Bee shot Thea a glare.

"I'm sure, Bee. I'll be okay, and the back window is boarded over with plywood, so no one can see in." Or shoot her through the window.

He nodded and looked at Thea. "I'll be right upstairs if you need me."

"Thanks, Bee." She waited for him to leave before turning to Thea. "So, what can I do for you?"

"I don't know where else to go." Thea cried softly. "The police are looking for me."

"So, why not talk to them?"

"I can't." She looked down at her untied work boots, slid her heel up and down, clunking the boot against the hardwood floor each time it slipped off.

The image of Thea standing over Elijah's body plowed into Cass's mind unbidden.

"I'm afraid they'll arrest me if I do." When she lifted her gaze back to Cass's, tears streamed down her face. "Please, you have to help me. I'm scared, and I don't know where to turn."

No way in the world could Cass turn this girl away. "Come on, let's sit down and we can talk. Do you want something to drink? Eat?"

She pressed a hand against her stomach. "No, I couldn't, thank you."

Cass led her to a seating arrangement nearest the front of the shop, then brushed the love seat off just in case any glass had reached it. She gestured for Thea to sit, then sat down in a chair on the opposite side of the coffee table so she could face her. "Tell me what's going on, Thea. And, please, tell me the truth. I can't help you if you aren't completely honest with me."

She nodded and sniffed.

Cass handed her a box of tissues from an end table.

"You have to believe me." She pulled out a tissue and balled it in her hands. "I didn't have anything to do with Mr. Anderson getting killed."

"Okay." Whatever had her so spooked, Cass would let her get to it in her own way. She studied the young girl while she waited for her to go on. The slightly too big smock dress, with heavy wool socks and open work boots, made her appear even more petite than she was.

"My friend, Cory, said the police were asking if he'd seen me. He's so mad, thinks I must have told them he was there, but I didn't. I didn't say a word to anyone. I kept my mouth shut, even though I was the one who wanted to call nine-one-one and wait for the police to show up." Once she'd opened the faucet, the words just poured out full force.

Cass held up a hand. "Slow down, Thea. What are you talking about? When did you want to call the police?"

She sucked in a deep, shuddering breath. Then another. And started again. "Okay. So, I tend to ride out past Twin Forks a lot, mostly just to see if anything's going on and to see if Ophelia tries to contact me. I don't always stop, just drive past to get a feel for the place, you know?"

Cass nodded. She did actually understand, had done the same thing just the night before. "And did you do that on the morning Mr. Anderson was killed?"

"I did," Thea whispered, then glanced up from beneath tear-darkened lashes. "And I saw you there, with your friend. You guys were unloading stuff from the car, and I was interested because I thought Ophelia might reach out to you."

"Were you alone?"

"No, my friends Cory and Blake were with me."

"Okay." Cass sat back, hoping Thea would take the cue and relax.

Instead, she continued to ball the tissue in her hands. "We went around back, parked on a dirt road that leads to the back of the property and walked up to the big storage shed out back."

Now she had Cass's full attention. She'd noticed the storage shed not far from where Elijah had been killed. "And?"

Her lower lip trembled and another bout of tears spilled over.

"We heard the shot. Saw Mr. Anderson fall. I ran over. Tried to save him. Honest."

And Cass believed her, because she'd seen her standing over his body.

"I wanted to call the police, wanted to help him."

"But it was too late." Cass would give her that much, because she knew all too well how it felt to shoulder the guilt of being unable to save someone. "I reached him a few minutes after he was shot, and it was too late to save him."

Thea sobbed harder, her shoulders sagging with either grief or relief, Cass wasn't sure which. Giving her a moment to process everything, Cass got up and grabbed a water bottle from the fridge and handed it to her.

"Thanks." She took it absently but made no attempt to open it.

When it seemed she'd recovered somewhat, Cass encouraged her gently. "So, what happened after you checked on him?"

"Like I said, I wanted to call for help." She opened the bottle and gulped half of it down, then screwed the cap back on. "But my friends, they were scared, said we'd get blamed if they found us there. So we ran."

Cass wouldn't mention the video to her, since that was evidence in an active police investigation in which Thea was a person of interest, be it as a suspect or a witness, but Thea's account of what happened did jibe with what Cass had seen on the tape. "Then what did you do?"

"I waited." She slid her boots off and tucked her feet beneath her skirt, hugged her knees, and rocked back and forth. "And no one came. So, later in the day, I went back out there to see if I could contact Ophelia."

"The police would have been there at that time."

"They were, but I didn't go near them."

Cass blew out a breath. She needed to collect herself, needed to figure out what to ask. "You said when you came last that Ophelia wanted to contact me. Was it about Elijah's murder?"

"I don't know. I told you, she can't just talk to me. I have to interpret what she wants, and all I could get was a strong sense of you. Cory researched you, after . . . you know . . . and he said you work with the police sometimes. Is that true?"

"Yes." Especially since Chief Rawlins had come to Bay Island and taken over.

"Do you think you could talk to them, tell them it wasn't me?" she begged.

"I think you should talk to them."

Her eyes went wide and she shook her head.

Cass moved to the coffee table and sat on the edge, where she could reach out to Thea. She took her hands. "Listen to me. First of all, I know two detectives you can trust."

"Friends of yours?"

"Yes. Very close friends. And they understand about me, about what I can do. They'll listen to you, I promise."

She chewed on her thumbnail, not looking convinced.

"But first, I want to know if you're willing to give something a try?"

"What?" She sniffed and blotted her eyes with the mangled tissue.

"I want to try to reach out and see if we can contact Ophelia." Because she had a sneaking suspicion Ophelia could somehow shed light on a clue if nothing else. And anything was better than what they had right now.

"I thought you said you wanted to wait until you could find out more about her."

"I did find out more, and it turns out you were right. She is actually an ancestor of yours."

"Really? Hmm . . ." As confident as she was when she'd come into the shop the first time, she still seemed to be contemplating the news as if she hadn't been quite certain.

"So, would you be willing to give it a try?"

She shrugged, seeming a lot more comfortable with the idea of talking to the dead than to the police. "Sure, why not. What do I have to do?"

"Just stay put a minute." She patted Thea's hands and went to a shelf at the back of the shop where she kept her crystal ball. While she'd prefer to sit at her regular table, the glass covering everything made it impossible, so she'd have to do her best. She moved back to her seat and set the crystal ball on the coffee table.

Thea grinned through tears. "Seriously?"

"It helps me focus."

"Whatever works, I guess, right?"

"Yup, and this does for me." Cass slid the ball between them and stared into its depths. "Just stare into the ball, focus on its center, let your mind wander wherever it does."

Thea studied her for a moment, maybe thinking she should book a room at Twin Forks, but she finally relented and did as instructed.

With a deep breath, Cass let her shields drop. When she spoke to Thea, she kept her voice pitched low. "You said the first time Ophelia made her presence known was five years ago, is that right?"

"Uh-huh." She looked up at Cass.

"Concentrate on the ball for now, okay?"

She shifted her gaze back. "What will that do?"

"Actually, I'm not sure it will do anything, but I'm hoping it will allow you to concentrate hard enough to help bring Ophelia to me." Because her jittery lack of concentration, as well as the curiosity Cass could completely understand, wouldn't be helpful.

She nodded and settled more comfortably, staring into the ball. "Okay. Got it."

"Now, when you were out there five years ago, what did you notice?"

Her brow furrowed in concentration. "The first thing I noticed was the smell of lilacs, which was weird because I didn't see any. There's not a lot of plants out there."

"No, there aren't." Other than what surrounded the outside of the complex. Wouldn't want to make it too easy for a patient to slip out undetected and disappear into thick underbrush.

"But I distinctly remember the scent of lilacs, too much, really. Overpowering." She frowned, staring deeper into the ball. "And then I heard it."

"Heard what?"

"Sobs. Faint, at first. Just soft sobbing, so I wasn't really sure if it was real or if I was imagining it."

Cold trickled in, surrounded Cass, enveloped her in its bitter embrace. And the soft sobs started again. The same as she'd heard when she and Bee had been out at Twin Forks. Ophelia? Cass let her mind go, tried to erase all thoughts and suggestions. She watched the ball, searched its depths for that telltale wisp of fog that would indicate something was coming. But nothing happened. Nothing . . . but that soft sobbing.

Something rapped against the door, and Cass jumped, startled, then laughed at herself when she saw a figure peeking in through the glass, a hand cupped around its face.

"Excuse me a minute." Sorry for the interruption, which may well have disrupted any attempt to reach Ophelia, Cass hurried to the door to tell whomever was out there she was closed for the time being to repair the damage to her window. She pulled open the door. "I'm sorry, we— Simone!"

Simone embraced Cass then stepped back, holding her by the arms and staring into her eyes. "How are you? I've missed you."

"I've missed you too." As always, Cass was struck by her beauty. Long dark hair hung in waves around her face, her dark skin and angular cheekbones a beautiful contrast to the white coat she wore.

"How long are you staying?" She stepped back and invited Simone in out of the cold.

"Only until tomorrow morning, I'm afraid. I'll have to catch the first ferry out."

Disappointment surged. Cass had hoped to have a day or two to catch up before the other woman had to head back to the city.

"I have meetings tomorrow, getting ready to start the tours up again for the spring." Her smile was contagious, as was her excitement about the haunted tours.

"I can't wait. I'm looking forward to it." Simone's tour company ran tours that included stops at Mystical Musings along with readings for her clients.

She sauntered into the shop, taking her time speaking as well as looking around, assessing the damage. Simone did everything in her own time, and Cass couldn't even imagine her rushing around in the morning, trying to hurry out the door while still hopping into her shoes with half a stale bagel hanging out of her mouth to free up her hands, as happened to Cass more often than not since acquiring Beast.

"I'm very excited. I'm planning to spend a week out here in April when we start up again. I'm going with a fresh new advertising approach I think will do wonders for business."

That's something Cass could definitely use.

"In the meantime." Simone removed her scarf and coat and hung them on a rack beside the door. Her yellow designer pantsuit brough to mind a ray of sunshine on a hot summer day.

"Is that Simone I hear?" Bee hurried down the spiral staircase, crossed the shop, and kissed Simone's cheeks. "Well, look at you, dear. You look like you just stepped off the cover of *Vogue*."

"Well, thank you, darling." She grinned. "And have you designed my new dress yet?"

"I'm working on it, and I'll have the preliminary sketches to you by the end of the week, but I've decided to go with a pastel, salmon I'm thinking, above the knee to show off those ridiculously long legs of yours, with an intricate strap pattern across the back. It's going to be amazing."

Cass had seen his initial sketches and had to admit she was jealous. "Amazing doesn't do that dress justice. It just might be the nicest one you've ever made."

Bee's cheeks turned purple. "You're biased."

"Maybe, but that doesn't make it any less true." Once Bee excused himself, Cass led Simone to the seating arrangement where she'd left Thea and gestured for her to take a seat. "Simone, this is Thea Newburgh, the young girl I spoke to you about."

"Yes, the one whose ancestor spoke to her." She reached across the table to shake Thea's hand then settled into a chair beside Cass's. "It's a pleasure to meet you, my dear."

"Nice to meet you too." Thea glanced nervously at Cass.

"No need to worry, Thea. Simone came to help me out, and her timing couldn't have been more perfect."

"Oh?" Thea studied her from the corner of her eye. "Why's that?"

"Because Simone is the strongest psychic I know." She was also the only other psychic Cass knew, but that was beside the point.

Thea sat up straighter, her gaze riveted on Simone. That caught her interest. "You think she can contact Ophelia?"

"I'm betting on it." Cass returned to her seat beside Simone and settled more comfortably. "Now, let's see if we can figure out what Ophelia's been trying to tell you."

145

Chapter Twenty

The sobbing returned almost instantly.

"Do you hear that?" Thea whispered.

Simone nodded, unflustered by either the sound or Thea's nerves.

"Those are the same cries I heard at Twin Forks right before Elijah was killed." Cass had been worried she'd been mistaken, that someone may have needed help and she'd overlooked it, thinking it was a remnant of the past, despite the fact that Bee hadn't heard anything. At least now she could let that fear go. The sobs wouldn't have followed them from Twin Forks if they'd originated in this world. "Have you heard them before when you were out there, Thea?"

Thea shook her head. "No. Just that one time."

"Did you hear them just before Simone knocked on the door?"

She shook her head again, eyes wide with that deer-in-the-headlights expression that made her appear so vulnerable Cass wanted to reach out to her, ease her fear. Sweat beaded on her forehead, yet she shivered and wrapped her arms around herself.

"It's okay, Thea. It's nothing to be afraid of." Cass did her best to reassure the young girl without breaking the tenuous connection with a woman she suspected might be Ophelia Wilson, though she doubted it helped much.

But Thea heaved in a shaky breath, nodded, and inched closer to the edge of the seat. She offered a shaky laugh and wiped her palms on her skirt. "I have to admit, I thought it was silly at first, but looking into the ball does seem to help me concentrate better."

"Hang on a minute." Cass jumped up and hurried to the display case behind the counter, then pulled out a black tourmaline and brought it to Thea. "Here, this will help protect against negative energy."

"Yeah?" She took the crystal from Cass, studied it a moment, then smoothed a finger over the cool surface and tucked it into her palm.

If nothing else, it would give her reassurance and something to fidget with. Even though Thea didn't know Simone enough to trust her, Cass did. And she had every reason to believe the other psychic could shield Thea from harm if need be. Psychic harm, at least.

Cass returned to her seat and glanced at Simone.

When Simone nodded she was ready, she and Cass leaned forward, focusing their energy into the crystal ball.

The realization the sobs had never abated while she'd been tending to Thea surfaced. Good, because Cass had a very strong suspicion those cries belonged to Ophelia. When Simone didn't say anything, Cass took the lead. "Look into the ball, Thea. Very deep, down into its center."

She rolled the black tourmaline between her fingers. "I don't see anything."

"Give it a moment. Longer if you need," Cass said.

"I already told you, I'm not psychic. Ophelia is just a strong enough psychic to reach me."

Curious if she could tell if that was true, Cass glanced at Simone.

Simone looked around the shop, then drew her brows together and frowned a moment before returning her gaze to Cass and nodding before addressing Thea. "If you didn't have any psychic ability of your own, she would not be able to communicate with you at all, no matter how strong she is. If you had no psychic abilities, while you might get a sense something wasn't quite right, or a weird prickling as if you were being watched, you would not understand any message someone who'd already passed over was trying to impart. And yet, you did."

The serenity in Simone's voice seemed to calm her a little. If Cass were being honest, she'd have to admit it calmed her too. Simone was one of only a few people Cass had ever met who was completely comfortable in her own skin, with all of her abilities, and in any surroundings. And that sense of peace emanated from her, surrounding those in her presence and enveloping them in harmony.

"Yes, I did." Thea nodded eagerly. "I knew without any doubt she was trying to direct me to Cass, though I don't know why."

"Then relax, my dear." Simone smiled and patted Thea's hand, which was fisted in a tight grip around the black tourmaline. "You've mostly already done your part. Cass and I will take if from here, as long as you're willing to answer any questions we might have. Yes?"

"Yes, thank you." Thea scooted back onto the love seat. "I could do that."

With no more need for the crystal ball to center Thea, Simone sat back in her chair and crossed one slender leg over the other.

Since she fully trusted Simone, in a way she'd never been able to achieve with anyone else, Cass relaxed as well.

"Then here we go." Simone closed her eyes.

Cass did the same and dropped her shields completely, confident Simone would watch over her and shield her from any psychic attack. With little information on Ophelia, other than that she'd been found at the scene of her family's murder, covered in blood, they couldn't know what to expect.

Cass floated in time, letting her mind wander, ridding herself of all awareness of her physical surroundings. Blackness encroached in her peripheral vision, invading the light swirling against her lids, a wave of dark threatening to overcome her.

She shied back, her shield threatening to slam back up, but Simone's warm hand on her wrist centered her, and she opened up again. "I'm here, Ophelia. You wanted to speak to me, tell me something, and now you can. I'm listening."

With that, Cass went still. Waited.

An image swirled in her mind, a blotch of gray and green, swirling, swirling, blurry, dizzying. She focused more fully on the gray-green splotch, ignored everything but the exact center.

An image, hazy but absolute, came to her, a building, gray, rusted with age. A field surrounding it, the grass green and lush, but Cass understood the memory was not as it would look now but as it would have appeared when Ophelia had wandered the grounds. Red fog intruded, spilled over everything, tinting the ground and everything around it.

A woman appeared. Sitting on the ground, hugging her knees tightly against her as she rocked back and forth, back and forth. Her forehead rested on her knees.

The sobs intensified.

Cass tried to reach out, tried to lay a hand on the sobbing woman's arm, offer comfort, but she couldn't get her hand to appear in the image, couldn't connect. "Is that you, Ophelia?"

The woman lifted her head, looked around, sniffed and wiped

her eyes with the heels of her hands. She stood slowly, as if aware she was no longer alone, but not sure what was happening. She faded slightly.

"No, please, I won't hurt you. I want to help. You sent Thea to me, asked for me to come, and I have."

The image steadied, and the woman lifted her hand, pointed to something behind the metal storage building.

Cass moved forward, slowly, still unable to see any part of herself in the vision. As she rounded the corner of the building, the green grass turned brown and brittle with time. A hundred years? More? Less? No way to tell. She inched forward slowly, kept an eye on the woman now at her back. When she chanced a quick glance away from the woman, who still stood perfectly still, arm and finger extended in Cass's direction, her gaze caught on something lying on the ground. A pile of dirt . . . deep, dark, brown.

Cass lurched back from the mound of dirt. A freshly covered grave.

A stone stood sentinel beyond the newly turned dirt, weathered and cracked with age, something etched into its surface. Cass moved closer, squinted in her mind to bring the one word into focus: *Cass.*

In her mind, she screamed and jerked away, whirled toward the woman—Ophelia?—who was now gone. Blackness surrounded Cass, thrusting against the green and brown and gray, shattering the image.

She screamed again and was forcefully ripped from the vision.

Simone stood over her, hands gripping both of her shoulders, gentle, but pressing Cass against the chair back, completely unruffled. "Are you all right?"

Was she? She had no idea. Pain from the bullet wound in her shoulder intensified with Simone's grasp, clearing any lingering vestiges of the vision.

Bee leaned closer, nudging Simone aside, one hand splayed against his chest, decidedly less composed than Simone. "What happened? Are you okay? Why did you scream like that? Are you hurt?"

Cass couldn't think, couldn't breathe, needed a moment to collect herself. "I—"

Simone handed her a cold water bottle.

"Thank you." She uncapped the water and took a sip, not realizing until that moment how parched her throat was. "I'm sorry."

"Don't be." Simone returned to her seat as if nothing odd had happened. Who knew? Maybe for her ripping screaming psychics from visions of death was all part of a regular day's work. "Did you find out what Ophelia was trying to tell you?"

"I'm not sure. You couldn't see?"

"No. Unfortunately, the vision was yours alone."

Cass nodded and took another sip of water, then gripped Bee's hand. "I'm okay, Bee. Thank you. I just needed a moment to recover."

"Well, don't do that to me again." He squeezed her hand, then released her and pulled a chair up beside her.

Thea still sat on the love seat, curled in a ball, rocking back and forth—much as Ophelia had been doing when Cass had happened upon her in the vision.

"She didn't do it." It was the first thing that came to mind when she relaxed enough to gather her wits.

"Who didn't do what?" Bee asked.

Thea sat up straighter, her gaze intensely focused on Cass.

"Ophelia." The certainty plowed through her with enough force to knock the wind from her lungs. She sucked in a slow deep breath. "She didn't kill her family."

"How do you know?" Bee frowned.

"I don't know how, and yet I'm absolutely positive. The woman had emotional problems, but she was no killer."

"So, who did kill them?" Simone sat forward, hands clasped, elbows resting on her knees.

Cass shook her head. That knowledge eluded her, perhaps because Ophelia hadn't known. "I don't know, and sadly we probably never will, since I don't think Ophelia knew and that's who contacted me."

Bee closed his eyes for a moment and sighed. Cass knew him well enough to know the knowledge that Ophelia had paid for a crime she didn't commit would haunt him, as it would her.

She lay a hand over his. "It's okay, Bee. We may not have all the answers, but at least we know she was no killer."

He nodded, having no choice but to accept the truth of it.

Cass's gaze turned to Thea. "It was important to her that you know that, that you believe it. I think having you know the truth will bring her the peace she's long sought."

Thea nodded. "I already believed it. I can't explain how, but after interacting with her, I just had a sense of it."

"Okay." Cass finished off the water in the bottle, then turned to Bee. "I need to talk through the rest of it now, but if it's going to upset you, I'm all right if you want to go back upstairs with Beast."

He rolled his shoulders and moaned. "I'll be all right. I'm starting to get used to the hocus-pocus. At least, a little bit."

"Yeah, well, that's not the part I'm worried about you freaking out about."

"Oh?" He lifted a skeptical brow.

Simone kept her attention on Bee. "Just remember, Bee, things are not always what they appear. We see something, view an image in our minds, but then we have to interpret its meaning. Think of it like a clue."

Cass had no doubt the reminder was meant for her as well as Bee.

"So, tell us." Simone sat back as if they were having nothing more than a friendly chat about the weather, rather than a discussion of a psychic vision, and Cass appreciated the calm acceptance.

It seemed the more she surrounded herself with people who understood and appreciated what she could do, the more she came to accept it herself. She set the water bottle aside and made an effort to relax. "I saw a mix of things, actually."

"That's not unusual. Can you separate them?"

"I think so." She thought back, reimagined the vision—the rusted storage building, clearly an image from the present, the lush green lawn, no doubt from Ophelia's time, the red haze overtaking it all. "I'm pretty sure Ophelia was trying to show me some time in the past, but not as long ago as she lived, if that makes sense."

Simone nodded but remained quiet.

"There was a grave. At least . . ." She tried to bring the vision back. The mound of freshly turned dirt. The stone. Even looking back there was no mistaking it was a gravestone. Her name etched so clearly. She glanced at Bee, wishing he'd gone back upstairs so he wouldn't have to hear that detail.

He rolled his eyes. "I'm fine, Cass, just sitting here imagining what Beast might be chewing up in your office as we speak."

She laughed, relieving at least some of her tension. "Okay. I saw what I'm pretty sure was a grave beside the old storage shed out at Twin Forks."

Simone studied her, looked deep into her eyes. "And?"

"My name was on the headstone."

Bee shivered. His gaze shot to Simone for answers.

She simply nodded. "It doesn't necessarily mean it's your grave, Cass, or even meant to be your grave. It could just be Ophelia is trying to draw your attention to it."

"Okay. That makes sense." And gave her some shred of hope to cling to.

"But, either way, you're going to go out there and check it out, right?" Thea asked.

She smiled, shaky but confident. "Absolutely. Since I have little doubt someone is buried out there who shouldn't be."

Chapter Twenty-one

Bee lurched to his feet, one hand planted on his hip, the other raised, pointer finger extended toward Cass much as Ophelia's had been when pointing out her grave. "Uh, no."

"Excuse me?" Cass turned to him.

"That is so not happening." He folded his arms across his chest and put on his best stubborn pout, letting her know he was drawing a line. "There's no way you're going out to Twin Forks so you can wind up in a shallow grave beside a storage shed."

"It's okay, Bee." Simone stood and faced him. "She's not going alone."

"You're darn tootin' she's not," he huffed.

A slow smile spread across Simone's face, and she stood on tiptoes to kiss Bee's cheek. "You are such a good friend, Bee. Cass is fortunate to have you."

"Hmm." Twin red patches popped up on his cheeks, and he lowered his arms to his sides. "So, I guess you understand then why I won't let her go."

"Not at all, dear, but I understand perfectly why you'll go with her." She patted his cheek and stepped back.

"Ugh . . ." His shoulders slumped, and he turned to Cass. "Why don't you just call Luke and Tank and have them go dig the place up?"

She thought about it for about a split second before shaking her head. "It has to be me. First of all, I can't ask the police to go dig up the property on the say-so of a ghost, especially when they might find nothing."

"Are they going to find nothing?" Bee asked.

"I don't think so. No, I'm pretty sure they're going to find something."

Bee opened his mouth to protest, but she held up a finger to stop him.

"And second of all, if there is a grave out there, I need to be the one to find it."

"Why's that?"

"Because if whoever it belongs to has something to say, I need to be there to hear it."

"Grrr . . ." Bee propped his hands on his hips and studied her. "Fine. I'll go. But only on one condition, and there's something else you have to do first, anyway."

"What's the condition?" She was only half paying attention, now that he'd relented and agreed to go with her, her mind caught on how to determine if there was an actual grave out there without having to dig up the whole place.

"The condition is that Luke and Tank provide security, even if they stay out of the way and let you do your thing."

"Okay." She could agree to that, as long as they agreed to stay back until she was ready for them to intervene. And if they didn't agree, she was pretty sure she could convince Chief Rawlins to go along with her.

"Sorry, honey, but that's . . . uh . . ." Bee started to argue, then paused. "Oh, okay, I didn't expect it to be that easy."

"So, what's the other thing?"

"Oh, right, you have an appointment with Salvatore Marcuzzio's widow."

Her thoughts skidded to a stop. "What are you talking about?"

"While you guys were doing your thing" — he gestured back and forth between the three of them — "I looked her up and called to see if she'd be willing to speak to you, and she agreed." He gestured toward the door. "We should probably get going. I told her we'd be there in about an hour."

Thea popped up from the love seat. "Well, on that note . . ."

"Not so fast, Thea." Cass turned to Bee. "I need you to do something for me, Bee."

He narrowed his gaze and looked at her from the corners of his eyes. "What's that?"

"Would you please stay here with Beast and Thea? Keep an eye on Beast while you wait for the insurance adjuster to show up, and sit with Thea until Luke or Tank can get here to question her?"

"I never mind doing you a favor, Cass, but I don't want you going anywhere alone, and I promised Luke I'd stay with you."

Simone stood. "I'll go with Cass, dear."

Bee seemed torn. Nothing would ever come ahead of Cass's safety where he was concerned. "Cass, you know I would do anything for you — "

"I'll keep her safe, Bee, I promise." Simone smiled. "Besides, we're only going to talk to a woman and then returning. When she goes out to Twin Forks, her pit bull will be with her."

"Well, when you put it that way . . ." He grinned but still looked undecided. "Oh, and about Twin Forks, I think I have an idea."

"What's that?" But Cass's mind had already switched gears. She still hadn't gotten Thea to agree to their plan, though she hadn't bolted yet, so that was something.

"Instead of digging up acres of property, which is completely unrealistic if not illegal, why not just go over the place with a metal detector and see what we come up with?" He shrugged. "At least then we can decide if we want to dig or let the police handle it."

She stared at him for a moment, then kissed his cheek. "That's brilliant, Bee. A much better idea than going out there armed with shovels and searching for something that may or may not exist. Do you have a metal detector?"

"I do, actually. I used to enjoy walking the beach in the early mornings, during the off-season, of course, in search of what the tide may have carried in and buried." He looked wistful for a moment. "I don't know why I ever stopped doing that; it's such a peaceful time of the day, before everyone else is up and about and cluttering the shore. A good way to relax and unwind before I go to bed."

"Maybe we can get in the habit of doing it again when it warms up a little. I never mind an early morning walk on the beach when I get up."

"Umm . . . yeah, we'll see about that." Bee's eyes rolled toward the ceiling. "I've seen what that beast digs up when you guys go for a quiet walk on the beach, and it's anything but peaceful."

Cass laughed, not in the least offended since his tone held only affection. "Yeah, well, I guess I can't argue that."

She shrugged into her coat and took her bag from beneath the counter, then fished out her keys and turned to Thea. "Are you okay with this, Thea?"

She picked what was left of the polish off one thumbnail. "It's not like I have a choice."

Cass sat beside her on the love seat for a moment and gripped her hand, then looked directly into her eyes. "You always have a choice, Thea. No one is going to physically restrain you to keep you here until the police arrive. But Bee is my closest friend, and I trust him with my life. He will take good care of you and make sure you're safe until my other friends get here."

"Your cop friends?"

"Yes." Though Luke had become something much more over the past year, especially since he'd moved to Bay Island to give their relationship a chance. "Two very good friends who will listen to what you have to say."

"They're gonna want to talk to my friends too, right?"

"I'm sure they will, just to corroborate your version of what happened, but I promise you they will be fair. As long as you're telling the truth, you have nothing to fear. And I've found it's much better to confront problems head on than it is to hide or run from them and allow that tension to hang over you and affect every aspect of your life."

She lowered her gaze to her lap and nodded. "All right, fine. I'll talk to them and tell them what happened."

"Good." Cass patted her hand and stood.

A tear dripped onto Thea's lap and she scrubbed at it with the heel of her hand then looked beseechingly into Cass's eyes, all the helplessness of her youth etched into the pained expression on her face. "You're sure they won't put me in jail, right?"

"They will question you, and they may ask you to go to the police department with them so they can make the interview official and record it and all that, but they can't and won't arrest you with no evidence that you did something wrong."

"And they'll be kind?"

"Kind?" Bee flopped onto a chair across from them and draped his leg over the arm. "Just you wait until you talk to Luke. He's got a killer accent that pours through you like warm sunshine on a cold day. I could listen to that guy talk for hours."

Thea laughed through her tears, and Cass shot him a grateful look.

"Here." He lifted his phone and tossed it to Cass. "I already called Luke, and he's going to meet us out there. Mrs. Marcuzzio's number is in there, if you need it, and I've already programed her address into the GPS."

When she leaned over to take it and kiss his cheek, he whispered,

"I told Luke what's going on, and he understands."

"Thank you, Bee." Confident Bee had explained the situation with Thea and how frightened she was, and knowing Luke would go easy on her, Cass checked the address Bee had typed in and headed for her car with Simone.

While they waited for the car to warm up, Cass ran through the suspect list with Simone. Who knew? Maybe a fresh perspective would come in handy, shake something loose Cass had missed.

"So, we have Liam McAlister, who wants to preserve the land, participated in a protest against its sale to Elijah Anderson, and seems to know or have some level of involvement with all of the players." Simone ticked off the point on one long, slim, maroon-tipped finger. "Then we have Cam Parker, who wants to develop the land, build condos, and went through the trouble of securing a seat on Elijah's board of directors after one of the other board members— Harvey Potts, was it?"

Cass nodded. "Yeah, he went missing, coincidentally, disappeared without a trace right before Cam took his seat. And I did find that photo of Cam in the paper with his arm slung around Elijah's wife."

"Yes, so either close friends or something more." Simone's thoughts obviously ran similar to Cass's own. "Which brings us to the grieving widow."

"Who didn't even hang around long enough to see what the investigation turned up or wait for the police to release Elijah's body." And left on her yacht after complaining relentlessly about the money Elijah dumped into Twin Forks and accepting Cass's return of the check Elijah had paid her, even though she'd done the job she'd been hired to do, for the most part. She could have at least offered partial payment.

Simone shrugged one shoulder, then aimed the heating vents toward her feet. "Everyone handles grief differently, so you can't condemn her for that."

A concept Cass understood completely, when she wasn't feeling surly and exhausted.

"Plus, she may have had family she wanted to notify in person before the news broke and they heard some other way," Simone added.

Feeling chastised, Cass relented. Simone was right. "Though, she and Cam both stood to gain the most financially. Evelyn, if she sold the property, and Cam Parker if she sold it to him."

"A fact I can't argue, but then again, so does Mercedes Dupont if she can talk Evelyn into selling to her."

Cass started to protest.

But Simone interrupted. "Believe it or not, Cass, no matter how you or I feel about her death museum idea, there are people out there who would be drawn to it. Probably more than you think."

"And she was also arrested for protesting the sale to Elijah."

"Which means all of these players have been actively involved with Elijah and the Twin Forks property for the past five years. So, the question you have to ask yourself is . . ."

"What happened five years ago, and how does it relate to Elijah's murder?" Cass finished for her as she pulled out of the lot.

"Exactly."

Well, hopefully, Sal's widow would be able to shed some light on that.

"I can't help but notice whose name was not on that list." Simone turned to her and lifted a perfectly sculpted brow. "I take it you no longer suspect Thea Newburgh had any involvement?"

Of all her suspects, Thea had been the only one she could be sure was present either at or right after the moment of Elijah's death. She had cause to want the place shut down, if she believed her ancestor had contacted her, which she seemed to. Unless the whole thing was an elaborate scam to get Cass to believe she had nothing to do with Elijah's murder, even though she was recorded at the scene. "No, I don't think she killed him."

"And her friends? The two who were with her that day?"

Cass was already shaking her head. "I think Thea spends a lot more time out there than she's been willing to admit. I think she's fascinated with the fact that Ophelia can contact her, and I think she was looking to increase her own abilities in the only way she could think of. And since she first realized her talent out there, I think she kept returning in the hopes she could figure it out. You don't agree?"

"Actually, I do. I just find it interesting that the one person you seem to have eliminated from the suspect list is the only one who not only has no alibi but was found standing over the body."

Hmm. That was interesting, and yet, Cass was certain, deep in her gut, that Thea Newburgh was innocent. Of course, the only way to prove that definitively was to find out who the actual killer was. "So maybe I'm looking at this the wrong way. We've already established who had motive, though some are stronger than others and some are still questionable, but I haven't given much thought to opportunity."

"Well, you know Evelyn was on Bay Island at the time of the murder." The sun peeked out from behind the clouds, and Simone squinted and reached into her oversized bag and pulled out a pair of Oakleys, then slid them on.

"As was Liam, though he might have been at work. I haven't looked into that yet." Cass grabbed her own sunglasses from the center console.

"But I'm sure the police have."

Cass made a mental note to ask Luke when she saw him.

"Mercedes and Cam were both on Bay Island soon after the murder was committed, but we don't know when exactly they arrived."

"But if I had to bet, I'd say Cam was here, since I saw him the night of the murder in the diner trying to make his way out to Twin Forks." The GPS interrupted with directions, and Cass silenced it. Though she didn't know exactly where Mrs. Marcuzzio's street was, she did know the general vicinity. Once they got close, she could just look for the house number.

It didn't take long to arrive, especially with the jumble of thoughts ricocheting around in her head, each one begging for attention. Cass spotted the number easy enough, turned into a narrow driveway, and parked beside a beat-up, older-model sedan. If the widow still lived in the house she'd shared with her husband, they'd lived a modest life. The small inline ranch with the postage-stamp lawn was well kept and boasted a lovely little garden beside the front porch.

Cass parked and got out, then started up the walkway with Simone.

The front door opened before they reached it, and a thin woman with brown hair and gray roots appeared. "Good morning, ladies."

"Are you Mrs. Marcuzzio?" Cass offered a hand.

"Yes." She shook Cass's hand then stepped back and gestured

them inside. "As I explained to your friend, I have to get to work, so I won't have long, but if there's any way to find out who killed my Sal, I'm willing to try."

"Thank you, Mrs. Marcuzzio, and I'm very sorry for your loss." She followed her to the kitchen then sat at one of the four chairs surrounding the small, scarred table.

"Thank you." She sat across from Cass.

Simone sat at her side.

"So . . ." Mrs. Marcuzzio clasped and unclasped her hands on the table. "What do you need to know?"

As much as Cass hated intruding on her grief, she tried to tell herself Mrs. Marcuzzio would be better off if she knew the truth. But was that the truth? Or was she just dredging up the pain of the past? Either way, she'd try to keep it as quick as possible. "If you could just run through what happened the day Sal was killed, that would be helpful."

She sighed. "As I told the police at the time, and each time I've contacted them for a progress report since, Sal was murdered. There's no way he fell and hit his head. It was too much of a coincidence that he died out there after . . ."

"After what?" Cass prodded gently when it didn't seem she would continue.

"He wasn't working that day. It was his day off, and we were supposed to go to the mainland to go furniture shopping. He promised we'd buy a new couch, since the old one was sagging in spots." She sniffed and pulled a napkin from a holder in the center of the table. "But he just couldn't let it go."

"Couldn't let what go?"

She blew her nose, got up to throw the napkin in the trash, then returned and grabbed another. "He saw something out there."

Cass stiffened. Could she be talking about Ophelia? "What kind of something?"

"He wasn't very specific about what he thought it was, but he did say he heard two people arguing a couple days earlier."

"Did he know what they were arguing about?" Cass's mind raced through the possibilities.

"That man who was buying the property, the one who got killed out there the other day."

"The two were arguing about Elijah Anderson?"

"Yes. Neither of them wanted the property sold, were extremely agitated about the whole thing, as if it would somehow affect them personally if the property were developed." She sniffed and wiped her eyes. "Let me ask you, in the end, do you really think it made enough of a difference for my Sal to be killed?"

Nothing would be worth losing someone you loved, but Mrs. Marcuzzio didn't seem to be looking for an answer. "Did he give any indication who he thought the two people were?"

"Nah, didn't even say if it was men or women. He didn't seem to think that much of it, at first, but then, the next day, while he was working, he noticed a patch of dirt that was freshly turned over then kind of tamped down; you know what I mean?"

A chill ripped through Cass, and she nodded. She knew exactly what she meant, because she'd probably seen the same thing in her vision.

"Anyway . . ." She shook her head and checked her watch. "He said he couldn't check what it was at the time, because there were too many people around, what with them getting ready to sell and all."

She was running out of time, no doubt. "Do you know who was there?"

"I'm sorry, especially if it would help find Sal's killer, but I don't know. Just that there was a lot of activity, a number of people interested in buying the property, a number there with Mr. Anderson to do whatever they were supposed to be doing."

"Mr. Anderson was there at the time?"

She frowned and narrowed her eyes for a minute. "I'm pretty sure that's what Sal said, but either way, he couldn't get to see why the dirt was dug up. And he was the only groundskeeper on duty out there by then, and he hadn't done it."

Cass nodded for her to continue.

But she only shrugged. "And that's it. Next thing you know, the police are knocking on my door sayin' Sal had been killed."

"Is there anything else at all you can tell us?"

"Nothing I can think of."

"If you think of anything else, you can call me anytime." Cass fished in her bag for a card and handed it to the other woman. "And if you'd like, you can come in for a reading, free of charge, and I can try to contact Sal for you."

"I could talk to Sal?"

"You can tell him whatever you'd like, and if he tries to get a message to you, I will try to interpret it to the best of my ability."

Mrs. Marcuzzio slapped a hand over her mouth as tears ran down her cheeks, and she nodded.

Cass patted the hand that still held the card. "You just let me know when you're ready."

She nodded again and soft sobs shook her. "Thank you."

"Thank you. And I promise you I will do my best to see to it Sal's killer is brought to justice." Leaving her to compose herself and get ready for work, Cass and Simone saw themselves out.

Once they'd closed the front door behind them and stood on the front lawn, Simone turned to her. "You think it was a grave he found."

"I do. And I think I know who it belongs to."

Simone nodded and looked back at the house. "You know, when you offered to contact Sal for his widow, you gave me an idea."

"Oh?" Cass unlocked the car, got inside, and started it up. Grateful for the rush of still warm air pouring from the vents, she just sat for a moment.

"The one thing you haven't yet tried to do, at least from my knowledge, is reach out to Elijah and ask him who killed him."

"You know it's not that easy." And if it were, she'd have already done so.

"I do know that, yes." A slow smile spread across her face. "But not everyone does."

Chapter Twenty-two

By the time they'd finished talking to Mrs. Marcuzzio, the insurance adjuster had already come and gone, and Luke and Tank had picked up Thea and taken her to the station for questioning. Bee had been chomping at the bit to get out of there. As soon as they'd picked him up, after a quick stop to pick up Bee's metal detector and a shovel, just in case, they headed for Twin Forks. Luke and Tank would meet them there as soon as they finished with Thea.

Bee leaned forward from the backseat, between Cass and Simone. "So, what is it you're hoping to accomplish exactly?"

Simone had just started to outline her plan to contact Elijah. "I want Cass to hold a group reading, let it be known she's going to try to contact Elijah and ask him to name his killer."

"But won't that be dangerous?" Bee asked.

"No more dangerous than the killer thinking Elijah already told her who killed him. Look at it this way, if she's trying to contact him to ask, it means he hasn't."

Actually, that made perfect sense. Cass watched Bee's reflection in the rearview mirror as he mulled that over.

"My way," Simone continued, "she has the upper hand."

"How do you figure she's not painting a target on her back? Someone already tried to kill her once." He rested his elbows on the front seats and linked his hands together, then rested his chin on them.

"Because we will know when and where the meeting will happen. If we can get it set up quickly, and get the rumor spread in time to draw any players who may be interested, we can have some level of control."

Bee snorted. "Well, I can make a hundred percent sure the news reaches all the right ears in a very short amount of time."

Simone pulled her appointment book from her bag and flipped through the pages. "I can free up some time on Saturday to come back, if you want to set a group reading up for then."

Bee nodded. "That could work, I suppose. But what if Elijah doesn't show up?"

"That's my concern." Trying to contact a specific someone in front of an audience gnawed at her gut. "The chances of me contacting Elijah, especially in the shop, are slim to none, at best."

"Ah, but who will know?" After jotting a few notes on her calendar, Simone dropped it back into her bag. "You are brilliant at readings. My understanding is you were good at getting to the truth even before you understood where your information was coming from."

Bee grinned. "So we get everyone together and let Cass work her magic, rustle the bushes and see if a snake pops out."

Cass had to admit, the idea had merit, and it might just work.

Simone held up a finger. "But there's a condition, if you want my help."

Cass glanced at her. "You didn't mention any conditions before when we talked about it."

"Because I knew you would balk."

Bee laughed and sat back. "A woman after my own heart."

"What's the condition?" Cass braced herself, pretty sure she knew what was coming, since Simone often worked with the police in New York and other places.

"You will involve the police."

"But—"

"But nothing. I agreed to go out to Twin Forks, even though Luke and Tank will keep their distance, because I do agree you're likely to gain more by going alone. And if we find what we need out there, then no harm done, we can forget about the reading. But, if we don't, and we decide to go ahead with the plan, you will have Luke and Tank there, inside the room, for protection, and you will have Chief Rawlins there, since she seems to be a great guide for you."

She couldn't argue that. While Chief Rawlins refused to treat her with kid gloves, she did seem to pull things out of Cass that surprised even her. Who knew? Maybe it was because she didn't treat her with kid gloves. She had certain expectations, and she pushed Cass to achieve them.

Cass parked in front of the gate at Twin Forks and turned off the ignition. "Fine. I'll talk to Luke and ask him to set it up as soon as we're done here."

She started to get out of the car, but Bee grabbed her arm.

Simone paused with her door open and one leg out and looked back at Bee. "Something wrong?"

"I was just thinking about last time we were out here. It seemed like someone . . ." He swallowed hard. "Or something . . . was dampening Cass's senses. We know now that Thea was out here at the time. Do you think it could have been her, maybe doing like whatever you did last time to shield Cass?"

She thought about it a moment, but shook her head. "No, there's no way. Thea's not strong enough for that."

"She couldn't be hiding it?" Bee persisted.

"I would be able to tell if she were a strong psychic."

"What about Ophelia? Is she strong enough?" Bee pointed toward the far end of the property. "There's Luke and Tank."

Cass had already seen them. True to his word, Luke had parked a good distance from them, and he and Tank leaned against the car, scanning the area.

"Ophelia might be strong enough, but for what purpose?" Simone continued. "It seems she wants Cass to have information, is trying very hard to pass on some kind of message. It doesn't make sense she would block her."

"Maybe the information she wants to pass on is selective. What if she wants to make sure no one else can tell her anything, like that Ophelia is lying through her ectoplasmic teeth?"

Hmm . . . Cass hadn't considered that. Nor had she considered that who or whatever was blocking her abilities might still try to interfere.

Simone waved one perfectly manicured hand. "It's irrelevant anyway."

"Not if something out here is trying to mess with her head, it's not," Bee insisted.

"If anyone, or anything, tries to . . . mess with her head . . . I can intervene." She started to get out of the car.

"You seem awfully confident about that."

Simone paused and shifted back into the seat. She pulled the door shut to study Bee. "How sure are you my dress is going to be beautiful? What if it doesn't come out good or I don't like it?"

Bee scoffed. "Your dress is going to be beyond your wildest dreams, sweetie."

"But how do you know?"

"Because I'm the best at what I do, and . . . oh . . ." He stuttered to a stop.

"And I trust you." She grinned. "I have been doing this for a long time, Bee, and I am very good at what I do. If someone is trying to interfere with Cass's ability to reach out, I will be able to help her identify and resist the threat. If someone tries to attack her psychically, I will be able to repel that attack."

"And if someone tries to attack her physically?" Though he still pressed the issue, he just seemed to be trying to reassure himself now.

"That's what Luke and Tank are for." Simone smiled and patted his hand. "And if anyone gets past those two, that would be your area of expertise, my dear."

And it wouldn't be the first time Bee had come between her and danger.

"And if someone takes another shot at her?"

Simone looked around. "That, there's nothing we can do to prevent, be it here, at the shop, or anywhere else. I can only hope I'll be strong enough to sense any danger before something like that happens. Please, honey, trust me. The only way to make Cass safe again is to find out who's trying to kill her."

"I guess I can't argue that," he mumbled. Still not seeming fully convinced, Bee finally relented, climbed out of the car, and looked around.

"Do you see anything?" Cass left her bag in the car, locked the door, and tucked the key into her jacket pocket.

"Nothing, but we didn't see Thea out here last time we were here either," Bee reminded her.

"Touché." Giving up on trying to convince Bee that she was as safe as she could be under the circumstances, she started up the walkway.

"The door is probably locked." Bee squinted against the sunlight streaming through the clouds and used his hand to shield his eyes.

Cass didn't think there was anything inside she was meant to see. Whatever path Ophelia would lead her down, she had a feeling it would be somewhere they hadn't yet explored. "That's okay. I'm not going inside anyway. At least, not yet."

"And if she should decide she needs to, I'm sure there are ways." Simone winked at Bee and walked away without elaborating, and Cass couldn't help but wonder how much she didn't know about the other woman. It seemed she might have more secrets than she let on.

Bee turned on the metal detector, fidgeted with it for a moment or two, then looked at Cass. "Ready when you are. Just point me in the right direction."

With one last glance to make sure Luke and Tank were in place, Cass took the lead, rounding the side of the building. As she turned the corner, a huge gust of cold wind pummeled her. She pulled her coat tighter and looked around. Deciding the best place to start would be where they'd found Elijah, she headed in that direction.

As much as she wanted to look around, search for any threats or any help Ophelia might decide to impart, Cass had to keep her head tucked against the wind tearing across the open field. She pressed a hand against her ear to keep the wind out. Too bad she hadn't thought to wear a hat. When they reached the spot where Elijah had fallen, Cass stopped.

Bee scanned the ground with the metal detector.

Simone stayed back, watchful, allowing Cass the space she needed to figure out what to do next.

Okay, now what, Ophelia? I'm here, but I have no idea what you want to show me.

Sal Marcuzzio's wife had said he'd seen freshly dug dirt; Cass had seen the same in her vision. But where? And what did it mean? They'd assumed a grave, especially with the addition of the headstone bearing her name, but what if it wasn't? What if someone had buried something else? Or maybe they'd dug something up.

A beeping sound pulled her back to the moment, as Bee bent to study something.

"Anything, Bee?"

He lifted his hand, with something caught between his thumb and forefinger. "Just a quarter."

"Leave it on the ground exactly where you found it," Simone instructed. "You never know what will turn out to be important evidence."

The advice seemed sound, if generic, until Cass studied the other woman more closely. Lines of strain creased her smooth skin, and a frown marred her usually serene features, as she watched Bee like a hawk.

He continued to scan the ground, occasionally coming up with an old nail or some other equally mundane item.

Cass moved around, closer to the woods, using the trees as cover to protect her from the worst of the wind . . . and whatever other threats might lie in wait. The change of perspective tugged at something in her. Mist seeped from the woods to her left. It flowed seductively across the field, enticing, tempting, daring Cass to follow.

She was halfway across the field before she even realized she was moving. A quick glance over her shoulder assured her Bee and Simone were following, though at a discreet distance. She came to another building, its brick façade ravaged by time and the elements. But still she kept moving forward, then began to angle back toward the main building. As she rounded the far corner, a metal storage shed came into view.

"There." She pointed toward the building, to the mound of dark dirt she'd seen in her vision, where it stood in stark contrast against what remained of the dried, dead grass, turned brittle and brown by time.

"Where?" Bee asked, metal detector at the ready.

But when she looked back, the pile of freshly dug dirt was gone, leaving no glimpse into the past. She approached slowly, hyperaware of her surroundings. Even knowing her name etched on the stone wasn't necessarily a portent of things to come, fear gripped her in its icy claws, squeezed. She choked, her airway cut off with the pressure.

"Cass!" Bee grabbed her arm and shook her.

"It's okay, Bee." Simone eased him back gently, then took his place, her hold on Cass's arm tentative, there if needed but not intrusive. "Talk to me, Cass. Tell me what's happening."

"Hard to breathe." She gulped in the cold air.

"Okay, just take it easy." She rubbed a hand up and down Cass's arm.

Cass couldn't feel her touch through her thick coat. Still, knowing she was there to offer support helped.

"Are you actually having trouble breathing? Or is it something else?"

Trying to ignore the feeling she was suffocating, which was no easy task, Cass inhaled slow, deep breaths. When she was able to fill her lungs to capacity before exhaling, some of the panic abated. "I'm not sure. Either something was trying to scare me off or it wasn't my discomfort I was feeling."

"Does it get worse when you move closer to the building?" Simone started forward, her hand still resting on Cass's arm.

Cass moved with her, Bee glued to her other side. "Yes. The closer I get, the more uncomfortable I feel. Pressure in my chest."

"It's okay, just take your time. Move slowly."

Cass unzipped her coat and rubbed her chest in an effort to ease the ache there. When she reached the phantom mound, she pointed toward where she knew it had been. "There. I think if you run the metal detector over that slight depression in the lawn, you'll find something."

Bee did as instructed, and the metal detector beeped. "Now what? Do you want to dig it up?"

Did she? She studied the impression, moved slowly around the perimeter of what she fully expected was a grave. Harvey Potts's grave, to be exact. "Not yet."

Bee moved out from the center in a circular pattern, but the metal detector remained silent. "It seems to be just something in that spot, but I can go farther if you want?"

Cass looked around. The storage shed, which hadn't seemed important until just that moment, caught her attention, suddenly filling her, consuming her. "Let's check inside."

Bee moved to the door and checked the padlock. "Broken."

Cass eased up beside him and pushed the door open a crack. Darkness stared back at her. They moved deeper inside, kicking up dust motes that danced and twirled in the few rays of sunshine that managed to squeeze through the door and force their way through the gloom.

The feeling of suffocating increased, but Cass had no doubt it was in her mind now. When she stopped to take notice, she was able to get a full, deep breath of the moldy air. "He was killed in here, I think."

169

"Who?" Bee frowned. "Elijah?"

"No. Harvey Potts."

"The board member who went missing?" Bee asked.

"Yeah. I don't know for sure it was him, but I have a feeling it was. I think he argued with someone out here, and that someone killed him."

"Freeing up his position on the board for Cam Parker to take."

She nodded. "We need to look around. There's something here. Something we're supposed to find."

"Something, or someone?" Bee's horrified expression brought a small smile.

"Something, Bee." She was pretty sure there was someone as well, but she'd leave that for the police to determine. At least Bee would be relieved to know that. "I'm going to call Luke and have him and Tank come in now."

"You don't need to dig first?" He pulled out his phone and made the call.

"No. Better to let the police take care of that." Simone wandered through the shed, searching among the deepest corners. "We don't want to disturb any evidence."

Cass looked at her. "Do you think someone's buried out there?"

"Oh, yes. It's definitely a grave, though I can't tell you whose."

Cass simply nodded, glad to have confirmation before bringing the police into it.

Bee finished the call, then knelt down, his phone light aimed at something on the ground.

Cass peered over his shoulder at something half buried in the dirt floor. "What is that?"

"I don't know." He held up the scrap of cloth between two fingers as if afraid it would rear up and bite him. "It looks like a handkerchief. And it's monogramed. Here, take my phone."

Cass took the phone from him and shined the light onto the mostly blackened cloth.

Bee used his thumbnail to scrape away some of the dirt caked on the corner to reveal the initials *EA*. "Elijah Anderson?"

"Possibly." Though how had it gotten there? "Maybe Elijah came out here the day he was killed? Either before or after he unlocked the door for us?"

Bee shook his head and examined the fabric more closely. "No, I don't think so. This fabric wouldn't be in this condition after only a few days, even if it has been humid. This is mildew-stained. It's been here for quite some time."

"Five years, to be precise," Simone said.

"Yes, I agree." Cass moved toward the doorway, to where Luke and Tank stood waiting. "Now, for the big question: what was Elijah Anderson doing out here five years ago, and did he have anything to do with Harvey's disappearance?"

"Well . . ." Simone pinned her with a stare. "There's only one way to find out."

"Right," Cass agreed, because she already knew she was going to do the reading as Simone had suggested.

Bee held the handkerchief out to her. "Ring up good ole Elijah and ask him."

Chapter Twenty-three

Cass looked in the mirror on the back of her office door for the tenth time, and for the tenth time she rubbed at the dark circles beneath her eyes, not that it had done any good the first nine times she'd tried it. Why was she so nervous? It's not like this was the first group reading she'd ever done.

The door eased open a crack. "Knock, knock."

She stepped back. "Come on in, Luke."

He stepped inside and closed the door behind him. "How are you doing?"

She shrugged. Because it was Luke, she could be honest. "I'm terrified."

He laughed. "You'll do fine. You always do."

She looked in the mirror again. She didn't know what she was looking for; her courage perhaps.

Luke moved up behind her, wrapped his arms around her waist and pulled her close. Resting his chin on her shoulder, he met her gaze in the mirror. "Captain Rawlins is here. She insisted on coming herself, was really thrilled you reached out to try to work with us on this. She's hoping you'll do so more often. She really believes in you, Cass."

Cass nodded and lowered her gaze. "I know she does. I just hope I don't let her down."

"You won't." He propped a finger beneath her chin and lifted it to return her gaze to his in the mirror. "You won't, Cass. I believe in you too. When I first met you, I didn't know what to make of your abilities, didn't know if I believed you actually spoke to the dead or that you were just extremely intuitive."

She smiled and turned to face him. She'd waited a long time to hear those words, but even as he finally said them, she realized he'd already shown her the truth of his feelings a million times, in a million different ways. "Heck, back then I didn't know either."

Keeping her close, he traced a finger down her cheek, slid her hair behind her ear so he could see her face more clearly. "I don't pretend to understand any of this, but I do believe in you. I know you are somehow able to determine things the rest of us can't. And if you do it by talking to the dead or by some other means, it doesn't matter to me. It's enough that I trust you can do it."

The admission warmed her. Luke had been trying to keep her out of his investigations since they'd met, though, in all fairness to him, some of the reason was for her own protection. "You and Tank will be inside the reading room?"

"We will. As will several other plainclothes officers in addition to the chief. If there's enough room for all of us, that is. It was starting to get pretty crowded downstairs, and Stephanie was keeping pretty busy behind the register." He tipped her head forward and massaged her uninjured shoulder, kneading the knots out of the muscles, moving up the back of her neck.

She tilted her head from side to side and moaned. "Stephanie's here?"

"Don't worry, Tank's keeping a close eye on her." He grinned and kissed her cheek. "He's actually pretty much sticking like glue, as is Bee."

"What about Aiden and Beast?" Not wanting to take a chance of Beast getting hurt, she'd dropped him off at Stephanie's earlier in the day. "Jess is at Stephanie's with them, and there's a patrol car parked out front, just in case. We've got this covered, Cass, trust us."

She nodded. Okay. All right. He was right. They had everything in place, and she was surrounded by people she did trust, people she knew were fully competent and had her back. She could get through this. Hopefully, it would all be over soon.

If she could just make this work.

The door plowed open, and Bee stuck his head in. "Oh, there you are, Luke. Tank is looking for you. Wants to go over a few things."

"Got it, thanks, Bee."

"Sure thing." He winked at Cass. "You go get 'em, girl."

For the first time that day, she actually started to hope they'd pull this off. "Thanks, Bee."

"I've gotta run, but first . . ." Luke turned her to face him and cradled her face between his hands. "I came in to let you know we identified the body you found buried out at Twin Forks."

"Harvey Potts."

"Yeah. Just like you figured."

No surprise. On a brighter note, it seemed her psychic talents were back on track. "Thanks for letting me know."

"I didn't know if it would make a difference in how you handle things tonight, but I just wanted to make sure you knew." Luke pulled her closer. He leaned in and kissed her, not a little peck on the cheek as she'd become used to when they were at public events, but the kind of kiss that surged through her and curled her toes almost as much as that thick Southern drawl he could evoke at will. Then he pulled back too soon. "Y'all knock 'em dead out there, ya hear?"

She grinned at him, and her fear melted away. "Let's hope not."

His deep rich laughter lingered behind him as he left her alone in her office.

It was time to pull herself together, time to figure out what exactly she needed to accomplish. Her first goal would be to contact Elijah Anderson. If she was able to do that, it would make her next steps a whole lot easier. Either way, whether she actually managed to contact him or not, she would have to convince those present that she had. And she wasn't quite sure how she felt about that.

She hadn't always known she was psychic, though she'd always suspected it on some level. She used to believe she was able to use her psychiatric training and good observation skills to "read" people, to help them figure out what exactly they were hoping to learn from those who'd moved on. In the past, even if she didn't think she was communicating with the dead, she'd always used whatever skills she had to help people. People sought to contact the dead for many reasons: to say goodbye, if they hadn't gotten the chance to do so, to alleviate guilt, if they hadn't been able to ask forgiveness before their loved one had passed on, to help them find something their dearly departed left behind, which given the right coaxing, they could often figure out on their own, or even just to say "I love you" one last time. It didn't matter why people came to Cass for help, just that they came, and that she was able to help them find peace.

But this . . . this didn't feel like she was helping anyone. What if Elijah had been present when Harvey Potts disappeared? What if he'd had something to do with his death? What if whoever had killed Elijah had also killed Harvey? Would she be able to get to the bottom of it? And even if she did, who would it help?

Someone knocked on the door.

She shook off any misgivings. No matter what Elijah may or may not have been guilty of, he still deserved justice. "Come in."

Stephanie opened the door only enough to slide in, then closed it firmly behind her. "It's crazy out there."

Cass crossed the room in a few steps and threw her arms around Stephanie. "Thank you so much for being here."

"Hey." She hugged Cass back hard, then stepped back. "You okay?"

"Yeah, I am. Just grateful you're here."

"Why wouldn't I be?" She punched Cass's good arm. "Have I ever missed a reading?"

"Actually, no."

Stephanie had attended every group reading she'd ever had. She grinned. "Wouldn't want it to look weird that I wasn't here, would we?"

In that instant, it hit Cass how much she'd missed her lately, though she couldn't regret keeping her distance if there was any chance a killer was targeting her. Putting Stephanie in any kind of danger wouldn't be fair to Aiden, or to Stephanie.

She fussed with Cass's hair, fluffing it a bit on top. "Anyway, I figured I'd let you know it's getting pretty packed out there. If you want time to mingle before the reading, you'd better get yourself out there."

"Do you know if Evelyn Anderson showed up?" Evelyn was the key. She was the one person who knew Elijah better than anyone. As long as Cass could keep an eye on her, gauge her reactions as she went along, she'd know if she was making a convincing argument for Elijah's presence.

"She's here. As are Cam Parker, Liam McAlister, Mercedes Dupont, and Thea Newburgh."

Hmm . . . if she could get Ophelia to show up now, she'd have everyone she needed present and accounted for. "How did you recognize them all?"

"Really, Cass? Did you think Bee, Bay Island's very own gossip queen, wouldn't have kept me in the loop about what's been going on?"

Heat flared in Cass's cheeks. Bee shouldn't have had to keep

Stephanie updated; Cass should have done it herself. Stephanie was one of her best friends, her oldest friend. Keeping her safe was more important than anything, but she should have kept in touch better. "I'm sorry, Stephanie."

She frowned. "For what?"

"I should have kept in touch, should have let you know what was going on. I was just so afraid you'd get hurt, or Aiden would, that I stayed away."

"Cass," Stephanie said. "You are one of my very best friends. There's nothing I wouldn't do for you and never a time I won't be there for you, and I not only understand why you kept your distance, I appreciate that you cared enough to do so."

Cass searched her expression and found only sincerity.

"But . . ." She grinned to soften whatever would come next. "You don't have to stay away completely. Next time, just keep me in the loop, let me know what's going on. Trust me, Aiden is my world, and there's nothing I wouldn't do to keep him safe. But just because things are a little different now doesn't change our relationship."

"You're right." She sniffed back tears. She'd missed hanging out with Stephanie, but even more, she'd missed having her to bounce ideas off of, missed having her to turn to when she felt anxious or sad or scared. "I'm sorry, and I'm so happy you came tonight."

"Me too. Now . . ." She gripped Cass's hand. "Let's go catch a killer."

Cass emerged from her office into organized chaos. Stephanie hadn't been kidding when she'd said the place was packed. There was barely room to walk. While Cass recognized a number of familiar faces, there were plenty of strangers she didn't recognize as well. Apparently, Bee had outdone himself.

"Cass, how are you holding up?" Chief Rawlins stood beside her in jeans and a sweatshirt.

Cass did a double take to be sure it was her. She'd never seen the woman dressed so casually, her dark hair spilling down her back and framing her face, rather than in its customary severe bun, softening her angular features. Undercover work suited her quite well. "Chief, thank you for coming."

"Of course, I wouldn't miss it." She leaned close enough to speak quietly, discreetly. "We have everything set up to record each of the players throughout the reading, so you don't have to worry about keeping an eye on all of them. Remember, you don't have to expose a killer tonight. We're just trying to watch everyone, see how they react, and maybe figure out who to focus on. You can go over the footage later."

She nodded. They'd been over this before, but Cass also knew she'd see more in the moment, feel more as things unfolded, than she would watching a video later on.

"I have to admit, I'm impressed you were able to get everyone together in one place, especially with so little notice."

"Actually, a lot of that was Bee's doing. I called and invited Evelyn, told her I was going to try to contact Elijah if she'd like to be present." A niggle of guilt crept in. She tamped it right down. It's not like she'd lied. She was going to try to contact Elijah. "I also asked her to reach out and invite the board members if they'd like to attend. We knew Liam would hear about the reading, since he's good friends with Tony and Gina from the bakery, and I asked Thea to attend, though I didn't explain why."

But she would seek her out afterward and talk to her. Bee had been harassing Cass for a while now to hire someone to work in the shop part-time so she would have more time to hang out with him, and she was thinking of offering Thea the position. With her working at Mystical Musings, Cass could work with her during the slower times to help her develop her abilities. She'd already spoken to Simone about it, and Simone had offered to give Cass some pointers on teaching another psychic how to open up.

Chief Rawlins angled her chin toward Mercedes. "What about Mercedes Dupont? How'd you get her to come?"

"I didn't. I invited those I could come up with an excuse to reach out to, but Mercedes must have heard about it from someone else. Liam, maybe? Although, with Bee hitting up every gossip hot spot on Bay Island to spread the news, she could have heard about it anywhere."

"Hmm . . . I'll have to keep him in mind next time I need to spread some news."

Cass laughed. Bee would be beyond happy to know that.

The chief moved on to make sure everything was in order, and Cass slid quietly through the crowd and made her way downstairs.

Usually, she'd be searching out those who seemed to be looking for something, those she could offer to read and help. This time was different. As she strolled through the crowd, listening to snippets of conversations, she tried to seek out those who seemed uncomfortable, those who seemed afraid she might actually contact Elijah, afraid of what he might reveal to her.

After she made a full circuit of the downstairs, she turned to go back up to the reading room and almost plowed right into Evelyn Anderson, and if the angry scowl on her face was any indication, the woman was not pleased.

"Good evening, Mrs. Anderson, I'm so glad you could come."

She snorted and looked down her nose at Cass. "Yes, well, that's all fine and good, but no one told me there would be assigned seating, and unless my seat is changed, I will most certainly not be staying."

Cass tried to think of a reason she could claim she couldn't change the woman's seating assignment. She couldn't very well tell her the truth, that she needed all of her suspects together in close proximity so the cameras would pick up not only all of their reactions but how they interacted with one another. She tried to remember who was seated next to Evelyn. She knew Cam Parker was on one side of her, since she wanted to see if they acted like they knew each other in a more than friendly way, but she couldn't remember who was on her other side. They'd played with the chart a number of times, and she couldn't be sure if it was Thea or Mercedes. "I'm sorry, Mrs. Anderson, what seems to be the problem?"

She contemplated Cass, then she pulled a handkerchief from her bag and took off her glasses. As she cleaned the lenses, Cass couldn't help but notice the monogram on the corner, the same as the one they'd found at Twin Forks. *EA* could stand not only for Elijah Anderson, but Evelyn Anderson as well. After tucking the handkerchief back into her bag and replacing her glasses, she straightened her spine and lifted her chin with a dignified huff. "I don't know what kind of game you're trying to play, dear, but you can forget it if you think I'm going to spend the next two or more hours sitting next to my husband's mistress."

Chapter Twenty-four

Cass took a deep steadying breath and smoothed her skirt, rocked by Evelyn's accusation that Mercedes Dupont and Elijah Anderson had been lovers. She still couldn't wrap her head around it. Though, she had to admit, if Elijah was going to stray, he'd strayed about as far from Evelyn Anderson as he could get with Mercedes. *If* the accusation was true. While Stephanie ran through her usual introduction, Cass watched Evelyn, who kept casting glares Mercedes's way.

Now that they'd moved her seat, Evelyn wouldn't be included on the video to watch later, so Cass would have to keep a closer eye on her during the reading. The fact they'd seated her between Chief Rawlins and Simone would help as well.

Cass's gaze returned to Mercedes. She assumed, if Mercedes really had been Elijah's mistress, the two had somehow connected after he'd bought Twin Forks, after Mercedes had been arrested protesting the sale. But who knew? One thing she did know, seeing Mercedes sitting at the round table, low lighting illuminating her face, Cass had seen her before. She recognized her now as the woman who'd gotten up and left during the reading Elijah had been present for. Had Evelyn known she was going to be there? Had Mercedes known Elijah and Evelyn would be there?

Thunderous applause from those seated, as well as those standing around the room because they'd run out of seats, alerted her she'd missed her cue from Stephanie. Tamping down her nerves and pasting on a smile, she walked to the front of the room and took the microphone Stephanie held out to her. "Thank you."

The applause continued. Boy, she sure hoped they'd be clapping this much when she'd finished tonight.

"I'm sorry we didn't have enough seats for everyone, but I'm very happy you all came out tonight." Dim lighting made it difficult to study everyone's faces, and she reminded herself she didn't have to. Her role tonight was to make Elijah Anderson's killer believe she contacted him and he would reveal who killed him. Beyond that, well, they'd cross that bridge when they came to it. "Though, I am sorry to have you all here under such sad circumstances."

After moving closer to the table where most of their suspects were seated, Cass asked for a moment of silence in memory of Elijah.

Thea, who by all accounts had never met Elijah, wiped away a tear, then clasped her hands together on the table and bounced them up and down.

Mercedes sat stone-faced, seemingly fascinated with the flames flickering in the candleholders in the center of the table.

Cam Parker bowed his head, so Cass wasn't able to read his expression.

Liam McAlister, who sat beside Thea, rested a hand on her clasped hands in what appeared to be a gesture of comfort. Or maybe he just wanted to still them.

"Thank you. And now, I will see if I can contact Elijah and ask him to join us." The line sounded off, scripted, not the way she usually did things. She needed her spiel to sound more natural. She needed to be able to wander the room, seek people out, talk to them, involve them. Learn from them. This wasn't going to work this way.

As she moved forward, a familiar face smiled up at her. She recognized the woman who'd come into the shop a few days ago in desperate need of sleep. As soon as their eyes met, the woman mouthed *thank you*.

Cass stopped beside her. "Amy, right?"

"Yes, and I just had to come tonight to say thank you."

"Sleeping better, I take it?"

"Oh, yes, so much so. I have more energy, and I feel so much better, even with just a couple of nights' sleep. I can't imagine how I'll feel in a week."

Cass grinned, happy to have been a help to the young mother. "I'm so happy to hear that. And I'm glad you came in to let me know."

Amy nodded. "I've never been to a reading before, but I'm definitely looking forward to it."

Cass moved on, the interaction helping her to relax, making her feel more at ease than she had earlier. Maybe she shouldn't just shoot straight for Elijah. Maybe she should take her time, work the room, do what she'd normally do.

Thea sat staring up at her, seemingly mesmerized. For a quick moment, she thought of speaking to her, asking if she was looking for a job, telling her she saw something new in her future, but she decided against it. She wouldn't start their working relationship, or their friendship, deceptively. That would be the quickest way to ensure neither relationship happened.

Instead, she zeroed in on Cam Parker. "Mr. Parker, is it?"

His eyes widened in surprise, and he looked around as if she might be talking to someone else.

"We haven't actually met, but I was in the diner the night Mr. Anderson was killed, when you came in looking for a ride out to Twin Forks."

"Oh, right, yes. I remember now. I was trying to make my way out there, but the roads were bad and I saw a plow in the parking lot so I stopped to see if I could get a hand." He didn't elaborate further, though there's no way he could have forgotten speaking to her, since she was the one who told him Elijah had been killed. Unless, of course, he'd already known.

She tilted her head as if listening to something, then frowned. "Did you ever make it out there that night?"

His jaw clenched. "Nope, never did."

She switched tactics. "Were you and Elijah close?"

He spread his hands on the table and pushed to his feet. "What is this? An interrogation?"

Bee, who was standing in his usual spot against the back wall, stepped forward.

Cass stopped him with one discreet head shake and decided it was time to be honest. "I'm sorry, Mr. Parker, I didn't mean to offend. This is not the way I usually do a group reading. I don't usually set out to contact a specific person. I usually wander the room and see who appears to need my assistance, and then I see what I can do for them. Since they are thinking about their loved one at the time, it's easier for me to reach out. It's easier for me to contact someone if I can learn a bit about them, and it's easier for them to respond if they know friends and loved ones are nearby."

A few of her regulars murmured and nodded assent.

Cam looked around, seeming more to be searching for something than responding to the crowd. Then he sat and clamped his mouth closed. Since he knew Evelyn was present, had, according to Bee, said hello to her earlier, Cass found it odd he didn't recommend she try speaking to her. But she let it go and decided to move on. For now.

She'd come back to him later, after he was more relaxed, more used to the way she did things. She turned her attention to Liam McAlister. "Mr. McAlister, you had several conversations with Mr. Anderson."

"I did, yes." He nodded, one leg crossed over the other, hands resting comfortably on his knee.

"Originally, you protested the sale of Twin Forks to him. Did you ever change your mind about that?"

Mercedes smirked and turned her head to look at him, seemingly interested in his answer.

Cam looked around the room as if he hadn't even heard the question.

"Yes and no, actually. I can't say I agreed with turning the property into a boarding school, which you well know, but I do think Mr. Anderson had good intentions. Better than some others, anyway." Liam slanted a glance at Cam.

Not wanting to draw attention to the fact that all those who knew Elijah seemed to be seated at the same two tables beside each other—they should probably have thought that out better—Cass weaved toward the back to where Evelyn sat. She didn't want to upset the woman further, but she did know her husband better than anyone.

"Mrs. Anderson," she said softly, "would you mind if I speak to you about Elijah?"

She pulled the handkerchief out of her bag and wiped her eyes. "Do you really think you'll be able to contact him?"

For the first time, Cass felt something stir. "Yes, actually, I really think I can."

She briefly wished she could have seen everyone else's reaction to that, but she'd have to trust the others to keep watch. Her focus now had to be on Evelyn.

Evelyn clutched the handkerchief tightly and traced a finger over the letters embroidered on the corner. She took in a deep breath and let it out slowly. "Yes, then, I'll speak to you."

Emmett, who was sitting two tables over, came to all of her readings, and knew how she liked to work, stood and brought Cass his chair.

"Thank you, Emmett."

"Sure thing." A man of few words, he simply set the chair facing Evelyn, held it until Cass sat, then went and stood beside Bee.

Evelyn turned her own chair until the two were sitting face-to-face.

"You were opposed to investing any more money in the venture."

She nodded.

"Elijah knew how you felt."

"Elijah knew how I felt about a lot of things, it just didn't matter to him." Her gaze skipped across the room and landed on Mercedes, and Cass shifted her chair a bit to the side to block her view of the other woman.

Sorrow filled Cass. Her own? No. She had no reason to be sorry. Elijah? Maybe. Was he feeling guilty that he'd cheated on his wife? Was he sad because he hadn't listened to her advice and had ended up dead? Maybe. But something seemed off. "He loved you. Very much."

Evelyn seemed surprised. "Elijah?"

"No." Cass frowned, waited, couldn't quite understand what she was sensing. Not Elijah, though. She should recognize his presence, since she'd met him, spoken to him. "I don't think so."

Cass stood, needed a moment to collect herself. Something wasn't right. Though it wasn't Elijah, an image began to shimmer in her mind. She moved back to the front of the room.

Silence enveloped her, taunted her, screamed so loud her head began to pound. No one made a sound, as if every single person in that room held their breath. Who knew? Perhaps they did.

Praying Simone and Chief Rawlins would keep their eyes glued to Evelyn instead of watching Cass when something obviously seemed to be wrong with her, she turned until she could see every one of her suspects with the exception of Evelyn. She couldn't see them all at once. Wouldn't be able to catch each of their reactions. And yet, she needed to. Had to, or she wouldn't know where to go next.

To give herself a moment, she uncapped a bottle of water from the front table and took a sip. She'd have to get everyone else's reactions later, on the video. She focused in on Mercedes and Cam, since they were sitting next to each other now that Evelyn had been moved. "It's not Elijah who's here with us, it's Harvey Potts."

Cam's eyes widened in surprise as he jerked back as if he'd been slapped.

Mercedes gasped, then folded her arms across her chest, sank back in her seat, and glared at Cass.

"Wait." Evelyn surged to her feet. "Does that mean he's dead? Harvey?"

"I'm sorry, Mrs. Anderson," Cass said gently. "But he is. His body was found earlier today."

"Oh, no. Oh, no." She sobbed softly and dropped back onto her chair. "No, no, no."

Simone squatted next to her and wrapped an arm around her shoulders and spoke quietly in her ear.

"I suppose I knew, on some level anyway. A man doesn't just disappear into thin air, leave the people he loves behind, but I always held on to hope he'd be found. Maybe turn up somewhere on a tropical island . . ." She lowered her face into her hands and cried softly.

Cam Parker stood, glanced at Evelyn, and turned to Cass. "Where? Where was he found?"

Cass wasn't even sure she was supposed to say they'd found him, never mind give details of his case, but it was too late to turn back now. And it seemed important, somehow, that she share the details. Some of them, at least. "I found him buried on the Twin Forks property."

"But, that's not possible."

"Why not, Mr. Parker?"

"I . . ." He once again looked at Evelyn, his expression pained. "Evelyn . . ."

She looked up from across the room, then met his gaze and nodded.

He blew out a breath and sank back into his seat. When he looked up into Cass's eyes, his pain was palpable.

And, for a moment, Cass wanted desperately to cancel the reading, just stop it right then and there and take him into her office to discuss whatever he had to say in private. But then she looked at Evelyn again, to where Simone was hunched over her, and when she looked into Evelyn's eyes, she saw nothing but steel.

Either Evelyn had the best poker face on the planet or she wanted her husband's killer caught at any and all cost to herself, even at the cost of admitting publicly to her affair with Cam Parker.

"Evelyn and I are the closest of friends, have been for more years than I can remember." Cam started off quietly.

Cass had to move closer to hear him. She wasn't about to ask him to raise his voice in the hushed room, respected the fact he would own up to whatever was going on between him and Evelyn if it meant getting justice for Elijah. But if both of them were seeking justice, then who was the killer?

Apparently resigned to the fact he was going to share his story, Cam sat up straighter. His voice hardened. "But, as close as we were, we could never be as close as Evelyn and Harvey were."

The breath shot from Cass's lungs. Some psychic; she hadn't seen that one coming.

Now that the tough part was out in the open, Cam deflated a bit. He propped his elbow on the table and cradled his forehead in his hand.

Evelyn stood and shook off Simone's hand. "Thank you, Cam, for telling the worst of it. At least, from a public opinion standpoint, if one cares about their reputation."

Cam turned to her. "You don't have to do this, Evelyn."

"Yes, I do. If I want justice for Elijah and for my Harvey — dear, sweet Harvey, who wouldn't harm another being for anything in the world — then I have to tell the truth, give Cass the ammunition to stop their killer. Because there is only one killer, and . . . well . . ." She pinned all of her hope on Cass with one look. "Let me tell what I know, and you can decide for yourself."

Cass nodded, afraid if she spoke it would shatter whatever spell had gripped her and compelled her to bare her soul.

"Elijah found out Harvey and I were seeing each other. I didn't know, not then anyway, neither of them told me. But when Harvey went missing . . ." She stopped and sniffed, struggled for composure. "When he went missing, Elijah told me what happened. He said they'd gone to Twin Forks on business, were intent on buying the property at that time. While they were surveying the property, alone together, Elijah confronted Harvey. According to Elijah, he told

Harvey to back off, told him he was going to destroy me, destroy the life Elijah and I had built together.

"And Harvey, being the kind of man he was, left and never returned. And I believed that." Her voice rose as anger swept in to add fuel to her grief. "For five long years I kept a vision of Harvey laying on a beach somewhere, enjoying his life, maybe even finding love, and all the while he was lying in a shallow grave on the grounds of Twin Forks."

When Evelyn stopped speaking, Cass started toward her.

Evelyn sneered. "So, imagine my surprise when I found out a few months later that Elijah, who'd chased away the man I loved, was sleeping with the woman who was competing with him to buy the property."

A collective gasp shot through the room. Everyone started to look around, search for whomever the woman might be.

But Cass knew exactly where to look, and she froze in place, feet from Mercedes's seat. "But she was at the protest, arrested for trespassing at the time."

"Of course she was." Evelyn scoffed. "She wanted the property for herself, and she was willing to stop at nothing to get it. So, when sleeping with my husband didn't work, and protesting the sale didn't work, she killed for him."

Chapter Twenty-five

"Are you saying Elijah's mistress killed Harvey Potts?" Cass kept Mercedes in view from the corner of her eye.

But the woman didn't budge. Instead, she simply stared at the centerpieces as if still mesmerized by the flames. As far as Mercedes knew, no one in the room knew she was supposedly Elijah's mistress, unless she'd heard Evelyn refusing to sit with her earlier. If that was the case, the woman had nerves of steel. But a cold-blooded killer?

"That's exactly what I'm saying. She killed him, took him out of the equation, and hoped Elijah would reward her by backing off and letting her purchase the property. And if that failed, I'm quite sure she wasn't above blackmail."

"But he didn't take the bait."

"No. No, he didn't. Instead, he went ahead with his plan." Evelyn gripped the table and slowly lowered herself onto the chair, apparently done talking.

Cass's head reeled. Where to go from there? She'd been following the wrong trail all along, so sure the killer had been motivated by business, though, in a way, Mercedes had. If Mercedes was the killer. Just because Evelyn made the accusation didn't mean it was true.

And, in her defense, Cass had considered the possibility the motive was more personal, had even asked Bee to research Elijah's personal life; they'd just lost track of that path when Luke had brought the picture of Thea Newburgh standing over Elijah's body.

Cass needed a moment to collect herself. She had to think, had to figure out where to go from there. Was it better to take a break? Give everyone, including herself, a moment or two to regroup? Or should she keep prodding while the iron was hot?

Mercedes answered that question for her when she slid her chair back quietly and stood, then started for the exit with her head down.

Cass panicked. She had to keep the other woman there. "Is everything okay, Mercedes?"

She stopped dead in her tracks and turned to Cass. "Why wouldn't it be?"

Her mind raced for a legitimate answer. "I was concerned. You left my last reading early, and now you seem to be leaving again. I'm starting to get a complex."

A ripple of uneasy laughter trickled through the room.

"Everything's fine. I just need to hit the ladies' room." She hooked a thumb toward the stairway.

"Sure thing, I need a moment to gather myself again anyway." Cass gestured to the table at the front of the room. "Why don't you all take a quick break, help yourselves to refreshments, and I'll be back in a moment? Then we can continue where we left off."

Luke, Tank, and Chief Rawlins all remained calm, their expressions neutral, though she had no doubt they were raging on the inside. If Evelyn's accusations were correct, Cass was about to leave the room with the woman who'd killed two men and possibly attempted to kill Cass.

Simone's attention was on Evelyn as they whispered together.

Stephanie sat on the edge of her seat, her gaze flitting between Cass and Tank and the door.

Bee propped his hands on his hips, his lips pressed into a firm line, and shook his head.

She tried to let him know with her gaze that she was sorry, that she couldn't take a chance Mercedes still carried the gun she'd used in the past, not in a roomful of people Cass had assembled. No. She had to diffuse the situation, had to get Mercedes out of there calmly before anyone could get hurt. And if she wasn't the killer, and the killer was still left in the room, there were enough officers present to take him or her down.

Cass plastered on the best smile she could muster. "Come on, I'll show you where the bathroom is."

"You really don't have to do that." Mercedes glared at her. "I'm perfectly capable of finding it myself."

"Oh, it's no problem, really. I'm headed that way anyway." She started toward the spiral staircase, hoping Mercedes would follow.

Mercedes only paused a moment, then fell into step beside Cass and walked out of the room and down the spiral staircase with her. Neither woman spoke until Cass reached the back room and slid the curtain aside. Thankfully, she'd left Beast with Jess, since they were entering the room he'd usually be in during a group reading.

Cass gestured toward the far side of the room, then moved to the counter and shifted some papers around, just to appear busy. Though, that probably wasn't the best idea, considering her hands were shaking badly enough to rattle the pages.

Bee's voice sounded in her head. *Way to be discreet, Cass.*

She pointed to a closed doorway beyond the couch. "The bathroom's in there."

"You know, I wonder." Mercedes made no move toward the bathroom. "Can you really talk to the dead?"

"Yes, more or less."

"What does that mean? More or less?"

"Well . . ." She had to keep her talking. If she could do that, it would give the others a chance to do whatever they had to to make sure everyone stayed safe. Cass gestured toward the couch. "Sit, and I'll explain."

"Thanks, but I think I'll stand."

Cass nodded and stood her ground, though, in hindsight, it would have been smarter to remain beside the doorway. Her psychic abilities really did seem to be on the fritz with this one. "While I can't just sit and have a conversation like you and I are doing, I can communicate with the dead, yes."

"It's long been a fascination for me, death, you know."

"I didn't. Can I ask what fascinates you about it?"

"Everything, really." She shrugged off the question. "So, did you communicate with Elijah or Harvey?"

"I felt Harvey's presence."

"Here?" She pointed to the ceiling.

"Yes, during the reading."

"And what did good old Harvey have to"—she made air quotes with her fingers—"communicate?"

This would be tricky. She wouldn't outright accuse Mercedes of murder, and yet, she needed to make her think Harvey could point the finger at her if she was the killer. "That his killer is present here tonight."

"Well, that sure is a shame." She pulled a handgun out of her jacket pocket and pointed it at Cass. "Tell me, can you contact Elijah?"

Cass's heart pounded painfully against her ribs. "Possibly."

"Well, no matter." Mercedes shrugged. "Even if you can't reach him from here, you'll be seeing him soon enough, so maybe you can pass along a message."

Cass swallowed the lump of fear clogging her throat. *Move away from Mercedes toward the doorway, or move closer to the other woman and go for the gun?* If she moved toward the shop and Mercedes fired, someone could get hit. Cass shifted to inch closer and whispered, "What message is that?"

"He should have kept his promise." She raised the gun.

Cass lunged. She grabbed Mercedes's wrist just as the weapon discharged.

The bullet went wide but way too close.

"Freeze!" Luke was first through the curtain, gun aimed squarely at Mercedes.

Tank was right behind him. "Drop your weapon!"

Cass grappled with Mercedes, clinging to her wrist for dear life. Her injured shoulder begged her to let go.

Mercedes shoved her back.

But Cass held tight. She couldn't get hold of the finger on the trigger, so she grabbed her middle finger and bent it back until she could feel the tendons popping.

"Drop it, Mercedes!" Luke warned again.

She finally looked away from Cass toward Luke and Tank, both of their weapons aimed right at her, and she loosened her hold on the gun.

Cass released her finger and took the gun from her hand.

Luke grabbed one arm and Tank the other. Once they had her hands cuffed behind her, Luke rushed to Cass. "Are you all right?"

"Yeah, fine, just a little winded." She handed him the weapon and pressed a hand against her shoulder wound, which throbbed unbearably after the scuffle.

Tank started out, pushing Mercedes ahead of him.

"Wait," Cass called, then limped over to Mercedes. Apparently, she was a little more sore than she realized. "I'm curious. What was the promise Elijah didn't keep? The one that cost him his life?"

She scowled and thrust her bottom lip out, like a petulant child who'd been sent to bed with no dessert. "He was never supposed to develop that land. He was going to sit on it for a while, then decide it wasn't profitable and sell it to me. That was the plan. That's what he told me right after I . . . right after Harvey disappeared. He said he'd hold on to it for five years or so, give things a chance to cool off, then decide not to proceed with the plans to use the property and sell it to me at a very reasonable price."

"Did he know? About Harvey?"

She clamped her mouth tightly closed and glared.

Not wanting to chance pushing her into a confession in front of two police officers without her lawyer present, Cass let the matter drop. "What changed his mind?"

"Who knows? Greed, I imagine. He thought he could make a profit. Although, he told me, right before he died, that he didn't want to see the past rebuilt, didn't want people to come and witness the atrocities committed there out of morbid curiosity." She shrugged and started past Cass. "In the end, I guess maybe he just wanted to do the right thing. But it's not like I didn't warn him what would happen if he crossed me."

● ● ●

Cass held her back door open for Luke.

He stamped his feet off on the mat, yanked his snow-covered hood off his head, and set a plate piled high with barbequed steaks in the center of her kitchen table.

Bee set out a bowl of potato salad. "Nothing like grilled steaks and good friends to weather a snowstorm with."

The storm Cass had predicted had finally unleashed its fury upon Bay Island, only a week late. Not too bad. She set out a pile of napkins and paper plates. "At least they closed down almost everything."

"True." After a final check that they had everything they needed, Bee took a seat at the table next to Aiden. "Here you go, honey, corn on the cob."

"Yay." Aiden smiled up into Bee's eyes. Corn on the cob, grilled on the barbeque, was his new favorite food. He'd eat it every day if he was allowed.

Cass sat on his other side, between Aiden and Luke. "And for dessert, we have apple pie."

Aiden's eyes went wide. The only thing he liked better than corn on the cob was apple pie.

Tank and Stephanie sat opposite them at the round table, getting to enjoy a meal while Bee and Cass spoiled Aiden.

Cass poured ice water into her glass, then handed the pitcher to Luke. "Did you ever find out why Cam Parker was trying to get out to Twin Forks the night we found Elijah?"

He filled his glass and set the pitcher aside, then forked a steak onto his plate. "According to him and Evelyn, in separate interviews, she asked him to go out there and try to talk Elijah out of going ahead with his plan, but he was too late."

"He'd have been better off all around to just sell the property to him to build condos, if you ask me." Bee added more butter to Aiden's corn.

"Probably, but you never know. Mercedes was pretty intent on getting that property. Her obsessions"—Luke shot a glance in Aiden's direction—"wouldn't allow her to let go."

"Do you think Elijah knew what happened to Harvey?" Cass figured Mercedes would have told him, whether to blackmail him into selling her the land or to make him fear he'd be next.

"According to Mercedes, she told him, and he was so appalled and guilt-ridden he kept it to himself, but we have no way to know if she's telling the truth," Tank said. "Unfortunately, some questions will probably remain unanswered."

Cass contemplated that. He was probably right. Of course, there was always the chance she could find the answers that had gone to the grave with Elijah, and Harvey, but that was for another time.

"So . . ." Bee said, his huge grin a portent of good news. "Have you looked at the vlog I posted from your encounter at Twin Forks?"

A niggle of doubt crept up Cass's spine. Though Evelyn had assured her it was okay to use the footage, Cass still wasn't completely sold on the vlog idea to generate income. "I've been afraid to look."

Bee's smile widened even further. "More than a hundred thousand views within a few hours of posting."

Thankfully, Cass hadn't had her mouth full, or she'd have choked for sure. "A hundred—"

"Thousand. Yes. And almost half of them subscribed."

"Wow." At a loss for words, she simply sat back, shocked, and grinned at Bee.

He grinned back sheepishly, then returned his attention to his plate. "There were also a ton of comments about the ghost that pushed you out the lighthouse door and onto your duff."

"What!" Heat burned up her cheeks. "You used that video, Bee? We didn't even finish the lighthouse video yet."

"We-eell, I may have used some of that footage, you know, clips from different places, for the introduction." He waggled his eyebrows. "Gotta have an intro, right? And it's staying, because people loved it."

Cass only groaned. What could she say? Bee was the one with the flair for drama. Plus, she couldn't argue the results.

"Public humiliation is a small price to pay for fame, dear." He winked.

Cass balled a napkin and threw it at him.

Aiden laughed and clapped and threw his napkin at him.

"Congratulations, Cass." Luke kissed her temple. "That's awesome."

"I knew you could do it," Stephanie said. And she had. Without her and Bee cheering her on, Cass never would have had the courage to try.

Though it still saddened her that Elijah having been killed out there had more than likely contributed to their successful first vlog, even though she'd been careful there was no mention of either Elijah's nor Harvey's murders. "Did you hear Evelyn Anderson decided to donate the Twin Forks property to Bay Island as a park."

Bee nodded. "You can't undo the past, but maybe something good can come out of it."

"Who knows? Maybe a hundred years from now, it will be a place of peace." Cass hoped that was true. Setting talk of murder aside, Cass scooped potato salad onto her plate. One look at Bee out of the corner of her eye had her pausing.

Bee studied her a little to innocently. "What?"

One glimpse under the table, at Beast happily munching on a piece of steak, told her why.

"What?" Bee asked. "He has to eat too."

"Herb says—"

"Oh, puh-lease, girl! Do not even tell me you are about to sit there and quote the dog trainer at me. Since when do you listen to

Herb's advice?"

"I listen." Cass sulked, because Bee, as usual, was right. "Sometimes."

"Yeah. Okay." He rolled his eyes. "That explains why, when Herb suggested you crate train him, I walked in and found you in the cage and Beast staring at you like you'd lost your mind."

Everyone laughed. Bee loved to tell that story, and Cass loved that he enjoyed it so much. She set a hand on Beast's head and slipped him another slice of steak. With the wind howling outside, Cass enjoyed the warmth of spending time with her family.

About the Author

Lena Gregory is the author of the Bay Island Psychic Mystery series, which takes place on a small island between the north and south forks of Long Island, New York, and the All-Day Breakfast Café Mystery series, which is set on the outskirts of Florida's Ocala National Forest.

Lena Grew up in a small town on the south shore of eastern Long Island, where she still lives with her husband, three kids, son-in-law, and five dogs, and works full-time as a writer and freelance editor.

To learn more about Lena and her latest writing endeavors, visit her website at www.lenagregory.com/, and be sure to sign up for her newsletter at lenagregory.us12.list-manage.com/subscribe? u=9765d0711ed4fab4fa31b16ac&id=49d42335d1.

Made in the USA
Monee, IL
17 July 2021